BLEEKER HILL

Also by Russell Mardell

Stone Bleeding
Silent Bombs Falling on Green Grass

BLEEKER
HILL

RUSSELL MARDELL

Matador
9 Priory Business Park,
Wistow Road, Kibworth Beauchamp,
Leicestershire. LE8 0RX
Tel: (+44) 116 279 2299
Fax: (+44) 116 279 2277
Email: books@troubador.co.uk
Web: www.troubador.co.uk/matador

ISBN 978 1783061 556

British Library Cataloguing in Publication Data.
A catalogue record for this book is available from the British Library.

Typeset in 12pt Bembo by Troubador Publishing Ltd, Leicester, UK
Printed and bound in the UK by TJ International, Padstow, Cornwall

Cover design by David Baker

Matador is an imprint of Troubador Publishing Ltd

For Kerry

PROLOGUE

ARRIVAL

They arrived just after dawn, the two old army utility trucks slowing and sliding on the icy road that cut through the forest and then broke on to the top of the hill. They came to rest neatly together whilst the small quad bike snowplough carried on down, cutting them a slithering path towards the house. To call it a house seemed an understatement of magnificent proportions. It was grander and more opulent than any of them had ever seen before – a great, sprawling mansion, a monument to a forgotten time. To see such a building in such a time as they were living in was almost unheard of and none of them could tear their eyes away. The house seemed to be all there was for miles; a forgotten life picked up and dumped down where nothing else could see it or touch it. It was the perfect place to disappear, the ideal place to start again, and it didn't take a genius to see why it had been chosen.

As the weak sun gave its token gesture above them, contemplating its position amongst the greying clouds, they saw the balloons in the sky that they had been looking for ever since cresting the hill; the sure sign that they were close. The balloons bloomed together in clusters as they rose up from beyond the great house, before breaking apart in the sky and then drifting away on the sharp breeze; red, and white and blue shapes, the only colour in the tired and washed-out skyline.

Everyone rechecked their weaponry for what felt like the hundredth time. Now, though, there was a finality and threat in every click of every gun as their nervous fingers and hands set to work. Their journey had been arduous; the many miles of travelling along the valleys treacherous, narrow roads had been bad enough, but the oncoming snow had caused long delays and improvised detours. The three-day trip had become a five-day expedition and now, finally at their destination, they felt spent, and ruined. But the real work hadn't even begun.

Lucas Hennessey held Mia in his arms in the cab of the lead truck, stroking her hair and gently rocking her from side to side, pulling the rug tighter over her shoulders and folding the ends over her bare neck. Her fever appeared to be getting worse, her face seemed to glow in the darkness of the cab, and the tacky, sweaty skin he could feel whenever he mopped her brow worried him. His daughter had been fine when they set out; she'd even taken turns at the wheel of the truck, her eighteen years seeming impossible, her boundless energy and enthusiasm an infectious encouragement. But by the end of the second day Mia had started to change, to seemingly age under his gaze and slowly shrivel in his arms.

Wallace had been a medic in the army back in the old country, many years before everything that had happened and he would tend to her as best he could, but medical supplies were pretty scarce and what was there seemed to be ineffective. By the third day he had all but given up on her, and by the fourth no one spoke about her any more, and everyone stared.

As Finn hopped off the snowplough and waved back up the hill to the two trucks, Hennessey looked down at his daughter to see her asleep against his chest. Wallace turned the engine over and shifted the lead truck forward as gently as he could, pumping the brake in short blasts. Behind them, Connor fired up the other truck and delicately edged forward in their tracks. With his free hand, Hennessey pulled out his mobile phone from his jacket and clumsily thumbed a number. The signal was weak, and the voice that answered the call faint, but between the rasp of the truck's engine and the angry crackle of the phone line he just about recognised Kendrick's voice.

'This is point team,' Hennessey shouted into the phone. 'The king has his castle. Repeat, the king has his castle.'

'Huh?'

'The king has…'

'Who is this?'

'This is Hennessey, you dickhead. We've arrived. Out.'

They cut the truck's engines before reaching the house and rolled the last few yards, coming to a stop in the snow-covered courtyard; the ploughed walls along the freshly cut pathway a gentle buffer against the tyres. Connor jumped down from the second truck and, with Finn, rounded the south side of the building, their machine guns primed in front of them, beckoning on whatever they were about to face. Wallace turned to Hennessey in the lead truck, and Hennessey waved absently in the air between them, urging Wallace on.

'Take position, I will be right behind you.'

'We go in pairs, Lucas. That was the deal. That was what you said.'

'Whose safety are you concerned about, Wallace? Mine or yours?'

'He's a madman.'

'We've got a job to do.'

'You've heard the stories about this place, I know you have.'

'After everything you've seen, now you're scared of stories?'

'What about Grennaught?'

'He's dead. What about the living?'

'People disappeared here.'

'Take position, Wallace.'

Wallace seemed to be trying to gulp down air in his throat. His right hand instinctively went to the side of his neck and seemed to hover there, the index finger tapping against the skin. 'I had this dream,' he started, before stopping abruptly and pulling his hand away, seemingly surprised by his own voice.

'Dream?' The word knocked Hennessey's calm demeanour momentarily and shook the authority from his voice. 'What dream?'

Wallace narrowed his eyes and seemed to be scrutinising Hennessey's face.

'What dream, Wallace?'

'I dreamed how I was going to die. I saw it. Felt it.'

Hennessey moved to speak but could offer nothing more than a grunt.

'You have too, haven't you, Lucas?'

For the longest of seconds they said nothing, though their eyes were quick to betray their silence. It was enough for Wallace and he answered his own question of his boss with a slow, purposeful nod of the head.

'Dreams and tall tales,' Hennessey snapped, stealing back his command and jerking a finger to the house beyond the windscreen. 'Do you really want this conversation, Wallace?'

'The way the country is, it's easy to believe in fate, right?'

'Take position.'

'I mean, it's normal isn't it? It doesn't make me a madman, does it?'

'Take position, Wallace. Now.'

Hennessey waved Wallace on again and turned back to Mia. Decision made, conversation over. Wallace shifted slowly around in the driver's seat, his hand pausing at the door, and then gently slipped out of the cab, landing with a soft crunch on the snow.

Staring at his daughter's sleeping face, Hennessey found Wallace's words echoing through his mind, trying to distort his vision and his control. He had dreamed deep and long these last few weeks. Ever since he was tasked with the mission, he had remembered his dreams vividly. He had seen things in his dreams, had felt them encroaching over his waking hours, and now, as so many times before, he took a hand to his heart and felt the pain his sub-conscious mind had already revealed to him. He refused to give Wallace's words space in that moment, he wouldn't allow questions that made no sense; he had got this far by controlling facts and acting on whatever truth lay before him, he wasn't going to succumb to any sort of madness now. That was for the rest of the country. Not him. As the pain in his heart slowly abated to it's usual nagging dullness, he took his hand away and gripped the certainty of his shotgun, and as he did, everything made sense.

Hennessey brushed away a knotted clump of hair from Mia's forehead and gazed at his daughter's face, aware already of the tears trickling down his own and hoping she wouldn't wake at that moment and see.

'I'm so sorry, Mia. This is my fault. I should have left you with your mother. But it wasn't safe there, you know that, don't you? Your mother is a very stubborn woman. But I will keep you safe here. I promise I will. When everyone else arrives we will get you seen to properly. Then sooner or later we will make this place home. We are going to start again. We are going to build everything from scratch. The Party will see that everything is okay. We will be happy here. Just you and me. I promise.'

Hennessey lowered his daughter down across the front seats of the truck's cab and readjusted the rug around her neck. For one brief moment he seemed to freeze, his hands clutching the end of the rug, not wanting to let go, wanting to hold on and pull it tighter. But, no sooner did the feeling come over him, than it went again, and then Hennessey was sat upright, staring out at the house through the snow-splattered windscreen, distracted by something at the back of his mind that wanted to be heard, grabbing at a thought and a feeling that he wanted to understand. The icy winter breeze came into the cab, whistling like the devil's own theme tune, and slowly, uncomfortably, Hennessey took his shotgun back into hands that didn't feel like his own and climbed down from the cab.

He followed Wallace's footprints in the snow, across

the courtyard and around to the north side of the building. A lifeless balloon hid in the snow under his feet and he jumped as it popped under him, fumbling the shotgun in his hands, his heart shooting through his body as if it had just been drop kicked. He stopped, waited, and breathed deeply, steadying his control. Pulling the shotgun back into his grasp he continued forward again, edging around the house and walking as lightly as he could in Wallace's path.

The north side was more exposed than the courtyard and the wind whipped up instantly and battered him, the heartless cold force probing every inch of exposed skin. He crouched down, gun in his lap, and tightened the toggle at the top of his coat. He looked forward towards Wallace's footprints and then craned around and stared back up the hill to the point where they had entered, between the trees. It seemed so far away at that moment, the forest on either side sucking the road out of sight. His eyes followed the snowplough's path down to the house and rested on the truck where his daughter slept. He had to keep Mia safe; somehow, amongst all that was happening, and all he had to do, nothing else would matter if he failed to protect her. Looking up, he saw the balloons floating over him and he suddenly wanted to take the machine gun from his back and blast them all out of the air, decimate them under a wave of brutal gunfire. Maybe he would, he thought. Once the mission is done, maybe he would do that very thing.

Hennessey pulled himself up and started walking in Wallace's footsteps again, the shotgun sweeping left to right in front of him, his painful eyes alert to everything, yet seeing nothing. He had gone no more than twenty feet when his left foot, instead of slipping neatly into Wallace's next footprint, crunched down through a patch of virgin snow and brought him to a staggering halt. Wallace's footprints had stopped and in front of him was nothing but untouched snow. Hennessey spun around on the spot, first behind him, then to the house. There was no trace of Wallace anywhere.

'Wallace?' Hennessey whispered into the air. 'Wallace? Get back in position, don't make me come find you!'

He moved on, crunching through new snow, his finger hovering over the trigger of the shotgun, and then he stopped again and was crouching down. In front of him, about ten feet ahead, a wide channel seemed to have been carved in the snow, running across his position and then away to the right, directly into the wall of the house. Looking back to the channel in the snow he followed it the other way and saw it break ahead, the smoothness becoming a large, body-shaped dent and giving way to a clumsy set of footprints scattering away into the distance. The first three footprints were splattered with blood, and after that they didn't look like footprints at all.

To Finn it was all a bit of fun. Here he was playing macho man with a gun and being encouraged to do so. Finn had been sprung from jail like most of the team, and instead of embracing his second chance of freedom he merely rode it as a licence to do as he pleased. No one liked him, and that was just how he liked it. He was the only member of the point team unconcerned about the mission, and the only one who volunteered. In fact, as far as Finn was concerned, he would have been happy if they had sent him by himself, strapped up in machine guns and carrying a machete between his teeth.

Finn was also the only one of the team who had witnessed the Wash firsthand, or at least he had been around it, and had seen people, fellow inmates, bagged up and bundled away. He had heard the stories like everyone else, but where many still believed it an urban myth, Finn knew all too well that rather than being a scare story, the Wash was, in fact, all too real.

Connor had asked so many questions about the Wash during their stops on the journey in, and Finn had been all too glad to be the centre of attention. It was only Hennessey constantly shouting them down that had stopped them. Now it was just the two of them, Connor wasted no time in piping up again.

'So, it's like some sort of electric shock treatment? Like they used to give the loonies, right? Or is it drugs? Schaeffer was a head quack, wasn't he?'

'Pills, potions and probes, reckon they have given

most things a spin at this place. Depends who you speak to. I heard Kendrick talk about some miracle drug that Schaeffer had got all long and tough about, that was what they tested out first. That was what I saw when I was still inside. He reckoned he could wipe their minds with one simple injection into the brain. Boom! Pump that shit right on in the old grey matter.'

'And?'

'Didn't work, kid. We lost about a hundred inmates in my nick alone to that first round of trials. Party plod would come for them in the night, we would hear them screaming, grown men I'm talking about here, hardened bastards and killers and they were screaming like little girls. Then they would be sent back about a week later. They would just be there, back in their cells, or shuffling around the courtyards, like they had never been away. But they were blasted, kid, I'm telling you. They looked carved out. Dead. Sometimes we would see some little dude with a clipboard standing there watching them, monitoring them. Man, they had messed them up good. First time I saw one turn he bit the neck out of one of the monitors, right there in the courtyard. It turned most of them psycho, the ones that didn't start bleeding out their ears and eyes that is, those never even made it back from this place, poor bastards. I've seen good men tear arms out of sockets, pluck out eyes…one guy even…'

'What?'

'Nah, better not say, thing is it didn't work. So they tried something else, then something else again. They stopped coming in the night then, they would just roll up, throw a bag over some poor bastard's head and drag them out of there. Never saw them again. Still, who knows, who cares? When we are done it will all be history anyway.' Finn slung his machine gun up over his shoulder and strode out past the side of the house, Connor tottering along in his wake. 'Schaeffer is a wacko, always was and will be. The man at the top may change, their legacy of carnage never does.'

'Don't want to let the Party hear you saying that. Party would kill a man for less than that.'

'Fuck the Party.'

'Didn't Kendrick say that Schaeffer reckoned he was close?'

'Not close enough to stop me shooting his winkie into the new world.'

'But what if he could actually do it? Think about it. We could get a grip on what's happening. We could start to rebuild the country.'

'Do you really want to live in a neutered world, kid? It is leaders want that Connor, not lackeys. What are you to the Party? What are any of us to them, for that matter? Expendable assets. Why'd you think they hire in cons?'

'Party have been good to me. Party like me.'

'They will be smiling like a freshly blown gigolo as

they pull the knife out your back, Connor. Now shut your trap. Let's go.'

Ahead of them the grounds rolled into the distance under sheets of brilliant white snow, glistening optimistically under a sun looking for a way through. It seemed to go on for miles; the forest running around the perimeter of the estate looked a long way off, like it were a trick of the eye. In the middle of the grounds was what appeared, from the distance of the house, to be a long concrete hut; a low building, like a bomb shelter, with a wide metal door eating up one side. Adjacent to the building was a large pen, fenced in by long wooden barriers, and topped off with barbed wire. Figures were wandering in aimless circles within the pen – they counted at least ten – turning their shambling gaits into one another before shuffling away again, all the time their eyes to the sky, and to the balloons belching up above them from an unseen point behind the concrete building. One of the figures tried to grab for a balloon in a clumsy, slightly hysterical wave of the arms, like a child desperate to be fed. Another figure tried to jump up but fell instead; a third figure tripped over the prostrate body and joined it on the ground.

'Balloons? What's with the balloons?' Connor asked, his machine gun pointing up to the sky as if Finn needed it explaining.

'Distraction.'

'What?'

'Keeps them occupied. Keeps them distracted. It means Schaeffer's come out his little hidey-hole.' Finn brought his machine gun down from his shoulder and into a rock-steady hold. 'Look at the stupid bastards. Just look at them. Kids. They're just like dumb kids.'

'Don't say that. Don't call them that.' Connor let his machine gun drop to his side, his eyes back on the pen. 'We got no business being here for people like that.'

'When you've seen what people like that can do to people like you, you start to lose any sympathy, kid. You know what it's said he used before balloons to keep them occupied?'

'What?'

'People like you kid, people like you.' Finn gave a short, brittle, cackle at the look of fear on Connor's face and then returned his gaze to the pen.

'Where are Hennessey and Wallace?' Connor muttered into the air, dropping to his knees and then to his front, pushing his gun to one side and scrabbling into his jacket for his binoculars. 'What do we do? We wait, right?'

Finn remained still, looking as likely to drop to his knees as do a jig. His face was fixed in a wiry, satisfied smile. He took one step forward and then stopped, his head tilted to one side, nodding up and down slowly as if he were counting the figures in the pen again. To Connor, he looked like a diner at the lobster tank, scrutinising the options and working out which he wanted to devour. Connor grabbed the binoculars from his jacket and pressed them to his eyes, though no sooner had he pulled them into focus and settled on the building ahead, than Finn had walked across his sightline, blocking his view, as he crunched through the snow towards the pen.

'Finn! What are you doing? Get back here! We're supposed to wait, aren't we supposed to wait?' Connor pulled himself up to his knees and fumbled across the snow to his gun. As he clasped the strap and started to drag it to him, a foot came down hard across his hand as a figure approached from behind. Connor spun his head around and a pistol struck him across the face, then, with a graceless thud, he was back down in the snow, a cold pressure growing against the back of his neck as pistol barrel met skin.

Hennessey saw Schaeffer slip out of a downstairs window as he turned around the north side of the house. He called to Connor and Finn, screamed at the top of his lungs, but could not be heard over the howling wind. He recognised Schaeffer straight away; a thin tree of a creature carrying a wild bush of white hair, which had now grown down his face. Schaeffer was a man not easily forgotten. Hennessey had been the one to study him, it was his job to lead these men here and his to understand, and eventually eliminate, the target. He knew all there was to know about Schaeffer and his wealth of information had done nothing to make him question the necessity of the job.

As the pistol cracked across Connor's face, Hennessey began to run, shotgun up before him, his machine gun clunking against his back. He could hear the three men's exchanges in small, stuttering gobbles of words, punching out through the persistent, whining wind, whistling into his ears. Schaeffer was calling after Finn, stretching up, yanking Connor with him by the hair, the pistol now against the side of Connor's head, and he was hollering, pleading, threatening, unaware with each word that he was appealing to quite the wrong sort of man. Finn hadn't even broken stride.

'You people must leave here…you go now, you turn away and leave!' There was fear in Schaeffer's voice, a genuine tremble. Finn wandered on, a raised hand over one shoulder, waving to Schaeffer. Then Schaeffer began to scream, a crazy, howling, barrage of words: 'Please, please…go…It will see…mustn't be here…kill…evil… here…evil.'

Hennessey was about twenty yards away when Schaeffer saw him. Both men fired together, Hennessey's shot veering wildly off course as he stumbled forward. Schaeffer shot twice and Hennessey let himself fall into the snow. The first shot missed, but not by much, and as Hennessey struggled up, readying himself to fire again, he saw Connor slump sideways into a red splatter of snow. Hennessey screamed nonsense into the air and staggered forward again. Schaeffer was moving across towards the pen now, his pistol in front of him, firing blindly towards Finn. Hennessey began to run, his feet planting deep, turning and pushing him over. He fell next to the prone body of Connor and fired off two quick blasts of his shotgun over Schaeffer's head.

Finn was now no more than a few yards from the pen. The figures were turning to him, one at a time, with wide-eyed curiosity; corrupted faces, growing blue from the cold, entranced by the stranger. Numbed hands reached out to him, gnarled fingers curled in the air before his face as they sought him out. Finn stopped and raised his machine gun. He glanced back once over his shoulder and saw Schaeffer charging towards him in a stupid, slapstick stumble, his gun waving around in his grip like a baton. He could see Hennessey in the distance trying to stand, and then, as if what he saw was a mere sideshow, Finn turned back to the pen, stepped forward and fired the machine gun magazine empty, reloaded and then turned to Schaeffer who was now bearing down on him, lunging forward, craziness in his face and fury in his screams.

As Schaeffer and Finn came together and their respective weapons cracked their shots into the air, Hennessey seemed to freeze on the spot. He saw them but they looked a hundred miles away, and he seemed to be watching from behind a dull screen. He stood wearily, turned uncomfortably and slumped down hard on to the snow, his fear and his fury ebbing out of him in one long breath as he gazed back at the magnificent and imposing features of the old house. He could feel a sticky smear of Connor's blood on his cheek and on his lips and he let his tongue out to taste it.

All around him the wind seemed to be pressing in, and it felt like the pressure of human force, it felt strong and firm and alive. It seemed to go up his nose and look into his brain, to seep in through his eyes and his mouth and his ears, almost through his very skin. Then it was a pressure at his legs and ankles and it was tightening around his feet and dragging him forward towards the house and he had no choice but to let it. He could hear laughing from somewhere, deep booming laughter, and then music; he could swear he heard music deep in his soul.

The building loomed over him, the gentle wave of balloons high above, gliding over the grandiose splendour. It was mocking him somehow, he was sure of it. But he had no fight to challenge the taunt. He had fallen into himself, sunk down deep to a place where the edges were blurred. The force that seemed to cover him had moved into him, stolen him, and then pushed him further back. The shotgun was in his hands yet he couldn't feel it, nor could he find the certainty it always gave him. Even as the barrel pushed down against his chest, right above his heart, it didn't feel real. He wanted to speak, he wanted to get up and run, but he was lost and had nothing left to give. Nothing but one word – one single, solitary name – an utterance whose importance would mean nothing to anyone, except himself.

"Mia…" he said softly in his mind, in perfect symmetry with the explosion that blasted out from the shotgun.

Mia remained asleep across the front seats of the cab, her light breathing breaking intermittently as the rug was slowly pulled off her. A pain in her right wrist had been growing, throbbing, for a few minutes and yet she didn't wake. As the right sleeve of her coat was unceremoniously yanked upward and the ghostly pale skin on her arm exposed, she merely rolled her head back and batted absently at her arm with her left hand like she were swatting a fly.

A pressure grew at her arm, a gentle hold breaking into a firm, unflinching grip; it was stirring her from her sleep, shaking her back to reality, demanding her attention, and as the first scratch slashed into her skin she flew out of her fevered dreams as if breaking through the surface of the deepest ocean. Blood was squirting into the air above her and splattering the roof of the cab and the snow-caked windscreen. She tried to pull her arm from whatever held it, but the pressure and the hold were too strong. Yanking herself crudely to a seated position, she screamed as more blood began lightly peppering her face and her left arm gave wild sweeps of the empty cab, hysterically trying to fight back against that which she couldn't see and couldn't possibly be. But at every swipe and each hopeless attack, the hold on her arm grew stronger and more persistent.

It was only when she finally looked down to her right arm that the pressure stopped and released its hold on her. It had been demanding to be acknowledged. To be seen.

Mia tentatively raised her right arm to her face, and through the diluted light of another weak morning she slowly connected the bloody scrawl that was there, carved in her skin. The word LEAVE was now written down her arm.

APART

1

The rat was next to his ear before he even realised it was back in the cell. Two long weeks of visits by this friendly rodent and it was now feeling comfortable enough in their burgeoning relationship to venture up to his pillow and whisper sweet nothings. The rat's fur was crusty and sticking up on its end in places, its tail stained black at the tip and its little paws devoid of their once baby pink colouring. It was another victim of the surroundings, Sullivan reasoned. He decided that if even those in this decaying country who were free to come and go were coloured by the putrid fear in the air, then there was actually little difference between jail and freedom after all.

Sullivan was too tired to pick the rat up or usher it away so just turned on his side and looked at it for a while. He always liked the way rats rubbed at their ears with their tiny little paws when they were cleaning themselves; a little twitch of the whiskers for good measure and the tiniest of winks from those beady little eyes. It was possible to befriend a rat, of that he was sure, he'd been closer to much worse back in the old country. Rats were intelligent, he had read that somewhere, maybe in one of those huge old books in the prison library that had pictures of creatures and arrows and footnotes and easy to understand chunks of information. Or maybe he had just imagined that any rat could care. He didn't. Why should this little fellow?

The rat seemed fixated by Sullivan's sad face, its whiskers quivering as its pinhead wine-gum nose sought out the human's odour and its paws shuffled forward across the bed covers. It was almost at Sullivan's chin when the footsteps began thudding on the metal staircase outside the cell door and then the rat was rearing up on its back paws, its neck craning up and its nose sniffing at the air, checking out what was headed their way, deciding whether it were friend or foe.

Sullivan recognised the footsteps approaching the solitary block as well as he recognised most sounds in the prison. People were becoming less and less human, far less a physical embodiment and more and more just a series of sounds and smells. Faces didn't matter any more. He heard the wheezing and small stuttering coughs that were Hudson's calling card getting closer, rattling through the hollow shell of the prison, then he heard the jangling keys bouncing up and down and then the chain dragging across the landing floor. It was all so very predictable. But there was something else behind these familiar sounds, something alien and troubling to Sullivan, and as the cell door screeched open the realisation of what it was hit him like a metal fist in the softness of the cheek. It was the sound of pure silence, a backing track to death.

Hudson was at the cell door, the strap and chain in one hand and more keys than necessary in the other. He tried to smile through his browned lips but coughed instead, spitting out blackened phlegm.

'The Party loves you.'

'The Party loves you too, Mr Hudson.'

Sullivan tilted his head upwards as much as he could manage and saw Hudson was nodding towards the rat.

'Rats.' Hudson said through the half of mouth free from chewing tobacco.

'Rat. Just the one. I'd never be that lucky.'

'Let's go, Sullivan. Walkies.'

Sullivan's daily walk amounted to endless circles of the small courtyard at the rear of the prison, under the south watchtower. When there had been someone to cook the prisoner's food, Hudson would walk Sullivan back through the kitchens and let him have a quick bite or two, but now, more often than not, he was kept alive on scraps past their prime and a small mug of water shoved through his cell door at odd intervals throughout the day. He had learned to conserve whatever food he was given and to not get angry if nothing came at all on some days. It was his own fault, Hudson was very quick to point out, and he should be grateful that anyone cared enough nowadays to feed him at all. Sullivan didn't argue. There was really no point. Even though he was in solitary confinement, and even though Hudson had never told him what he had done to warrant that punishment, at least Hudson spoke to him, looked after him, and gave the pretence of concern. That in itself reminded Sullivan that he was still a human after all, albeit one of no great importance.

Sullivan knew from his wife's letters that things had gone funny back in the real world, he could even remember it crumbling and breaking before he got sent down – the riots, the looting, the anarchy – and, he supposed the very little Hudson did for him, at the very least, set him above the average. Sure, Hudson had once enjoyed his job, he had got nourished on the cruelty and the power, "the little man with a lot of keys complex," Wiggs had called it before Hudson had beaten him to death, but really, these days Hudson was just little. He wasn't immune to what was happening beyond the prison walls either; the fire wasn't there any more and he was working from routine. Sullivan knew that Hudson was probably grateful to be at work and to have a purpose, no matter how unimportant it and he had become. It was frightening to question what a man like Hudson would do without a purpose. He would almost certainly have to create his own, and that was a dangerous prospect as far as Sullivan could see.

Old man Mandrake was already in the courtyard as Sullivan was led out. Mandrake was turning his shambling circles; his eyes to the floor and his gnarled feet falling out of badly taped leather work boots. There was no guard standing over him so Sullivan guessed Hudson was probably pulling everyone else's shifts again. Nowadays it seemed it was only ever Hudson that walked him, fed him, and locked him in again. It was always Hudson's footsteps he could hear on the landings and the staircases, always Hudson's voice echoing around the ever-emptying space of the prison. Wiggs always used to say that when the Wash is all out of prisoners that they were going to come for the screws next. Sullivan decided they probably had.

He gazed around the wide courtyard, left and right and back again, but saw no other prisoners. He knew numbers were dwindling – even in solitary, word got around – add in those taken by the Wash, those who had escaped or naturally expired, and more recently the ones taken to diving off the top floor balcony, and there could be little more than a handful left, but somehow that early morning emptiness suggested otherwise.

Sullivan walked his well-worn path around the courtyard, the chain locked to a metal pole bolted into the ground and fastened at the other end to the leather strap that was tied around his neck. He never liked to shuffle – which was the action the set up naturally lent itself to – but a quick pace was beyond him. Besides, anything too fast and the endless circling would make him dizzy and if he fell Hudson would probably beat him. It would be violence through habit rather than sadism, of course, – "give a small man a stick and he will beat you before he ever contemplates using it to pick the wax outta his ears," Wiggs used to say, and he should have known – but Sullivan knew his body wouldn't stand the scrutiny of abuse these days and tried to give Hudson no reason for it, and besides, Mandrake always shuffled and Sullivan had never liked him. Even in this situation, in this corner of the world, having your own identity seemed to matter.

Sullivan was on his tenth turn of the courtyard when he realised Hudson was not there any more. Looking to his right at Mandrake, he saw Hudson just beyond him, scuttling towards the watchtower in a flustered waddle like a man late for a first date who has forgotten the flowers. A tall man was standing on the edge of the shadow spilt by the watchtower and Hudson stopped before him, his little arms waving around as if trying to direct the man into the light. Incoherent words, tied up in Hudson's nervous laughter broke the silence, and it was immediately clear to Sullivan that whatever power Hudson had at Thinwater prison, or thought he had, it had just been transferred to the stranger.

Mandrake was trying his best to turn his shuffle into a jog and was failing miserably, landing with a heavy thud on the concrete and then hobbling up again before the inevitable repeat performance. Mandrake had been at Thinwater long before Sullivan. He'd been arrested under Party outlawed practices no. 117a – the facilitation of false hope. Mandrake, like so many others, claimed he could speak to the dead. It was nothing new. After the country broke and so many fell, preying on grief and offering hope to the hopeless became big business. Mediums, fortune tellers, psychics and soothsayers; suddenly everyone claimed the touch and possessed the power. They were working street corners, back alleys, door to door, and people were buying. Some still traded money, but usually it was food or water, clothing or sometimes a room for the night. That so many were willing to believe terrified the Party and so such practices were soon outlawed, punishable by a ten-year stretch, if they were lucky; Party Plod had been known to shoot dead on sight. The Party was strong and powerful, but even they couldn't control the dead. "Bet they are working on it." Wiggs would say, and Sullivan couldn't disagree.

That Mandrake could have either the touch or the nous to work the con amazed Sullivan. The old man barely seemed capable of knowing the day. He was hunched and pathetic, his long and matted hair crudely framing a pruned face, his dirty rags swinging from a disjointed skeleton. Occasionally, Sullivan would hear him calling out from his cell at night, long and guttural moaning hiding disconnected words and soft pleading. Such noise never lasted long, Hudson would see to that. "Didn't see that coming did you?" he would often hear

Hudson scream from Mandrake's cell on the floor above. Then would come the old man's sobbing and Sullivan would have to bury his head into his pillow so as not to hear.

Hudson was now in heated conversation with the stranger, his arms gesticulating wildly between Mandrake and Sullivan and from the prison block to the wall of the courtyard. The stranger remained still, cushioned in the shadow and towering over Hudson much as the old watchtower towered over the prison. Mandrake fell again in front of them and this time Hudson took up the slack of the chain around his strap and began to whip him with it; an unleashed fury in each swipe, and in each grimace on his sweaty little cubed face. Mandrake struggled up and the chain caught him around his mouth and shattered the few old teeth that had been holding on. He tumbled down again and his face hit hard on to the concrete.

'Get up old man! Get on up and walk. Face us.' Hudson barked the words, spitting them out, chewing on every full stop.

Suddenly, as if waiting for a cue, the stranger stepped forward out of the shadows, pushed Hudson to one side, walked one quick circle around Mandrake as if he were eyeing up a car to purchase, and then drew a small pistol from a holster on his hip and shot Mandrake through the head. The casualness of the act, if not the actual act, made Sullivan retch, his heart sagging like a carrier bag filled with warm water, and suddenly it hurt, everything hurt, and his body felt like it would escape him. He quickly turned his eyes away, looking back down to his feet, to his own path that led back to where he started, and he began turning his circles just that bit more quickly. Across the courtyard, the stranger had moved away from Mandrake and was striding towards Sullivan the way only a man in charge of something worthwhile could. Hudson was trotting along behind with the horrid look of a pupil trying to impress a teacher. The stranger, for his part, didn't even seem to know Hudson was there.

'Keep walking,' the stranger said to Sullivan through a closed mouth. Sullivan hadn't actually stopped walking and so read the instruction as it was really meant – "walk faster!" Sullivan knew the stranger must have been an important man as they were the only people who said what they wanted by saying something else. It was the little runts like Hudson that had to scream it at you in capital letters.

'Good build isn't he?' Hudson panted. 'All things considered.'

'Does he speak?'

'Oh yes. Yes he speaks. Don't you, Sullivan?'

'Yes, Mr Hudson. Yes, I speak.'

'Give you any trouble?'

'Nothing he hasn't learnt from, isn't that so, Sullivan? You learn the right from the wrong don't you?'

'Yes. Yes, Mr Hudson.'

'Is he educated?'

'Oh yes, regular at the library is Sullivan. Bit of a bookworm.'

'So he can read?'

'Yes. He can read. Can you read, Sullivan?

'Yes I can read, Mr Hudson.'

'Good enough,' the stranger said, stepping closer. 'Untie him.'

Hudson leapt forward and yanked the strap from Sullivan with such eagerness it made Sullivan gag and he had to fight the urge to buckle forward. Hudson was then at his back, shoving him clumsily, trying to straighten him up to face the stranger. Sullivan tried to smile but soon thought better of it. He thought of offering his hand but not for long. The stranger's demeanour made cordial greetings seem like the ultimate offence.

'The Party loves you, Mr Sullivan.'

'The Party loves you too, Mr...'

'My name is Frankie Bergan. Have you heard of me?'

Hudson shoved Sullivan in the back making his reply stick in his throat and show itself simply as a shrug.

'I guess not. Good. I am a man light. Grennaught caught a bullet. He was a good man. How do you feel about that?'

'Well...' Sullivan began, arching away from the sweaty fist of Hudson that was hovering at the base of his spine.

'I prefer complete honesty. Rare as that may be in this world,' Bergan continued, rolling forward on the balls of his feet briefly before settling back and fixing Sullivan with charcoal eyes.

'I really don't care,' Sullivan replied, with complete honesty.

Bergan smiled, a warm and genuine smile. Had that warmth transferred anything, even the most remote flicker, to his dead eyes, Sullivan might have felt at ease rather than terrified. But Bergan's face was a contradiction, a mask to keep you wary and on edge and ultimately confused. Even the contrast between his jet-black hair and his greying beard seemed to be a deliberate ruse to throw you off the truth of the man.

'Good. You'll do. Grennaught was strong and skilled. I'm sure you can find a way of filling that void.'

'I'm a lag, Mr Bergan. A lifer. Been here over five years.'

'You're vertical aren't you? Right now, that qualifies you.'

2

Bergan led them back into the prison, turning corridors until coming out on to the staff landing and kicking open the door to Hudson's office, a small once-white room now a vulgar yellow-brown colour thanks to Hudson's tobacco and, probably, some form of universal decay.

Bergan sat and put his feet up on Hudson's desk, which made the little man wince before he gathered his well-rehearsed pupil character again and stood to Bergan's shoulder like a soldier on parade. Bergan ushered Sullivan to sit and took a wrapped sandwich from inside his jacket and tossed it on to the table.

'Cheese and salami. I think it's still edible. Eat it,' Bergan said and waved a hand towards Sullivan and then to the sandwich. Sullivan didn't need telling twice and ploughed into the hard cheese and curled salami sandwich with super speed, salivating from one corner of his mouth and coughing bits of bread back to splutter on to the table. Sullivan nodded his gratitude, Bergan shrugged, a smile on his lips, death in his eyes. 'Petrol canisters,' Bergan said into the air, almost as if to see which of the two men would grab the words. Predictably it was Hudson.

'Pardon me?'

'Find me some petrol canisters. And some rags.'

'I don't understand?'

'That's why you are you, and I am me. Go away.' Bergan flicked a finger to the open door and set an expression that ended the conversation with inarguable finality. Hudson rocked from one foot to the other before scuttling away, head bowed and shoulders hunched. Sullivan took a moment between bites to allow a smile out. 'A tedious individual if ever I stumbled across one,' Bergan said, and leant back in the chair fixing Sullivan once more with those dreadful eyes of his. 'You and the old man were friends?'

'No. I never liked him.'

'You don't think me a bastard for doing what I did then?'

'I'm trying not to think anything, Mr Bergan.'

'There was really no other option. In fact, I really did him favour. We live in harsh times. There is very little room for the weak. Of course I could have turned him out, back into the world, but really, how long would such an old man last? He was of no use to me, no use to the Party, no use to society, not the way it is now. So really, I merely expedited the inevitable, and I did it quick. He felt nothing. No, very much the thing to do. Wouldn't you agree?'

Sullivan nodded timidly and returned to devouring his sandwich.

'What do you know about the way the country is, Sullivan? The real world, outside these walls?'

Sullivan swallowed hard as the last bite of sandwich caught on his dry throat and coughed violently before holding up a hand of apology. 'My wife used to tell me things when she visited, then they stopped letting people come here. I heard bits and pieces from people. My wife used to write me letters. When that was allowed. They were heavily edited at the start, but I got the gist. My daughter always used to say that things had got funny.'

'Funny? Curious sense of humour children have these days.'

'Funny…weird, you know?'

'Yes, Sullivan. Yes. I know what you meant.'

'Sorry. We are at war, aren't we?'

Bergan fell silent and stared through Sullivan at the open door behind him. 'That's what she said, is it?'

'That's what she thought.'

'Out the mouths of babes.'

'Are we?'

'We are in a lot of shit, Sullivan. Country has gone to the dogs. Dogs don't want it. Who can blame them?'

'I remember things before I got sent down. But they feel like dreams. Little fragments of dreams. Like they don't really belong to me any more. Does that make sense?' Bergan's face said nothing. Sullivan continued. 'I remember the fires before I got sent down. Everywhere seemed to be ablaze, every building and every house. I still dream about that. Almost every night my dreams are of fire. Sorry, that's…'

'Meaningless, yes, go on.'

'There were riots. There were curfews. I remember all that. I remember my wife being scared, then I remember her getting excited because she had heard that the system was falling apart, government I mean, the law, courts, all of it. I remember her telling me that I wouldn't even stand trial, that no one would care any more and that it would all crumble. I guess I left the party before the cabaret?'

'You left the party before the Party.'

'Oh yeah, that's right. The Party is going to make it all better.'

'You're not a Party man, Sullivan?'

'I'm not anything, Mr Bergan.'

'True.'

'Is that who you work for? The Party?'

'We all do, Sullivan. One way or another. Even you. Even here. You got off lightly. It's not pretty out there.'

'It's not pretty in here. Still, it's better than the Wash, right? That's what Wiggs used to say. "Better than a bag on the head and a hypodermic up the jacksie."'

'What do you know about that?'

'What I hear. I'm not daft. People talk. I knew something was happening. Every night we expected them to come for us. I guess I got lucky.'

Bergan seemed to flush a translucent colour and

shifted in the chair. 'A vicious practice from a quack with a god complex.' He wafted a hand in the air as if trying to swat away the words Sullivan had just spoken. 'Right, let's get to the bones, time is short, my desire to be here even shorter and my patience non-existent. You have an offer here, Sullivan. I assume you aren't stupid enough not to see that? You have a choice. You have options. Something you haven't had in a long time. Say thank you.'

'I beg your pardon?'

'Thank me.'

'Thank you.'

'You come with me and you work for me. You do as you are told and follow me, without hesitation or question, or, and I stress this is the only other option open to you now, I waste another bullet. Here and now. Through your head. Bang! I will drop you like litter and leave you here. Speak. Tell me how it is going to be.'

'I don't see what I have to offer you.'

'Don't question a good deed in a bad place. Personally, I'm totally indifferent to your plight. But I need someone to fill Grennaught's shoes. Circumstance gives me you. So that's what is on offer. I need a shooter who will do whatever is asked of him without question. You are ignorant and you know how to fire a gun. I'd say you were over-qualified for what I need. Of course, you don't have to. You don't have to do anything. It can end here if you really want it to.'

'How do you know I know how to fire a gun?'

'I've read your record. You were sent here for shooting someone. A young kid, so it goes. Quite the nasty little bastard, aren't you?'

'It was self-defence.'

'It was still murder.'

It never failed to get Sullivan where it hurt. He could barely remember what he had done the previous day, yet he could remember that day as if he were still there living it. In many ways he was. He had left all that was good lying on the floor of his living room that day, mixing in the blood of that kid. He could piece every detail together with crystal clear clarity, could see it all, smell it all – the furniture polish in the house, the smoking embers in the fire in the hearth, his wife's perfume, the soft scent of his daughter. Then there was the waft of death mixing with those joyous smells, invading all and overpowering them with brute strength, brought forth on the tang of the gun barrel – he had never touched a gun before, never would again, he vowed. Now, suddenly, all he wanted to do was lie down on his bed and close his eyes. He needed to think of his family without interruption. It was what kept him going and he felt Bergan was trying to wrestle that from him. He was beginning to sweat and to twitch, the barely chewed sandwich lying in his throat, tasteless and harsh. Bergan seemed to be scrutinising every tick and droplet of perspiration, those lifeless eyes roaming every inch of his body. Sullivan thought back to the speed with which he had stepped from the shadows and put a bullet into old man Mandrake, and the silence that had fallen between them now seemed dangerous. He looked to Bergan and was about to speak, say anything to him, when the sharp smell of petrol flooded his nostrils and charged into his brain, dragging him back to the here and the now, shutting out the never again.

Hudson was out of breath, weighed down with four petrol canisters and a bundle of rags – old prison uniforms. The clothes of ghosts. He dumped them at the table and stood panting, pointing down at them and struggling to speak.

'Very good, Hudson. Now pick them up and follow me.' Bergan stood and pushed past Hudson, slapped Sullivan on the shoulder and walked to the door. 'You've five minutes to get anything you want, Sullivan. Then we are going to burn this bugger down.'

The words seemed to squash Hudson on the spot. To Sullivan, Hudson had never looked smaller than he did at that point, prison rags bundled under one arm and the petrol canisters wobbling in the other.

'But, the other prisoners, Mr Bergan?'

'What others? You're it. The last one out the door.'

The realisation smacked Sullivan hard across the face, reverberating through his mind in waves of understanding.

'What? Mr Bergan…please.' Hudson's voice was

small and weedy, drained of any power or force. In another circumstance, another world, Sullivan could have pitied him. 'Why would you…but, my job, Mr Bergan? What about my job?'

'You have no job any more you rancid little cock botherer, or hadn't you noticed? No more animals in this zoo, Hudson. You're nobody in particular in charge of nothing much at all.'

As Bergan turned out of the office, Sullivan could see the truth creep over Hudson. In all his posturing, in all his sycophantic platitudes and grovelling at Bergan's feet it had not, even for a moment, occurred to Hudson that the very man he was trying so hard to please, had just swept in and made his own life meaningless.

Sullivan stared back through the open door and into the dark hall outside, towards the sound of Bergan's slowly descending footsteps on the metal stairwell. To his side, his mouth hanging open at a slant, much as it did when he was chewing his tobacco, Sullivan's jailer wept.

3

'Hurry up, Hudson! Bring them here!' Sullivan could hear Bergan bellowing up above, as he stumbled down the staircase to the lower floor, towards his cell, his home. His head was swimming with the idea of possibilities, the last half an hour's activity making his brain scramble to catch up. He hadn't allowed himself to believe what Bergan had said, and even peering over his shoulder and watching Bergan empty the first petrol canister on to the floor he still believed it a warped joke between people unprepared to share. It was Hudson's tears and wailing that finally turned Sullivan around to the truth. The sheer heartbreak in each incomplete, warbled word that fell off his tongue and landed unheard next to Bergan was the most honest Hudson had ever been. Thinwater prison was going down, and Sullivan's heart charged into his throat as his face broke into the widest sort of happiness.

The rat was back on his bed looking at him as Sullivan arrived in the cell. Could it sense what was happening? The cell seemed darker than ever to Sullivan at that moment, so dark that he struggled for longer than he dared in the small wooden cupboard on the wall, looking for his wife's letters – the only things five years in this hell had offered worth a damn. His hands probed the murky depths, catching splinters and combing through cobwebs until finally his fingers caught on the string he'd tied them with and he plucked them up and held them to his chest. Sullivan looked back to the rat on his bed and smiled. The rat, Sullivan believed, returned it.

'Time to go,' Sullivan said and held out the palm of his hand, which the rat sniffed before climbing on to. They turned out of the cell for the last time and never looked back.

Sullivan hopped and staggered back up the stairwells, his legs throbbing with each over-exuberant bound, his head floating somewhere above him, alive with childish, grabbing ideas. As he turned out on to the main landing he pulled up and came to a quick stop, the rat squealing as the momentum caused Sullivan's hands to close to fists. Hudson was kneeling in the middle of the landing, his short box shape jittering as his body shook from great tides of tears, and his arms reached out to the air in an over-dramatic pleading gesture. His wheezing was now a harsh rasping sound and the coughs came in great loud blasts between the sobs. Bergan was at the far end of the landing, whistling a catchy tune and wrapping the rags around an old chair leg.

Hudson met Sullivan's gaze and Sullivan could see the pleading in his eyes, his mouth almost, but not quite, forming the word "please" as Sullivan stood over him. He thought instantly of Mandrake and his night-time sobbing, his calls, his pleads and his harsh treatment at the hands of this sorry little mess now knelt in the middle of his derelict kingdom, and Sullivan felt nothing. He wanted to. He wanted to be human and feel what humans should, but he knew there was no point even trying to find the emotion. He passed Hudson and walked on, loosening his fists and raising the rat up to his face as if he were about to kiss it better.

He hated himself for it. Hated Hudson for making him face what he had become, hated Bergan for starting the whole damn circus. He had resigned himself long ago to slowly fading away from sight, and the one benefit he had managed to chisel out of that unfortunate end was the fact he no longer had to feel anything about anyone. He was a slave to his memories – they were his fuel – but he had managed to all but shut out any care or concern for his neighbours and his jailers. Now, at the sight of the fearsome man who had ruled his life through threat and fear for five years, broken and defeated, he felt a deep fear grab around his ribcage and his confident stride collapsed into a weedy shuffle. Suddenly the disruption to his life seemed like thievery, seemed like a callous offence. Something was going to be expected of him, people would ask questions and he would have to find answers, or even worse, opinions. He had been exposed and the very idea of freedom suddenly terrified him, so much so that he thought, for the briefest of moments, that perhaps he should have taken a dive in the courtyard in front of Bergan and then perhaps all this, whatever this was, would be playing out a million miles away from him. He would be truly free of everything.

Crossing the landing, he started to walk like a drunkard, each step in need of a guide, an instruction or an order. The thought of leaving prison, the undiluted excitement of it, was slowly being eclipsed by his reality and the knowledge that whatever was outside the walls these days, it surely was not for him. Then he looked at the rat sitting in the palm of his hand, looking at him with curiosity and expectancy, twitching its nose to the air and Sullivan knew what he had to do. Wiggs always used to say the secret to getting through life at Thinwater Prison was to find little goals, even the smallest things, even something you would view as irrelevant back in the real world. Find one and see it through. Each goal was a stepping-stone to survival and that was all that mattered. So it was to the rat's safety that Sullivan eventually turned, and towards Bergan that he walked.

'Please Mr Bergan! Why must we do this? Why?' Hudson started shrieking, his hands clenched into fists, beating on to his head and his red-raw childlike face. 'He can't want this! He can't want you to take the prison. Leave me something. I can stay here and secure it for you. It can be a haven for you all. With some money, some reinforcements, we can…'

'All this place is good for now is tactical misdirection.'

'But no one would come here, no one has been this way for weeks. We are quite safe here. Yes, you should all come here. We can secure it, that would be my pleasure, and then we can…'

'There are two groups at the city border. Large groups. Hundreds. They will come to the fire. We want them to come,' Bergan shouted back, his elbow barging Sullivan to one side as a hand probed his pocket for a lighter. 'It might buy us time. That's the only commodity that matters now, Hudson. Time. Now get off your fat arse and shut up.'

'But…but…'

Bergan dipped the bound rags into the nearest pool of petrol and then held the chair leg aloft like a sword. 'Shall I torch him along with it? What do you think, Sullivan?'

Sullivan laughed lightly, nervously, then realised Bergan wasn't joking, that he was perhaps, with those eyes, incapable of it. Sullivan quickly shook his head. 'No, Mr Bergan. Please don't do that.'

'Why not? He's a scumbag. There is no real point to him any more. He's done his job. You were his job. His pet. His justification.'

'His justification for what?'

'Living.'

'What do you mean?'

'I don't understand you, Sullivan. I find it curious

that you should want to spare him. Are you sure?'

Sullivan thought for a moment, but the thoughts wouldn't hold. He shrugged them off him and nodded.

'Why look so unhappy, Sullivan? Smile. This is what freedom feels like.'

'Please Mr Bergan! Please!' Hudson screamed again, staggering slowly to his feet, his arms waving around his head. 'Please don't do this!'

'Make your choice, Hudson.'

'But…'

'Now!'

Hudson, slowly and delicately, started hobbling towards them; the simpering and smug teacher's pet of before now nothing more than a snot-nosed infant on his first day at school. Bergan took the lighter to the rags and let the fury of the flames into his eyes for the briefest of moments before launching the chair leg up and across the staircase and on to the landing.

Hudson was the first out of the door, the stark deviousness of the winter wind hitting him as if from another world.

There was snow in the air, just light freckles, but enough to excite a child Sullivan thought. His child, his daughter, she would have been excited by it. The surroundings would have made no difference to her, she would have danced and skipped around with her arms to the sky, catching snowflakes in her hands and on her smiling face. To Sullivan, it was merely an irritant; the cold day now just those few notches chillier, the flakes of snow a mocking threat that promised coldness that would seep into his bones and make him shiver.

Bergan led the way. Hudson, on a zombie like autopilot, followed and, chain of command obviously still standing, Sullivan brought up the rear. Sullivan wouldn't look back at the prison despite his great rush of exhilaration as the flames caught their first. Something had locked inside him and at every sound of breaking glass, at every snap of the vicious crackling flames, Sullivan felt a jab in his mind, as if someone was plucking things from his subconscious and tossing them away to the wind. His dreams had come alive, that was his thought, his concern. Had he dreamt this? Was this always what was meant for him? Burning paper fell around them and the smell was sharp and pungent.

Sullivan caught a cough in the back of his throat and swayed as he tried to clear it.

The great iron gates to the prison were parted like the yawning mouth of a trapdoor on the gallows. Beyond, only a bruised inhuman sky was visible. A jet black BMW was parked across the entrance, neatly tucked between the doors, and a figure in tatty army fatigues strolled around the vehicle in a perfect circle, a large hunting rifle rested in his arms, his face turning left to right and back again, looking out into the real world beyond the gate and giving the raging inferno of Thinwater prison nothing more than the most cursory of glances. The man looked young, little more than a teenager, Sullivan thought. But he had the wiry edge in his eyes of one who has seen too much.

The rat was trying to wriggle free from Sullivan's hand as if frightened by the world beyond those iron gates and for that moment Sullivan didn't want to let it go. He looked down into those dark eyes, eyes so similar to Bergan's yet graced with a twinkle of light that Bergan had yet to find and, with difficulty, he hunched down and opened his palm full so as to let the rat make its decision. The rat looked back once, sniffed at the grease on Sullivan's palm, decided it wasn't for them and then scurried off his hand and away into the car park, zigzagging a path towards freedom or at least something similar.

What if it had a family in there? A Mr or Mrs Rat and a couple of kids. What if I've taken it away from its family? Why would it be so eager to escape?

Sullivan let the thoughts go. It was easy. Far too easy. As he stood and turned back towards the great gates of the prison he suddenly felt life drain from his brain and down his body. He rocked back and forth on unsteady feet, once more the drunkard looking for guidance, and then he began to fall forward, his limbs empty, his body hollow; an Easter egg with a disappointing gift inside.

Humpty Dumpty had a great fall...that was her favourite nursery rhyme. She'd sing it aloud to me and I could never tell her how much I hated it and how I found it ever so slightly creepy. There was beauty in the difference though, real beauty, I should have told her that. I assumed she wouldn't understand.

He was stopped by a hand that felt like a pitchers glove, grabbing at his collar and spinning him around. Bergan was at his side and propping him up, Sullivan's head flopping on to Bergan's shoulder as he was dragged forward to the car. Bergan had managed to catch him, turn him and start marching him toward the car without breaking stride. If Sullivan had had any great capacity for thought left he would probably have conceded it was an impressive manoeuvre.

Sullivan was tumbled on to the back seat of the car face first and Hudson was shoved in crudely behind him; the heel of Bergan's boot making the jailer fit just that little bit better. The smell of the leather seats was strong and smelt unspoilt but Sullivan would conclude later, when he gave time to look back, that it was probably just the brief reacquainting of an old memory that made the smell so keen. There was, surely, nothing unspoilt in this world.

Sullivan lay there for a moment, gathering himself, inhaling the leather seats and allowing his head time to float back to his shoulders. He could feel Hudson pressed up against him, could hear his wheezing and his coughing. Hudson's mighty ring of keys was pushing into Sullivan's backside and one kneecap was pushed up into his ribs. Sullivan readjusted and raised himself to a seated position.

Bergan was against the boot of the car talking to the man with the rifle and Sullivan caught a few words in every sentence, the two men talking quickly and urgently, nothing making much sense. The man with the rifle was called Kleinman, that much was obvious, and something over the road had caught their attention, for it was there they were looking, Kleinman occasionally pointing with his rifle and Bergan craning forward, squinting those blackened eyes.

'Like a scuffling noise...' Kleinman was saying. 'Leaves...a breaking branch.'

'A straggler...'

'Why torch the place, Frank?'

'If we can't control it, kid, we torch it. What have I taught you? They…come across to the fire. It might buy us a day.'

When Sullivan looked back into the car he saw that Hudson was sitting bolt-upright staring at the headrest of the driver's seat. His face was blank, his mouth tightly closed and his body rigid. Looking at him, Sullivan was reminded once more of that dreadful day; the day he had last held a gun, the day that had changed everything for him. He remembered feeling that all that had defined him had seeped out of his body that day, on to the floor and away from him, free to mix in with the blood at his feet. He knew Hudson was having the same feeling. Hudson was Thinwater prison, and now, whatever was left to stand up in his clothes when he stepped out of the car, would never fit them quite the same way.

Kleinman was stepping forward, the rifle trained in front of him. Bergan was at his shoulder, the pistol drawn from its holster again and aimed ahead at a clump of diseased horse chestnut trees across the road. Sullivan wiped the growing condensation from the car window nearest him and tried to see what they were looking at, but as the two men advanced Bergan blocked his view. Sullivan shifted himself on the seat and tried to look from the back window, craning his neck across the headrests. Kleinman was edging sideways, his finger clamped over the trigger of the rifle, his face scrunched in concentration. Bergan was holding his free hand to him, stopping him from moving forward.

'Only if you are sure...we need to preserve ammunition. Don't fire unless you are sure.'

From the corner of the window an orange glow was growing around each man as the window began reflecting the fire of the prison. It was only now that Sullivan looked back at his home for the last five years; Thinwater prison, the last place he thought he would ever see. The kitchens had just caught alight and were crumbling under great dancing flames, smoke pouring from the punctured eyes of the windows and swirling outwards into the car park. One wall of the main prison block had fallen outwards, spilling its brick guts down into an orangey blood pool. The blackened landings inside, twisted and bent, comical almost, poked out like broken metal ribs. A solitary car in the car park had been dragged into the enveloping flames and popped and juddered as the fire began to dismantle it, looking for the drink of petrol it would greedily swallow.

He looked back at Kleinman and Bergan and saw that Bergan had holstered his pistol and was just staring ahead, hands in his pockets. Kleinman was down on one knee, the rifle butt against his shoulder, one supporting arm rested on a raised knee, his finger rock steady on the trigger. For a minute there seemed to be no noise, nothing anywhere, from the broken road ahead of them or the ice cold sky above, even Thinwater prison appeared to be falling apart without fanfare or complaint. Then, suddenly, one quick rifle shot cracked and blasted into the air and Sullivan jumped back so quickly he hit his head on the roof of the car and then fell forward into the window. Almost instantly Kleinman opened the door and Sullivan tumbled out, slipping down to the ground like a limp rag doll.

'Jeez Frank, guys a wet lettuce. Maddox would have him for breakfast.'

'Come on, kid, you know Maddox wouldn't ever touch salad. Raw meat all the way!'

There was laughter and then the fading smell of leather upholstery as Bergan and Kleinman each took one of Sullivan's arms and lifted him back into the car. Sullivan was aware of the car starting and the orange glint at the side of his eyes, then he found himself in a fitful sleep before waking up three hours later screaming. He had been dreaming of fire.

5

Sullivan was lying on a bed in the centre of a brilliantly white room and his screams bounced off the walls and echoed back to him. He shook his head trying to focus but a greasy, uncontrollable sweat was falling from the lines on his forehead and dropping like tiny darts into the corner of his eyes. He could feel hot piss staining one leg and he felt colder than he had ever been before. Snot fell from his nose like limp tusks and as he tried to wipe it clear he realised his hand was numb. Scrunching his toes against the metal bar across the base of the bed, he realised his feet were the same way. His wife's letters lay scattered over him and above the bed water was coming in from some unseen place, carried along with an icy breeze that threatened to burrow to his core. All around him, all over him, the feeling of emptiness hung like a huge cage swinging on a frayed wire, groaning on its last effort to remain in place and threatening to fall at speed and shut out whatever feeling there was left.

A mouse under a trap. That's me, baby. Look at me now. How she hated the mousetraps I used to put down. She scolded me for that. Wouldn't speak to me for days. She loved the mice. Rats. Rodents. Tough cookie, my girl. That time she found one in the garden and let it run over and under her cupped hands...that was joy, right there, that was what it was all about. Fucked up world.

Sullivan pulled himself up on his elbows and slowly felt his head come back to its natural position. A shape, fleetingly and tantalisingly the shape of his wife, hovered into view at the base of his bed, shadows finding a form, colours mixing as his eyes sought the truth. The memory of his wife faded as the shape stood and became instead, the rock carved bulk of a man in army fatigues – these black rather than the camouflage colourings of Kleinman's cut and paste clothing. The man was a brute by even the most forgiving person's standards; cuts and grazes plastered his heavily-stubbled face as well as his scalp, all too visible under the shaven hair, and a crazed fury lit brilliant blue eyes, sucking out any hint of friendship. He held a hunting knife in one hand and one of Sullivan's wife's letters in the other which, having satisfied himself Sullivan was awake enough to see, he began to screw up into a ball. Sullivan jerked forward to grab the letter but collapsed back on to the bed in a heap. The man laughed, a horrid, loud and spiteful laugh and dropped the balled letter on to Sullivan's head, and then he rounded the bed and crossed to the door, leaving the laugh behind him like a bad smell. Sullivan could feel the prickly promise of tears but kept them locked away until he heard the door to the room slam shut and the man's footsteps walking away. With the safe release of the tears he rolled over on to his side and gathered up as many of the letters as he could see on the bed, clumsily dragging them to his chest and wrapping his body over them for protection.

The door to the room swung open and footsteps approached the bed, two people had arrived and were standing on either side of him. Sullivan remained motionless, scrunched up as best as he could, covering the letters and waiting for the fists or the screams, but for several seconds there was just silence, an awkward silence that seemed to demand someone to clear their throat simply to help usher in some conversation. Sullivan wasn't going to be the first to speak, that much he was sure of, for despite the many questions spinning around his head, at that precise moment he had simply nothing to say.

'Mr Sullivan?' the man to his right said in a soft, slightly clipped voice, as close to gentle as Sullivan had ever heard. 'Are you okay, Mr Sullivan?'

Sullivan opened his eyes and slowly rolled towards the voice. A friendly face, half smile, half smug, looked down at him from above a small body tied tightly in an expensive suit and below a perfectly groomed hairdo. Even his thin beard seemed to have been styled. He jutted his hand down to Sullivan in a greeting and Sullivan caught sight of his watch – garish and gold.

Cheap in the circumstances, Sullivan thought. Yet Sullivan wasn't beyond civility, so he smiled and nodded at the man, his numbed hands too busy guarding the letters to attempt a handshake.

'My name is Joe Kendrick. Am I right in thinking you don't know who I am?'

Sullivan shook his head.

'No, Frankie suggested you wouldn't. No matter. The Party loves you, Mr Sullivan.'

Sullivan mumbled the well-rehearsed response into the space between them.

'We've tended to your bumps and bruises as best we can. We will get you some food and clean clothes if you would like. I understand it has been a stressful day.'

Sullivan laughed and looked away from Kendrick's face and down to his shoes – equally expensive and out of place. Sullivan wanted to spit on them to see what he would do, but he didn't think he had any spit left. It would have to keep. Kendrick was saying something else but Sullivan had stopped listening and was staring down at the bunched up letters on the bed, desperately trying to grip them in hands that didn't feel like his own. He started raking them up in his arms, bringing them to his nose and inhaling, looking for something in the smell that wouldn't come, a memory that wouldn't stir. Again and again he brought the letters to his face and breathed them in, the last time so strongly that he began a coughing fit that doubled him up. It was then that the other man spoke, a barely concealed impatience in his voice and a long sigh cushioning the words as they tumbled out of his velvet mouth, perfectly formed but short and direct.

'And you don't know me?'

Sullivan was already shaking his head before he opened his eyes. The coughing was severe and his body was jerking back and forth, tears plucked out by the letters mixing seamlessly with tears of pain. It took every ounce of effort he had left to look at the man, and even then it took a few seconds for Sullivan to recognise him. With recognition the coughing seemed to pass, scared into submission perhaps by what the eyes were trying hard to believe. The man crouched down beside the bed and held one beautifully manicured hand to one of Sullivan's stubble scarred cheeks, before taking it to his greasy forehead.

'You're burning up, Mr Sullivan.'

'But I'm freezing cold.'

'Yes, it is a very strange world, isn't it?'

'Yes. Yes Mr...yes, Prime Minister, it is.'

'Well, let's see if we can't fix you up good as new, Mr Sullivan.'

Edward Davenport, Prime Minister of Great Britain, rocked back on his heels, and stared intently at Sullivan, a thin smile creasing out on his face.

TOGETHER

1

Frankie Bergan walked out into the TV studio car park and stood staring at the electric fence crossing the main entrance. The huge NO TRESPASSING sign hanging off it, held up by one thin strip of wire, bobbed about in the stiff winter breeze, clanking and sighing on its last. He crossed to one end of the fence and turned the isolator switch, waited until he could convince himself he heard the gentle hum of electricity, and then, satisfied, or at the very least, willingly deceived, crossed to the small security hut next to the fence. The fence was tall, just shy of twenty feet, but it was deceptive. Back a few years, it would have been an ample deterrent for anyone, but now, now that the country had changed so dramatically, it was worthless and Bergan knew it all too well. Nothing stopped people nowadays beyond a bullet, but that being so, there was something in that light throbbing of electricity that calmed him. The fact it still worked, he had decided, was also reason enough to use it.

He caressed the butt of his pistol and entered the hut. A window was smashed and blood caked the wooden walls. Files and bits of paper lay about soaking up the mess and at his head flies investigated the worth of everything left. Pulling up a small stool he slumped down and stared back through the jagged glass in the window to the empty street beyond. He liked the quiet but he feared it. Ever since things had collapsed and the country had broken, he knew that silence was more often than not just a prelude to chaos. The attacks were frantic, and deadly, but they always came through the most unearthly quiet. There was no rhythm, no timetable and no plan. They just came, whenever they came – in groups, often in armies – attacking on sight and devouring whatever gave sustenance to their fury. For the last however many months, the only answer had been to keep moving, trundling towards that last safe place, and to keep one step ahead. He had led his merry band of misfits back and forth and kept them alive, most of them, but there was something in his bones that made the next step, the journey to come, seem like one of hopelessness. For the first time he had found himself questioning what he was doing. He was a man who played the odds and a betting man knew that they couldn't get away with it forever. Not with an enemy this size. He had considered that the feeling may be born simply from his dreams and was nothing that belonged in reality. Yet how many times can a person die in their dreams before it starts to feel like fate? He would always find himself asking his subconscious that particular question whenever he looked like brushing the feeling off. He took one giant hand to his throat and rubbed the fingers against the beard line. The choking feeling that came to him in his dreams was there again, just for a second.

The road ahead was lined with chestnut trees either snapped at the base or shorn of their branches and leaves. The pavements intersecting the main road to the studio were dotted with rubble and charred car parts, and the buildings that still stood within eyeshot were all but defeated. In the distance a blackened warehouse, looking to Bergan like a rotten chocolate cake, stood across the tip of the road swallowing it up. He let his eyes rest there for a moment, gently sweeping across the warehouse's wide body and then darting up and down at the many blown through windows, before finally stopping at the beams that poked out of the battered roof and then returning to the start and taking it all in again.

Everyone, even his wife, would always say that he had dead looking eyes, but there was no one whose vision was more alive. Davenport used to joke that Bergan could see through walls, such was his ability to sense danger before it chose to show itself. Whatever it was that so primed Bergan's instinct, it was in play again now as those black eyes landed with a graceful swoop at the top right window of the warehouse and waited. Something was in that warehouse; somehow to Bergan it was obvious, so very blatant indeed that it may as well have hung a sign over its head and given him a wave.

Pulling his pistol from its holster and resting it in his lap, and plucking his walkie-talkie from its pouch on his jacket, he waited, stock-still and calm, his body ready for the reveal his eyes had already seen.

Seconds became minutes and the gloomy clouds above bloomed together and seemed to press down on the road ahead making him squint his eyes as they burrowed deep into the darkness of the window. He didn't move, not an inch, one hand cradling the walkie-talkie, the other on the pistol. He could see a flash of light, something in the increasing gloom; he convinced himself he could hear voices, low scratching growls of voices, inhuman and angry. He willed the window to show its secrets, his eyes threatening and encouraging in one blank stare, and then, finally, almost as if dragged forcibly into the fading light by his sheer command, a small dark cloud of pigeons erupted clumsily from the window on the top floor and scattered like buckshot into the sky. Bergan shot up from the stool and trained his pistol from the broken window of the security hut, the walkie-talkie at his lips, thumb on the button. As the pigeons scattered in their graceless formation and the silence fell once more, he took a step back and walked out of the hut, crossing to one side and staring out between the wires of the fence. The pigeons hadn't quelled his senses. He wasn't satisfied. A coward would be relieved; Bergan wanted to know what had made the pigeons fly away.

Thumbing the button of the walkie-talkie, he spoke into it in a low whisper. 'Maddox? Get on the roof. Eyes on the warehouse to the east. Get ready to move.' Without waiting for an answer Bergan put the walkie-talkie back into its pouch, and with one final look down the road, entered the building and mounted the stairs to Davenport's office, three at a time.

2

Bend Lane television studios had once been home to the great and the good, or at least television's version of the myth. Like a permanent reminder of worth, framed photos lined the walls as far as the eye could see. Almost every side room Sullivan walked past seemed to be a dressing room of sorts; dismantled self-worship holes each with a huge mirrored heart. There were so many mirrors. So many smiling faces. Even without all that was happening, had happened, and threatened to continue, the sight of the photos and the stench of the cheap would have turned Sullivan's stomach. Sullivan was not much of a one for TV but even he recognised some of the faces staring back from the walls; magicians, comedians, soap stars, singers and the curious tuxedoed jack-of-all-trades known simply as entertainers. Some of the photos were autographed, some foxing, some ripped and smashed, but all had the same vulgar pang of a trapped desperation, caught in a moment for generations to see. He saw a photo of the old comedian that his wife loved so much hanging over the door to one dressing room and struggled to recall his name. He'd stood in line at a book signing to get him to sign his autobiography for his wife, many years ago –

monosyllabic, drunken, self absorbed old fool, Sullivan remembered vividly – but the name escaped him, the ultimate insult for this parade of fading whores.

The squat man with the hat led Sullivan past the last dressing room and turned into a cafeteria where he presented, with pride, two bowls of leek and potato soup and a broken, brittle baguette. The room seemed to stretch for a mile, never ending wooden benches splitting the cracked tiled flooring, sitting under a fug of smoke and the horrid congealing smell of burnt food. The man took a seat opposite Sullivan and watched intently as Sullivan devoured both bowls, stopping only to belch and nod an occasional thank you, and then began mopping the dregs clean with the stiff bread. It was the satisfied smile on the man's face and the questioning eyes that made Sullivan realise the man was in fact the chef. The chef's hat on his head was so flat and squashed that Sullivan had thought it were a beret.

The chef was called John Delmarno, but was Turtle to his friends, and Sullivan was told that was how he should refer to him too. As Turtle watched him eating, Sullivan was put in mind of a parent on sports day watching their child come first in the sack race; the beaming smile, the clasped hands, the expectant excitement in his eyes. Cooking, for Turtle, was a fine art, the finest maybe, and he was quick to tell Sullivan that he had complained to Bergan from the start about what he was expected to work with. As the food supplies had dwindled, so Turtle's temperamental artistic rage had flourished. No one liked to sit near Turtle when they were eating, and not just because he had been serving twenty years for poisoning his former employers when Bergan happened upon him, they also found the fact he wouldn't stop talking rather an unhelpful aid to satisfactory digestion.

'How many have you met? You met Maddox yet?' Turtle asked, as Sullivan finished the bread and began attacking the plastic bowls with his tongue. 'We're a sorry bunch of bastards, but it's not all beyond hope.'

'I met some guys. Bergan. A kid. There was some short bloke in a suit. And the Prime Minister, y'know? This is really great soup. Thanks.'

'Limp leeks, lacks bite. But you're lucky it's not a chicken night.'

'How long have you been here?'

'I've been with Frankie almost from the start; after all, a chef is about as important a role as there is to any team and Frankie knew that. He didn't deliberate long, he didn't have the luxury, and he took to me as easily as he takes to anyone, which is to say I didn't question anything and so Frankie felt able to tolerate me. Don't ask him too many questions, okay? He doesn't like that, it gets him riled. Just be grateful you aren't still banged up, that's the way to look at it. I reckon that's why Frankie sprung most of us from prison, at least this way we have a purpose, right?'

Turtle continued talking for another quarter of an hour – his machine gun rattle of a voice something Sullivan knew he was going to tire of quickly – firing off names of people Sullivan didn't recognise, places he'd never heard of and recipes for food he didn't care about. When Turtle finally shut up and gathered the bowls on the bench, Sullivan felt like he'd been woken from a dream. Coughing away a touch of heartburn he stood and followed Turtle to the kitchens at the back of the cafeteria. They were chatting lightly about some large breasted singer who was hanging in a lopsided photo frame next to the freezer – her Hollywood smile now more a post-box to an empty house – when Sullivan saw Hudson sitting alone at the other side of the cafeteria, eyes fixed down into a coffee mug, his hands clasped around it as if it were holding him anchored to the world.

'What's the deal with him, Turtle?'

'I don't know how Frankie expects me to keep any kind of standards when he keeps changing things,' Turtle sighed as he scratched one chubby hand against a hotchpotch beard of black and grey. 'He didn't want anything anyway, but I gave him a coffee, don't think he's going to drink it. He's been looking into it for nearly an hour. Don't know what Frankie was thinking.'

'He was supposed to leave him there?'

'Well, yeah. I suppose.' Turtle was at the sink now, his hands working away at the bowls beneath a small field of bubbles. His eyes never left Sullivan as he spoke, never once ventured toward the subject of the conversation, he seemed almost unable to acknowledge him. 'I did a spin at Thinwater when he was starting out. Between you, me and the kitchen sink, I don't care for the man. I got no beef with screws, a man's gotta earn a crust whichever way he sees fit to do it, but your man Hudson is a bastard of the first order. Seen him beat a man to a pulp. Man with a family. Man with kids. You gotta be tough these days, you gotta have the steel, man, you really do. But there's no one that should enjoy it. It's survival. Not entertainment. Fuck him. Frankie should have left him to burn. C'mon, I will give you the guided tour.'

Sullivan turned back towards Hudson and watched him gazing down into his mug. His face was rigid and stony, his hands much the same. He was so pale Sullivan wasn't sure where his face ended and the curdled cream coloured walls of the cafeteria began. 'Give me a minute, Turtle, will you?'

While Turtle hovered at the door to the cafeteria, flashing looks to the clock on the wall above him and strumming the doorframe with his fingers, Sullivan approached Hudson. The nearer he got to the former jailer of Thinwater prison, the more inhuman he started to look; his pale skin made Sullivan think of a chalk cliff face, the deep furrows on his forehead, of leaking ink.

Sullivan suddenly didn't know what to say. 'Mr

Hudson, are you okay?' The very words made Sullivan scrunch his face up in contempt at himself. 'I mean…can I get you another coffee? That one seems to have gone cold.'

Hudson didn't move. Behind them, Turtle coughed and knocked loudly on the cafeteria door. Sullivan moved across to Hudson's side and bent down to him. 'Hello? Mr Hudson?'

'Where's my wife?' The words came in a whisper but still took Sullivan by surprise. 'She's late.'

'Do you know who I am, Mr Hudson?'

'Sullivan. Five years, two months. Shot a man. Bang. Bang. Bang.'

'Do you know where you are?'

'It doesn't matter where I am. Where are we going?'

'I don't know.'

'Do you ever…do you ever feel like…you remember at school, the kid that always got picked last for sports? Do you ever feel like that kid, Sullivan five years, two months?'

'I don't understand, Mr Hudson.'

'Where's my wife?'

'I don't know.'

Hudson's words were dreamy and distant, a weedy mimic of the barking brute that had ruled Sullivan's life for so long. 'I always used to get picked first for teams. But I think we're losing, Sullivan five years, two months. I think we're on the wrong team.'

'I don't understand.'

'You should go back to your cell now, five years, two months. I will tell you when you can come out. When the time is right. I know what I will do then. Do you know what you will do when the time comes?'

Hudson turned slightly to Sullivan, his eyes moving across the bench, his hands leaving the coffee mug and rising to his face, the index finger on his right hand resting clumsily against his forehead, his mouth creasing into a crazy smile. Hudson's thumb cocked the hammer on his loaded finger and the last words Sullivan heard him speak came out with the finality of a snapped branch from a felled tree.

'Bang. Bang. Bang.'

3

Davenport paced the office on the top floor of the studio, flashing intermittent looks at himself in a long mirror propped against the back wall. He'd put his jacket down in the office the day they arrived, marking it his own during their stay there. It was the biggest office on the top floor and both those facts made Davenport feel at home. It was a small thing; in their current situation such gestures were fairly redundant, but Davenport had developed the habit of self-importance a long time ago and it was hard to accept irrelevance. They had arrived at the studios in such a hurry and through such chaos that no one else had thought to question it. Bergan, Maddox and Kleinman had been too busy attending to Grennaught's injuries to care about their boss and the rest were too preoccupied with securing the building and working the watch in shifts to have any time to worry about where Davenport pitched tent. It was only Kendrick that could see it for what it was, gazing around the room as he did with a wide, beaming smile and winking at Davenport like a conspiratorial lover. At times Kendrick made Davenport cringe. They had been together so many years, long before Davenport took office, long before they joined the Party and politics was even a realistic goal, but they were never actually friends. Acquaintances certainly, allies perhaps, but they had never really made the time to like each other.

As Davenport strode around the office once more, Kendrick lifted his feet on to the long oak table in the middle of the room and started gazing admiringly at his shoes. Bergan remained stoically at the door, his stillness in body and face somehow saying all that was necessary. A large map was pinned to the wall by the one window in the room, a crude black line drawn in pen from the point where they now stood to the point they needed to be, and Davenport rapped a fist against the wonky black circle drawn around their planned destination as he passed.

'Suddenly looks a long way away, don't you think?'

'A day, tops. Weather permitting.'

'Just weather? You said there were groups at the edge of the city. Hundreds you said. You are confident that torching Thinwater will…'

'Look, who knows? There are no givens any more Eddie. Frankie thought it worth a shot and I'm inclined to agree with him.'

'Any reason to change plans?'

'We move out at first light. We stick to the plan, no reason to change anything. Right, Frank?'

Bergan shrugged, nodded and looked away from the two men and towards the window.

'Communications?' Davenport continued.

'Fucked. Everything is fucked. Baxter's been beavering away at it, but there's nothing there. Nothing that really works. Still no word from the hill.'

'Nothing?'

'He's getting nothing on the radio but static, says he hears faint voices every now and again but can't make anything out. I dunno.'

'What about radio stations? Has he picked up any radio stations? Is anyone still broadcasting?'

'I don't know.'

'You don't know?'

'That's right. I don't know, Eddie'

'Isn't that just the truth? You don't know a damn thing. Neither of you. My great advisors! That's a joke. You two couldn't advise piss up a wall.'

Bergan moved across the room so quickly and purposefully that it took Davenport by surprise, and he jumped back out of his path as if he had just stepped out in front of a juggernaut.

'Don't mind me, Frankie!' Davenport bellowed. 'Just you pretend I'm not here!'

'You okay there, Frankie?' Kendrick asked across his footwear.

Bergan said nothing as he took position at the window, resting his giant hands either side of the frame and gently leaning his forehead against the glass. The city looked so quiet from up there on the top floor of the studio. The battered skyline, torn through by half demolished buildings, was covered in a misty grey hue and the snow they had left behind at Thinwater prison was already settling across the city and moving closer. Clean patches of white peeped out on the far away hills making the shadow choked city streets all the more oppressive. Bergan's eyes fell back on to the warehouse. Outside the window a pigeon swooped past, turned in the air and flew back to where it had come from.

'What if the safe house has been compromised?' Davenport was at Bergan's back now, peering around his giant frame at the city skyline. 'What if the point team didn't secure it? You would have us move out to an unsecured location, Joe? Particularly that place.'

'That place?'

'With all that's happened there?'

'Nothing happened there. Ten workers screwed the Party, that's all that happened.'

'Ten people disappeared there, that's what happened, Joe.'

'I see no reason to change anything. The months we have invested in that place, the work that's been done. Eddie... there is nowhere else. Right now it's probably the most secure place in the country.'

'Hardly saying much is it?'

'We're here to keep you safe, Eddie. Perhaps you should start trusting us to do that? Right, Frank?' Bergan remained silent, his giant hands moving from the windowframe and rubbing at the condensation building up on the panes of glass. 'Besides, even if the point team failed, even if a group found the safe house, so what? We can deal with that. And even if we can't, which is a big if, because…'

'It's a big "if" is it?' Davenport barked back, his hands grabbing at the top of his hips and his chest thrusting forward in one last attempt to look important. 'We have enough ammunition left to feel safe walking into that do we? Just how much do we actually have left, Joe? Frank? And food for that matter? Do we have enough food to see us past tomorrow if there's a problem?'

'There is food at the safe house, and weaponry too. At least there should be.'

'Should be?'

'Look, what do you want from me?' Kendrick yelled. 'Yes, there should be. That was part of the plan. The plan, Eddie, do you remember the plan? The safe house? The bunker? All that money the Party squirreled away just to shove at that place? All this ringing any bells? We go to the safe house. As planned. At first light. If it's been compromised, if it's been found, if Schaeffer has…'

Bergan's right hand suddenly shattered the pane of glass it had been rubbing and he titled forward at the sudden change in pressure, his great body pushing into the remaining glass as his wrist flopped out of the hole between two toothy shards. He stood motionless for a second as the snow-flecked wind swirled against his bloody slab of a palm, and the jagged piece of glass that now sat plum in the centre. Grabbing it roughly between the index finger and thumb of his left hand he yanked it out and tossed it down to the ground below, then retracted his hand and stared back into the room as if someone had just insulted him.

'Frank?' Davenport said gently, backing up a few steps.

Bergan moved around the edge of the table, past Davenport and towards the door, the blood on his hand now oozing between his fingers and dropping in trickles to the floor. He stopped in the doorway and looked back into the room, first to Kendrick, already back gazing at his shoes, and then to Davenport, stood framed by the window and the ever-darkening gloom outside.

'We move out. As soon as possible.'

4

Turtle led the way out of the cafeteria and up a large flight of stairs to a room that Sullivan assumed must have once been used for hair and make up in the overgrown child's playground. The light bulbs lining the mirrors and a large collection of wigs in a huge cardboard box gave the room's past life away. Beyond that it was all decay; the walls were crumbling and the roof was leaking, small yellow puddles gathered in the uneven floor, the electrics were exposed, windows smashed. Damp was in the walls, woodworm in the floors. A heavily bearded man in washed out khaki was leaning over an old transistor radio in the corner of the room. Kleinman, looking like the other end of the evolutionary scale, was standing over him, a wretched copper wig sitting at a slant on his head, watching Sullivan with a child's curiosity. Sullivan saw for the first time just how young Kleinman looked and found himself thinking again of his daughter. How old had she been? He desperately tried to remember, to scrabble back something of that that had been lost, but, as with everything else it seemed, it wasn't easily to hand.

She wanted a rat for her birthday one year. Where do you find a rat?

'This is Sullivan then,' Turtle offered the others, waving an arm around the room as if there were a hundred Sullivan's. 'New blood. Ex of Thinwater, Grennaught's replacement.'

'We've met,' Kleinman said as he gave Sullivan a quick, disinterested nod, the wig slipping off his head and landing in a puddle on the floor.

'Kid here is Kleinman, he was in a young offenders outside the capital, back in the old country,' Turtle continued, seemingly oblivious to the animosity Kleinman was making no effort to hide. 'Got busted for car jacking. He's our wheels. The grizzled old walnut on the floor there is Baxter. He's our communications king.' Baxter raised a hairy hand in a half-hearted wave but didn't look up. 'He was twenty years in the army. One of the last ones out the door, eh Baxter?'

'Are you saying we don't have an army any more?' Sullivan asked the room.

'Shit man, where you been hiding yourself? Jail?' Turtle said with a loud laugh. The room didn't take up the joke.

Kleinman stepped forward and drew up to Sullivan. 'What were you in Thinwater for, square peg?'

'Frankie says he shot a man,' Baxter said into the floor just as a crackle and whine screeched out of the radio and died amongst the stale air of the room.

'That true, Sullivan?' Kleinman asked. 'You shoot a man? You a badass? Or are you innocent like the rest of us?'

'Life screwed me, kid.'

'Screw it back. It makes you feel better.'

'I will remember that.'

'Grennaught was a good man. Good shooter…'

'Police marksman before…all of it…' Baxter chipped in.

'…You think you can replace him do you?'

'Ok, let's not swing dicks in a confined space,' Turtle said stepping between them and nudging Sullivan back to the doorway. 'I'm just giving Sullivan the guided tour Kleinman, put your macho posturing away. You haven't the hair on the balls to pull it off. What have you heard from the top, we still moving out at dawn? Maddox seems to think so.'

'You met Maddox yet, new boy?' Kleinman asked Sullivan through the sort of cocky grin only the young ever seem capable of pulling off. The more he spoke, the more he postured, the more Sullivan saw a sense of self-confidence bought from the strength of others. Kleinman was the sort of kid on the playground who holds the bully's coat for him. 'He's gonna love you, Sullivan.'

'I'll be sure to bend over for him, kid.'

Turtle turned Sullivan around, planted his hands on his shoulders, and marched him from the room and back on to the stairs. Kleinman remained in the doorway, his arms crossed petulantly over his chest, cocky grin fading with each step Sullivan took. As Sullivan and Turtle disappeared at the turn in the stairs, Baxter's radio fizzed and crackled and died again.

Turtle and Sullivan came out on to a long landing with window-lined offices running down one side. Bloodied bits of paper and shredded folders lay on the floor, a filing cabinet was on its side and chairs and bits of broken table lay here and there, all around. As they passed the first office, Sullivan saw a man walking across a fire escape outside the window – submachine gun slung over one shoulder, cigar clamped between his lips – and then begin to casually climb a ladder to the roof. Sullivan recognised his black fatigues instantly, the bulky frame, the cuts and scars on his shaven head, and suddenly he was back on the bed in that impossibly white room, hugging his wife's letters. The hatred he felt for that man then, was bubbling back inside him, spilling over his heart. Turtle turned Sullivan away from the room and offered him a gentle shake of the head. Sullivan chanced a look back and saw the cigar smoke breaking apart on the harsh November wind, and then Turtle was in front of him again, pushing him on.

'Theo Maddox,' Turtle said, like it was meant to mean something. 'There's not one of us, at one time or another, that didn't wish Frankie had left him to rot in jail.'

'That desperate for numbers is he?'

'The man can shoot. Man, he can shoot. Maddox could shoot a rogue eyelash off you from a different postcode with one hand on his dick and his trousers round his ankles. Never seen anything like it.'

'Good guy to have on side then.'

'Maddox is on his own side. Don't think you're getting anything more than a cold shoulder from him. Story goes he said to the judge at his trial that adding attempted murder to his list of crimes was an insult to him. He says he said to the judge, "Your Honour, when I attempt to murder someone I succeed and I strongly disapprove of your insult to my career." You get the picture. Anyway, we're not all that bad, wouldn't want to give you the wrong impression and have you running for the hills. I mean, if you could, if you had a choice.' Turtle gave a small, overly polite cough, and steered Sullivan forward again. 'You ever been in a TV studio before? I'm a little underwhelmed if I'm being honest. Anyway, they want a word, come this way.'

As they picked a route through the debris on the floor and made their way toward Davenport's office, Sullivan started stacking up the many questions in his mind, sorting them into some priority, trying to claw back some semblance of reality that he could understand, but in the end the one question he knew that he would have to ask again sooner or later was a simple one – why me? He had nothing to offer, he was nothing to these people, was not a thug or a killer, he couldn't work a radio, read a map or shoot a gun like any expert – despite what his history may report – he had no special knowledge to impart, no opinions to share, stories to tell or advice to give. He had nothing. Indeed as far as the real world was concerned, he was nothing. But hadn't there been something in Bergan's eyes as they had talked in Hudson's office? Sullivan had thought so, but with Bergan it was so hard to tell. When a man's eyes are dead they don't ask questions. They already seem to have all the answers.

5

Davenport was sitting at the table in his office staring into the dregs of a glass of whisky. He barely lifted his eyes as Bergan ushered Sullivan in and shoved him crudely into a seat at the opposite side of the table. Bergan, his hand freshly bandaged, returned to the broken window and continued his silent watch.

'The Party loves you, Mr Sullivan.'

'The Party loves you too, Mr Davenport. Sir.'

'Can I tempt you to some whisky, Sullivan? It's not very good but it's a wise man that learns to find pleasure in the substandard. Keeps you going, don't you find?'

'Little goals, sir.'

'Yes, little goals. I suppose so.' Davenport raised an empty glass to Sullivan.

'No, thank you. But thank you all the same.'

'How are you? Feeling human again?'

'I'm not sure I would go that far.'

Davenport laughed to himself and looked up to face Sullivan. Wordlessly they felt each other out, groping their way into the conversation both knew they had to have.

'You have questions, I'm sure?'

'I do. Many. If I may?'

'Time is short. We are about to move out again. Have you met everyone?'

'Most people, I think, I don't know. May I ask…'

'Why you were picked?'

'Yes.'

'Frankie needed a replacement for Grennaught. He found you.'

'Simple as that?'

'If you like.'

'Forgive me, but I'm not sure I've got what you need. I'm not a killer.'

'Your records would suggest otherwise.'

'I was protecting my family. It was self defence.'

'I see.'

'I don't expect you to believe me.'

Davenport shrugged and swirled the whisky in his glass. 'I'm not sure that really matters anymore.'

'It matters to me. I'm no murderer.'

'At the risk of stating the obvious our pool of available talent is somewhat shallow these days, Sullivan. However you choose to tag your offence, we haven't the luxury of great choice.'

'That's it?'

'Is that not enough?'

'No. Not really.'

Davenport looked back to his whisky glass and sighed. At the window, Bergan had his walkie-talkie to his lips again. Above them footsteps thudded across the roof and the ceiling moaned in its response, its bare light flex swinging like a hangman's rope under the vibration. Bergan started plucking the loose shards of glass from the pane and then leaned his head out, looking east, breathing in the sharp air.

'Anything?' Bergan whispered into the walkie-talkie. 'Maddox? You got anything?'

'Nothing, Frank. Nothing here,' came the response from the walkie-talkie. 'Can't see anything out there.'

'Keep on it.'

Davenport eased himself from his chair and walked a full circle around the room, past the map on the wall, past Bergan, behind Sullivan, stopping where he started and perching on the edge of the table, whisky glass turning in the effeminate grip of beautifully manicured hands, wrong in style, symbol and sin. He looked down at Sullivan, his face caught by the slip of light slicing through the musty darkness from the outside corridor, and he spoke in soft tones, fragile enough to shatter at the wrong ears, and when the words came they violated Sullivan, piercing his heart with cold assurance. 'Your wife loves you very much, Mr Sullivan.'

Almost instantly Sullivan felt dizzy; the room tilted and fell back out of step with what he had seen before. Those lethal words repeated in an echo, each louder than the time before, and they infested him. Davenport was floating over him, beaming down through the cut of light and trying to straighten the old lag's body by resting those clean hands at his shoulder. His wife's face came to him, her smell washed over him, her hands, her arms, their touch was against his skin, pressing hard and trying to hold on. Then she went again, back to where she hid, back to the safe part of Sullivan that no one could ever find. His eyes lifted to those of Davenport and they asked the question better than he could ever have spoken it.

'She worked for me. In the last weeks, before… before we had to take flight…you don't even know what's happened to the country do you, Mr Sullivan?'

'It's gone funny.'

'Funny?'

'Even before I went down things had… your predecessor…'

'Yes. Dreadful man.'

'There were riots and everything went nuts…I remember that. That government, that joke of a party that we all created, they broke apart and got ousted. There was anarchy on the streets. No law. No recourse. By the time you and yours got into power, people had fallen too far to care. The country had broken and you were too late to fix it. People didn't want it fixing.' Sullivan shifted in his chair, his eyes never leaving Davenport's wandering own. 'My wife wrote me letters…' he could feel the tears again, those wretched bloody tears, but he held them back, he was on a roll now, the questions and the memories, everything tumbling up through him and spitting out in quick garbled words. 'Someone edited her letters. Why would they do that? Why take her words? They stopped allowing visitors there before long, so why take people's words too? Haven't you people already taken enough? You people took everything we had that mattered in that place. Fuck freedom, that prison took our purpose. It took my heart!'

'Well, you were paying your debt to society, Mr Sullivan. You had to be punished.'

Sullivan knew Davenport wasn't really listening, that he had nothing but cue card responses to give him, but he blundered on regardless, Davenport had reached in and opened him up, Davenport would just have to deal with it.

'I don't care what's happened to the country, I never did, what does it matter to me that things have folded and people are killing each other? Why should I care about you and the Party? You want to try and rule this mess of a country, you go ahead and try, but I just don't care anymore. My wife and my daughter, they are my country, my whole world. You know what? Once they stopped letting people into Thinwater, once they closed the doors, if I had known that was how it would stay, that that was as good as it was going to get, then the Wash may as well have had me. They may as well have fucking had everything left.'

'I know it's hard to believe, and I know you won't want to understand, but you must take my word for it, you were in the best place, Mr Sullivan. The things that have gone on…'

'You will forgive me if I don't agree?'

'Sure, yes, okay, it sounded a touch cheap when I said it. But there is truth in it. Believe me. There is so much left for the Party to do to get this country back. There has been so much bloodshed, Sullivan. We've all seen too much, far too much that no one would wish to see. We are trying, we really are. The Party are trying to start again because we care about our country. We care about our people. We believe in civilization. There has to be something left when all this madness passes. There simply has to be. There has to be answers. There has to be a future.'

'You mean the Wash? Did that not give you the answer you wanted? Did that not create the people you needed?'

'Not a practice I ever subscribed to. Not the Party's finest hour. We are an ever-evolving beast, Sullivan and so mistakes will be made on the path to the right answer. When we took power there was anarchy on the streets, pure anarchy, like you said, it was a crazy time. Madness. We had to find our way, we had to try and get a grip with what was happening and retain some semblance of order. We had to forge a path for rebuilding the country. Though I may not agree with what went on, I can understand how my predecessor was sold on it. The Wash was a desperate measure because we were living in desperate times. When I took charge I outlawed it immediately. There were still some that advocated it and it went on for a while, I know, against my orders, but he...he is a very persuasive man. You have heard of Ellis Schaeffer, of course?'

'Who?'

'You haven't heard of him?'

'No.'

Davenport squinted, his expression one of doubt, he looked to be scrutinising, disbelieving, staring into Sullivan for a truth that wasn't there.

'Are you sure?'

'Yes. I'm sure. Why, what did I miss?'

Bergan looked around momentarily, first to Sullivan, then to Davenport and then back to the window and the walkie-talkie in his hand. 'Anything?'

'Nothing Frank. Think you called it wrong,' Maddox's tinny walkie-talkie voice replied. 'This place is dead.'

'Keep looking.'

Davenport was smiling back at Sullivan. A smile in itself, a sign of enjoyment in these awful surroundings, was suspicious enough, but Davenport wore something inhuman in that grin and Sullivan hated it. Hated him. 'Schaeffer was the instigator of the Wash. A madman, some say. A scientist. He believed he could cure our country's ills and make us human again. He convinced others that he could wipe people's pasts and leave them open to a new future.'

'Steal their memories, you mean?'

Davenport shrugged and smiled again. 'I'm not a man of science. I can't pretend to understand how it all works. I just saw what it did. "Empty vessels" he would call them. But these people were of no use to man nor beast. He had damaged them beyond anything humanity could save. Who knows, perhaps he could have achieved what he claimed in time, but I couldn't allow what he was doing to play out to proof. You kill a hundred, five hundred, and maybe you find the answer, or maybe you are just a mass murderer. I couldn't allow it to continue. You had friends taken for the Wash?'

'I don't have friends. Where's my wife?'

Davenport let a long and weary breath creep out of him, and slid the whisky glass on to the table. 'She worked as a secretary for the Party. She was a good woman, a fine person. She talked of you often and with such love. I know she only applied for the job so she could have time with me, time to talk about you, to argue your case, plead your release. She loved you very much.'

'Loved?'

'With all that's happened...'

'My wife is not dead, Mr Davenport. I know she isn't.'

'The simple truth is, I can't say either way. My offices were destroyed, people died there. Good people. You understand? I have no way of knowing whether she was there at the time. She made me promise to search you out. She asked me to find you and make you safe. To make sure you didn't die in that prison. You wonder why Hudson was so attentive, why he kept you from the Wash and the riots, the murder and the mayhem? It was because of your wife Sullivan, and the debt I felt I owed her. It was our friendship. Such a thing can still exist, even in times like these. I find optimism in that. I find hope. Maybe you do too? I only wish we could have got to you sooner. So you ask me why you are here, that is all I can give you. Is that enough?'

Sullivan sat there soaking it all in and as he did, as the pretty picture of his wife, that timeless photo he kept locked away for safe keeping developed in his mind, he broke into deep, uncontrollable tears, and this time he made no pretence, and no effort to stop. The emptiness that had consumed him since arrival at the TV studios was now total and complete, and he felt as if he were floating through space, with nothing to see and nowhere to land.

'We have been moving around for months, from one hideout to another,' Davenport continued, slipping off the table and turning away from Sullivan's tears. 'We were a great many more at the start, friends, family and colleagues. The Party have pockets of people throughout the country, but for now we must remain apart. We must stay alive until it is safe for us again.' Davenport trailed off, distracted by the heavy footsteps on the roof, growing stronger, walking faster. He looked to the map on the wall and then back into the room. 'We continue to head west now. We have a secure place, a safe house. Probably the only place left now that is. The Party worked on it for many months. As soon as things started to break, they started to build…'

A second set of footsteps began charging up the staircase outside the office. Bergan was leaning from the window, bellowing into the walkie-talkie. 'What's happening up there? What do you see? Talk to me!'

'It was decided that it would be where we started again. Where we would start to rebuild. Its purpose was corrupted by the Wash, by Schaeffer, but we will save this country from itself, Sullivan. We will be victorious over this madness. I sent a point team ahead…'

'We are at war then?' Sullivan yanked himself from his chair and wiped his face with a sleeve, his words quiet and broken, but forceful enough to break into Davenport's' well-rehearsed speech. 'We really are at war?'

'Yes. Yes, Sullivan. We are.'

'With whom?'

'With each other dear man, with each other.'

There was a thud on the roof, and then a bang on the door, and then a bullet – the first of hundreds that were to be fired at them over the next quarter of an hour – broke through the windowframe just above Bergan's left shoulder and embedded itself into the far wall. In all the ensuing confusion and panic, past the gunfire and the screaming, the one thing that would stay with Sullivan as clear as day was the sight of a bullet hole in the map on the wall. He saw it as he fell and the image seemed to imprint itself on his mind. The small dark hole was neatly centred in the middle of the recently drawn black circle, and just above it, flecked with blood, and scorched with heat, were the bold letters on the map spelling out the name BLEEKER HILL.

AIR

1

They poured from the warehouse in droves, wave after wave of small black shapes; ants breaking out of that rotten old chocolate cake at the end of the road. They came out of windows and through the damaged roof, from the doors and across the empty grounds, swarming together into one congested blur, moving forward towards the TV studio. Some had guns, most sticks and clubs and other makeshift weaponry. Some screamed, raw, primeval wails, whilst others just charged forward, heads bowed in an ominous, threatening silence. A group broke away looking for other ways in, but the main mass just ploughed on, rolled through the deserted road and towards the fence that would not hold them.

Bergan was out of Davenport's office in a flash, barging into Kendrick and Kleinman on the other side of the door, and then shots came again and Kleinman was hit in the back, the blast spinning him around on the spot and throwing him roughly against Bergan, pushing him into the wall and then down to the ground. Baxter was running up the stairwell toward them, Turtle puffing away behind him. What was left of the window in the office fell inwards and the foundations shook as half the wall came away with it and the room was peeled open across one whole side. Sullivan was knocked backwards on to the floor, falling arse-over-head and landing with a heavy thud on his front. Hands were on him in a flash, clean and beautiful hands, and as he looked up he saw Davenport had him in a tight hug and was dragging him toward the door. Kendrick was behind him, leading him out, one hand at the collar of Davenport's suit jacket.

'Burn the map! Burn the damn map!' Kendrick was yelling as he crawled, pulled and guided them to the door.

Baxter dived across them into the room, rolling over and stopping on his haunches. Turtle was darting down to his knees, skidding across the office floor and then coming to a stop next to Kleinman. They tipped the giant oak table on to its side, ducked behind it and pulled the screaming Kleinman to them just as more bullets tore into the room through the gaping hole, tearing into the flesh of the walls and across the exposed lip of the table. Bergan scrabbled across the floor and ducked through the door, narrowly avoiding being struck as it sheared off its hinges and landed at the feet of the retreating Davenport, Kendrick and Sullivan. Bergan waved them on, hunkered down and craned back into the room at his trapped men, his corpse eyes alive, searching for a way out.

Above them footsteps pounded across the roof and

angry blasts of machine gun fire cut though the sky to the ground below. Maddox was easily heard through the broken wall screaming abuse to unseen people, the horrid joy in his voice every bit as vicious as the explosion of fire from his weapon. The ceiling started to crumble, dropping bits of plasterboard to the floor like oversized confetti, and as Maddox's footsteps came again, a second torrent of gunfire blasted down from the roof making the room rock, the roof buckle and Maddox even more excited.

'Baxter?' Bergan was half in the doorway, half out, pistol raised high, rigid in his grip. 'Can you get Kleinman out?'

'Have to drag him by the feet, I dunno Frank. How exposed are we?'

Bergan looked to where the far wall used to be and where now just a broken, jagged hole stood, beckoning the world in, and slowly shook his head.

'Turtle? You hit?'

'I'm okay, Frank.'

'We don't have much time. We need to move.'

Another wave of gunfire hit the room and broke into the side of the wall above where Bergan was crouched and he flinched to the side, dropping flat to the floor. The table, that fragile shield, suddenly broke down the middle as if sliced in two by an invisible chainsaw and a bullet ripped through Kleinman's right shoulder sending a jet of blood across Baxter's forest of facial hair and another childish scream from Kleinman's mouth as his shoulder bone snapped and broke through his skin. He started to jig and spasm in Baxter's grip, the one hand strong enough to move slapping at Baxter's beard in limp desperation.

'Frankie, we have to get him out of here! I have to try.'

'Wait!' Bergan bellowed into the floor as the gunfire from above started again and Maddox's whooping and name-calling reached a pitch of hysterics.

'Frankie! We have to move him!' Baxter shouted back, Kleinman's hand probing and pulling at his mouth and hair. 'Shield me!'

'Wait!'

Baxter was up into a crouch and grabbing at Kleinman's ankles. Almost instantly a bullet chipped off the corner of the table and entered Baxter just above his heart sending him flying back across the room and into the empty doorway where he struck the frayed border and spun around, his back to the room and the next blast of gunfire. A second and third bullet entered the back of his skull and he dropped like a lead weight in front of Bergan. As if for a final flourish, a terrible curtain call, the following wave of gunfire brought the roof in; the cheap ceiling spewing its contents on to the heads of those in the office as if pulled inside out by a giant's hand. With it came Maddox who landed just in front of the table with a mighty thud, a large submachine gun following him down and finding its way into his grip before anyone even had a chance to blink. He rolled over on to his side, arched the machine gun up over the broken wall and then, preceded by a defiant scream, unleashed the remaining bullets down on to the massed enemy below.

Bergan bounded back into the room and grabbed Kleinman's ankles, pulling him, yanking him, unceremoniously to the doorway. Turtle crawled along behind, trying to support Kleinman's head, pushing past Baxter like he were just another part of the furniture, not affording him a look, knowing not to allow it. As they turned into the stairwell, Bergan shouted back over his shoulder, struggling to make himself heard over the incessant gunfire. 'Get the map! Maddox! Destroy the map!'

Bergan's words remained unheard. By the time Maddox had fired empty and backed from the room, reloading and turning out into the stairwell, following the others down, it would have been too late anyway. The cold fury in Maddox's brilliant, blue eyes was already sold on the next enemy.

Kendrick led Davenport and Sullivan to the ground floor, turning them into a long office lined corridor. Behind them the stairwell shook and shuddered as it echoed out the ferocious gunplay above. The three men hunkered down, tucking themselves into an office doorway momentarily as a rain of concrete and metal showered the corridor in front of them, spat through the throat of the stairwell, shattering in deathly loud blasts in front of them. Kendrick was the first up, tugging at Davenport's arm, pulling him on. Davenport, in turn, was grabbing at Sullivan and doing the same. There were footsteps behind them, more loud thudding blasts, and as Sullivan chanced a look back he saw Maddox bouncing down the stairs towards them, three steps at a time, rifles slung over each shoulder, submachine gun under one arm and an impossibly fat cigar clamped into his mouth.

The offices around them suddenly began to take their turn; the steady wave of gunfire from outside the walls crashing into them, puncturing through them and punching out the windows, as each room they stumbled past was slowly dismantled, eaten alive and spat back out by the enveloping tide of bullets, a force that seemed to surround them, follow them and nibble at their heels, looking to chase them down and swallow them whole. Maddox began responding in kind, his huge bulk of a body swinging left and right as he strode the corridor, the machine gun blasting one way and then the other, his curled lips casually sucking deep on the cigar, savouring the taste whilst he savoured the violence.

Kendrick dragged Davenport and Sullivan around a corner, through a fire exit and then down a small staircase, through a second exit and out into a long empty corridor that led to a set of double doors at the end. He pulled them on again, his heavy-handed hold making Davenport stumble and Sullivan slip out of his grasp and on to the floor. Kendrick was on him in an instant, giving no time for him to readjust, his hand in his hair, grabbing him to his feet and shoving him crudely on.

They stopped at the doors, and Kendrick rested his head against them, turning an ear to the frame, straining to hear anything other than the rain of bullets that was pounding on the studio walls from all sides. As they all paused at the door and fought to establish their breathing again, Davenport rested a hand on Sullivan's arm and raised his eyebrows to him, enquiring – even in this madness – as to his well-being. Sullivan had nothing to return in that moment, instead choosing to look back with little more than the dumb expression he knew he was wearing. Kendrick was squeezing his head against the slit in the door, gently pushing them apart with one expensive shoe and then stopping again, convinced he'd heard something, holding a hand to the others and then craning his head forward once more.

Behind them the heavy footfall of Theo Maddox was rumbling their way as he thudded along the corridor with the confident stride of a lunatic king. The huge machine gun was up in front of him and Bergan and Turtle were trailing in his wake; Kleinman swinging limply over Turtle's shoulder like wet laundry. Maddox walked through them, booted the double doors open and walked inside, his cigar smoke gathering around his head like a broken halo.

They stepped out into a large underground car park, which opened out around them leading to a small break of light at the far end. The rest of the car park was pressed hard with a heavy darkness that felt like paperweight thunderclouds pushing down on them, making a mockery of the two orange strip lights that tried to paint each of them with a fiery glow. At the opposite end of the car park a running engine purred with the growling satisfaction of a kill fed wildcat, and Sullivan could feel Davenport's hand on his shoulder tensing slightly, his fingers digging in. The old army utility truck – their wheels – one of the three trucks that the dear departed Baxter had procured for them with great difficulty, and a little bit of bribery, was slowly falling into view, its canvas-covered shell catching just enough light from the open entrance to give it away. Next to it the black BMW that had brought Sullivan to Bend Lane TV studios, the one Bergan had jemmied open and hotwired, was parked at an angle, the front doors open invitingly.

'Let's go, we're nearly there.' Kendrick hurried Davenport and Sullivan on, but Bergan was quickly in front of them, blocking their path and pushing them to the ground, deep into the shadows. 'What the hell are you doing, Frank?'

'Gate's open.' Bergan waved one huge slab of a hand towards the slit of light at the end of the car park, just beyond the truck. 'Don't move.'

'Yes, I know the gate's open, how did you want us to get out of here? Hope, will and wishing?'

'If the gate is open, someone opened it, whipdick,' Bergan snarled back.

'More to the point, who turned the engine over?' Davenport chipped in.

'A valid point, Prime Minister,' Maddox said, swinging the two rifles from his shoulder, handing one to Bergan and the other, barrel first, to Sullivan. 'Pleased to meet you, killer.'

'What am I supposed to do with that?' Sullivan asked, his eyes meeting Maddox's own, the hatred he couldn't stem brimming at the surface.

'Aim for the head.'

Sullivan grabbed the rifle and swung it the right way round. 'Whose?'

'Well not yours, killer. Not yet anyway.' Maddox

smiled and started walking forward slowly, deeper into the shadows. 'Take the truck, Frank. I will flush any stragglers.' Bit-by-bit, the thick shadows swallowed Maddox and only the echo of his footsteps remained, the cigar smoke trailing behind him and then slowly drifting out into the damp, cold stench of the car park.

'Give it to me, Sullivan.' Kendrick's hand was in front of him, the palm flat, the fingers clicking, and waggling. 'Give me the rifle.'

Sullivan wasted no time in a second thought and clumsily shoved the rifle into Kendrick's waiting hand. 'Thanks. Thank you, I…'

'Don't worry about it.' Kendrick's voice carried a bounce, a lightness that had no place where they hid. 'Stay out of sight.' Kendrick half-stood, half-walked to the nearest pillar, leant against it and then slowly pointed the rifle out toward the black heart of the car park.

Silence seemed to have fallen without anyone noticing. The gunfire had stopped, the screaming too. Only the sound of the truck's engine remained, and as Bergan fed the next bullet into his rifle's chamber the heavy clunking sound reverberated around the car park. Bergan took a step forward, Turtle right behind him, struggling with Kleinman and trying hard not to show it.

'Get ready, Turtle.'

'I'm there, Frank.'

They passed Kendrick and stood at the edge of the

pillar, staring out across the car park at the truck.

'Too easy, Frank.'

Bergan nodded and raised the rifle higher. In front of them the truck was starting to edge forward, the purring engine getting louder, angrier. 'I doubt it, Turtle.'

3

Fear the quiet. That's what Bergan had always told them. It was what he feared more than anything. The quiet preludes, the eerie calm, the sheer deepness of silence. He had drilled that into each of them, had taught them to respect the quiet and to fear it, and he could tell that at that very moment each of them did, though none more so, he was sure, than he himself.

The utility truck gently curved between two pillars and began backing toward them. The tailgate was down, the darkness in the heart of the truck foreboding yet inviting. It slowed to a crawl, trundling backwards another few feet, before finally coming to a dead stop about twenty yards ahead of them. Bergan trained his rifle to the driver's side of the cab. Next to him Kleinman was moaning and mumbling incoherent words, Turtle shifting his weight to stop from tipping over. Kendrick remained against the pillar, his rifle aiming into the car park, and next to him Davenport and Sullivan were tucked in behind, resisting the impulse to hold each other. Somewhere further into the car park, Maddox was wandering through the shadows looking for something to destroy, and all around them that damned silence hung like the worst enemy they could ever meet.

When the face peered around from the driver's window, it was so sudden and quick that it was a miracle Bergan didn't plant a shot right through it. His fingers twitched, pulled on the trigger and then quickly jumped off just before connection.

'Son of a bitch,' Bergan breathed into the air, as the truck's horn sounded three times and the cubed bull-like head of Hudson stared back at them. He wasn't smiling, not quite, but he seemed happy. He had a madman's look of simple pleasure.

Suddenly, as if called to action by the sound of the horn, the car park seemed to stir awake, the hanging silence breaking with the steady echo of footsteps, the slow rumble of forming human screams and then, finally, the heavy, vibrating boom of gun fire. The deep, dark corners of the car park were quickly ripped open as staccato bursts of angry colour flared out from all sides. Figures were charging forward, seemingly swarming out of the walls, massing together and coming at them as one. Maddox, tucked behind a pillar further into the car park, was firing left, then right, then back again, sweeping his machine gun fire in all directions. Figures were falling, breaking apart under his swarm of bullets, but no sooner did they disappear than another seemed to replace them. Kendrick was firing off his rifle into the darkness, shooting blind with nothing to find in the gloom, no definition or shapes, just the quick tantalising reveal that came at each burst of gunfire. The massed roar thundered through them, ate into them like they were caught in a storm cloud they couldn't break. The sound seemed to want to cover you, suffocate you, pin you to the ground.

'Move!' Bergan screamed as he sprinted to the driver's door of the truck, yanked it open and roughly shoved Hudson to one side. A bullet shattered the side window and then more tore into the canvas.

'Give me a gun! Let me kill them! I want to kill them!' Hudson was almost bouncing in the seat, his crazy face distorted into lunatic logic, fat tongue flicking at his upper lip and one sweaty hand grabbing at the rifle now in Bergan's lap. Bergan swung one huge hand at Hudson and swatted him into the passenger side window. Turning back to the wheel, he lurched the truck back further towards the others.

'Now!' Bergan yelled out of the truck window, as another shower of bullets peppered the steel cab. 'We leave now! Move!'

Hudson seized his moment with Bergan distracted and grabbed the rifle from his lap. Swinging around in the seat and kicking open the passenger door, he fired off the first shot into the darkness before his feet even touched the floor. Turtle was at the tailgate now, tilting Kleinman over it before clumsily pulling himself up to join him. Turtle didn't even spare Hudson a glance as he ran past him at the tailgate and unleashed another two shots into the car park before jumping into the waiting BMW, reaching under the wheel and fumbling at the exposed wires.

A jagged shard flew off the pillar and hit Kendrick, cutting a cheek. He stumbled backwards, spinning around, his hands flying to his face as he landed in Davenport's arms. Davenport was tugging him to the ground, wrestling him down and hugging him and Sullivan close.

'My face! Not my face!' Kendrick was gibbering, his hands smoothing over the cut and coming away blood red. Across from them another rifle shot sounded, ushering forth a delirious whooping from Hudson as the BMW's engine fired and the ex-jailer of Thinwater prison brought his weight down on the accelerator, quickly moving through the gears and ploughing the car forward towards the oncoming hoards, screaming like a madman from the window.

'Sullivan! Get off your arse!' Bergan's voice blasted from inside the truck.

'Get them in the back! Move!' Turtle screamed.

Sullivan pulled Davenport up by his collar, shoving him forward towards Turtle's waiting grasp. Kendrick was still in a state of shock at the blood on his hands and terrified for the mark on his face, and he struggled and fought as Sullivan turned his attention on to him, yanking him up by his suit jacket lapels. His weedy, short arms flailing around in a windmill of panic.

Bergan was starting to edge the truck forward, pumping the bite. 'Get in! Move it!'

Sullivan followed Kendrick over the tailgate just as more bullets tore through the canvas covering. Across the car park Maddox started to retreat, firing low and ducking back to the nearest pillar, trying to weave a safe passage to the truck. Bergan lifted his foot from the clutch and the truck started to gather speed, the engine snarling in front of them. Maddox backed further away and unleashed the rest of the magazine before discarding the machine gun and turning, running flat out towards the departing truck.

Hudson had made one circle of the car park and was coming back for seconds. Figures pinged off the car as he mowed through the nearest crowd of people, others were sucked under the car and squashed, or thrust head first into the bonnet, and yet more still managed to mount the car and were hanging from the windscreen and the roof. Hudson didn't seem to care, didn't seem to want to see anyone, charging the car on in a series of crazy, improvised turns, weaving in and out of pillars and taking corners as fast as he could. He was a joyrider on one last fix, delirious and sucking on the high. He didn't see the figure crawl in through the sunroof, nor did he feel the hands on him until it was too late. The car swerved expertly past one more pillar and then thudded pathetically into the next, the airbag blowing up in Hudson's face and pinning him to the seat. Figures were at the car doors instantly, yanking them open, they were smashing windows and crawling through, and Hudson was screaming into the big white balloon pressed into his face. The car was swamped, outside and inside, and Hudson was steadily blocked from view.

Maddox was about twenty feet from the truck and gaining. Bergan moved up another gear and they shot out of the gate and into the meagre light, only a shade brighter than what they had left. Sullivan found himself at the tailgate, silently volunteered to be the one to offer Maddox a helping hand up, being the only one not now cowering on the floor of the truck, and as Maddox's hand came to him, as the burly brutes expectant look came and then slowly fell away, Sullivan found himself backing off, looking down at Maddox and shaking his head.

What was left of the enemy were now coming out of the car park; scattered clusters of rag-tag clothes and gaunt, ghostly bodies, and across from them even more were running out from the front of the studios, joining their tribe, returning to their flock. Maddox wasn't stopping, and he wasn't losing ground. Those brilliant blue eyes seemed to wash white as they looked back up at Sullivan, and the mouth beneath it pulled into a grimace.

The truck picked up the road in front of the studio and began scything through the carnage of the earlier battle, ploughing over bodies fallen to Maddox's gunfire, scattered limbs catching under the tyres and slowing them, threatening to stop them, and then as the truck pitched over the flattened electric fence, bounced up and broadsided a fencepost, it slowed just enough for Maddox to jump on to the tailgate, haul himself over and then punch Sullivan square in the face.

4

They drove the city out in silence, the broken shells of houses and offices, factories and warehouses, finally falling away to wide stretches of snow-splattered wastelands and fields. They passed burnt out cars and swerved around bodies. They drove through a small village where the dead had been stacked on to a large pyre. A priest was standing to one side offering prayer. He signalled to them as they passed and assured them that the Party loved them. He was given no such assurance. At the far end of the village a barn, half standing, presented passers with a giant poster of Edward Davenport. He looked young, handsome, dynamic and thrusting, a stark contrast to the man he was now; a matinee idol at a midnight show. Beyond the barn a snow-caked field was dotted with the fallen carcases of cows; crows scattering, seemingly from inside their torn bellies, as the truck passed them.

The snow was coming down at a steady speed, the feeble windscreen wipers brushing the gathering flakes aside with increasing ineffectiveness, the torn canvas shell of the truck offering little protection to those in the back, huddled up, their coats and jackets zipped up and pulled close. The sharp winter wind was a thousand little spikes firing in from the back of the truck, through the sides, the roof and every conceivable empty space.

Kleinman lay under a makeshift duvet of coats, drifting in and out of consciousness, mumbling words, moaning strange sounds and then falling back to nothing. The others sat around him in a circle, staring down, nothing to say, flashing intermittent looks to each other, hoping another would break the silence. Only Maddox sat apart from them, leaning against the tailgate, staring out at where they had just been, sucking deep on a cigar and fondling a rifle. It was he who finally broke the silence, and after he did, everyone else found themselves wishing the silence back.

'He's dead,' was all he said, spitting the words out through the corner of his mouth free from cigar.

'No he isn't,' Turtle returned, not looking up.

'Kleinman is still alive, Theo.' Davenport said in a low whisper. 'I will thank you for keeping such statements to yourself.'

'Nah,' Maddox said in a casual, laconic drawl, his eyes returning to the view behind them, and then to the cold, unforgiving sky above. 'He's dead.'

The truck started to circle around, stop, and then begin a slow ascent, crawling steeply and then pulling off to the left. From the back of the truck the road seemed to dangle beneath them like a tail before feeding back out. They had reached the start of the valley into Bleeker Hill and the terrain was getting worse, the tyres sliding on slick ice patches as they picked between and trundled over smatterings of rock and felled branches.

Bergan was sighing and growling in the driver's seat, the odd swear word tossed into the silences between. The truck skidded wildly as they crested the first hill, the rear right tyre slamming hard against a rock, and then Bergan was moving down a gear and trying to hold the truck as it began to move down the other side.

Two smaller hills followed, and then finally the road broke into a long plateau, a snake line running between huge valley walls to their right and a sheer drop to their left, and the truck settled into a slow crawl. Turtle moved away from the others and clambered over into the cab, plonking himself down next to Bergan, and on seeing the drop just beyond his door, fastened his seatbelt as tight as he could.

'How far, Frank?' Turtle asked, fiddling in vain with the heater on the dash, which had long since given up the ghost.

'Half a day, maybe more. Somewhere you need to be?'

Turtle leant forward and tapped the fuel gauge with an index finger; it was already in the red. Bergan spared it a look and simply nodded.

Kendrick shuffled from the group in the back of the truck and leant against the cab, staring out at each man in turn, delicately stroking the cut on his face and then the beard growing beneath it. 'Weapons. What we got?'

'I'm out,' Turtle said from behind him. 'Frankie too.'

'Theo?'

Maddox didn't respond, didn't look back into the truck, merely raised the rifle slightly and continued puffing on his cigar.

'Is that it?' Davenport said, straightening himself and rubbing at his back. 'Do we have nothing else?'

'There's weaponry at the safe house. The point team carried enough to level a small country.'

'Wonderful. If we get there, that will be wonderful. Wouldn't you say, Joe?'

Kendrick said nothing and settled down against the cab, gave the cut one last caress and then closed his eyes. Silence fell between them again like a default setting and beyond Kleinman's moaning and the persistent trill of the wind, there was nothing else on offer until, half an hour later, the truck rumbled with an ugly gurgle and began to swerve and skittle across the road, pinging off rocks, slipping on ice and then finally front ending the rock wall and stopping completely, and then the rear of the truck came alive again in a series of sighs, and grunts, and questioning looks.

'Fuel,' was all Bergan said, over the side of the cab, was all he really needed to say, and then they were stepping out of the truck, through the doors, over the tailgate, and gathering together in one tight huddle.

'Well, isn't this just fine and dandy?' Davenport

snapped, pulling his coat collars tight over his face, muffling the rest of his words, but not the venom they carried.

Bergan shoved Davenport to one side and leant across the open tailgate, looking in at Kleinman. 'He said anything?' He asked everyone, and no one.

'Moans and groans, he's in and out of it,' Sullivan said joining Bergan at the tailgate. 'How far we got left?'

'Far enough.'

'Kid make it that far?' Turtle asked, drawing up to them both, staring in at Kleinman and then looking away.

Bergan seemed stuck on a thought, staring in at the prone body of Kleinman, his mind working over the situation. A hand went to his neck and brushed the stubble. He could feel the tightening in his throat, the pulsing echoes of a constant dream. 'Find us a path out of the valley, Turtle. A track, a rockfall, anything.'

'On it.' Turtle turned away, slipping and sliding as he went.

Bergan reached up a hand and hoisted himself into the back of the truck, moved across to Kleinman and then crouched down beside him, lifting one shovel hand under his head and resting it against his lap. Kleinman slowly opened delirious eyes to him and coughed a small splat of blood on to Bergan's sleeve.

'Hey, Frank…think I messed up…we kill 'em Frank?'

'Sure did. Every last one.'

Kleinman tried to smile but it seemed to bring a pain. He scrunched up his eyes instead, summoning up the last drop of a waning, puny strength to fight it away, and then rolled his head to the side, almost as if he couldn't bear to watch his own miserable defeat. Bergan reached over and brought his young charge's head back into his lap, his free hand gently cupping Kleinman's right cheek. His skin was almost completely smooth still; Kleinman the only one of the group not sporting facial hair, the only one still groping at his youth with hands strong enough. The smooth skin made Bergan smile but there was an unbearable sadness behind it, Bergan could feel it knocking at him, but he knew the kid couldn't see it, and then as he slowly moved his hand across Kleinman's mouth, he made sure the smile was broad, and bright and believable.

'It's okay, Kleinman. It's all okay.' Bergan took thumb and index finger to Kleinman's nose and then clamped them over his nostrils, pressing his palm down hard over his mouth as he did; his weight brought forward, strength pushed down. He looked away, staring through a rip in the canvas, focusing on the rock wall visible through it, and the steady snowfall that came down and freckled and ate it up. He could feel Kleinman struggling briefly, his head trying to rock back and forth in the grip of his hand, his legs kicking out, and then Kleinman went soft and limp and he tumbled out of Bergan's hold as soon as he opened his giant hands.

Bergan could sense everyone's eyes on him, he knew, even without looking, that the others were all still gathered at the tailgate, he could feel them and he wanted to scream at them. He wanted the sadness and the fury that had just come into him to blast out and he wanted one of them to feel it, to know what it would do, but he held it together, he suppressed it, he screwed the top back on and fell back into his role. The ease at which he could was the most worrying thing to him, and the greatest sign, if ever he still needed one, that he was too far gone now to be the man he was again. Once more something seemed to tighten around his throat. He was going to dream again when finally he slept, he knew it, felt it.

'Maddox?' Bergan turned slowly to the others, and there they were, like he had pictured them, grouped together at the open tailgate, his merry band of worthless rabble. 'Gather up the coats, and anything else we might need and can carry. Then get the canvas off the roof. When you're done, you put the truck over the edge. Sullivan? Get up here and get Kleinman out. Then find a spot and bury him.'

Bergan stood and jumped down from the truck. Maddox stepped forward and joined Sullivan at the tailgate. Maddox had said very little since planting the punch on Sullivan, but as they stood there, hands on the truck, ready to hoist themselves up, Maddox turned slightly and breathed quiet words laced with menace:

'I'm gonna break you, killer,' and then he climbed up into the truck and said no more, gathering up their belongings and bundling them out over the tailgate like they were rubbish.

Davenport and Kendrick retreated to a long, flat rock and slumped down, Davenport rubbing his hands together against the cold, and Kendrick dabbing lightly at the cut on his face. As Bergan approached, Kendrick stood quickly, too quickly; his posh shoes slipped on the ice, and then he tumbled back to the rock, wincing as his backside connected firmly and precisely.

'And?' Kendrick said in a loud, pompous bleat that was trying to paper over his little slip.

'And what?' Bergan said into the air, moving away from Kendrick and rounding the truck.

'And now what, Mr Bergan? Now what?'

Bergan looked down the valley path and saw Turtle at the mouth of what seemed to be a cave, waving his arms over his head and beckoning them to him. High above, drifting lonely in the wind, a single red balloon floated over them and then fell out of sight behind the valley wall.

'We move on, Mr Kendrick. We move on.'

BLOOD

1

To Sullivan's mind, the cave entrance looked like a rotten corpse mouth. It fed through the limestone rock face, opening out further along its throat to two different paths and a multitude of stalactites and stalagmites hanging down or jutting up like giant, perversely vicious teeth. The widest path led them further up into the valley wall and through a fragile patch of flowstone towards an even floor about twenty feet across that sat directly underneath a ragged hole on the other side of the valley wall. It was a hole that would, Bergan assured them, open out in the opposite wall directly above the forest around Bleeker Hill. It would shave off hours of travelling and, after assessing that everyone would fit through the second hole, they settled on the stroke of fortune, didn't dare question it, and decided to bed in for the night.

The canvas roof from the truck was strung up across the mouth of the cave yet with the rips and tears and numerous bullet holes it offered scant respite from the howling, snow-flecked wind. Davenport and Kendrick sat together, huddled close just beyond the opening, with Maddox on sentry next to them, sitting on a rock with his legs pulled up to his chest, rubbing the back of his neck absently. No one had asked him to take that position, but no one had wanted to tell him otherwise either. Bergan had said he would take over the watch after three hours and Maddox had just shrugged. As it was Bergan slept through until dawn and Maddox didn't even move.

Sullivan and Turtle were charged with guarding the second hole, though, as Turtle was quick to mention "guarding" was a slightly wishful term without any weaponry. Bergan had just stared at him as he said it and Turtle had said no more about it, merely fastened his coat as tight as he could and followed Sullivan on his hands and knees across the flowstone to the even ground before the final angled feed up to the hole.

'We could do with some rope, that's got to be about twenty feet to the hole,' Sullivan said, assessing their exit.

'PM's going to have a problem with that. Kendrick too,' Turtle offered, shivering into his coat and burying his mouth into the collar. 'No place for sensible suits and expensive shoes. You okay, Sullivan?'

'Define okay, Turtle.'

'Yeah, I know. I hear 'ya. But, shit, don't bother yourself with it. You get used to it.'

'Killing people, you mean?'

'They're not people, not in the real sense of the word.'

'What is the real sense of being a person?'

'You seen what they do. Baxter? Kleinman? They're dead, man, they're not coming back.'

'I've also seen what Maddox does, where's the line and what side am I supposed to be on?'

Turtle laughed into his coat and nodded slowly. 'I hear you, man, I do, but we are where we are and we survive how we survive. You know the way the country is now.'

'Do I? I'm not sure I know much of anything any more.'

'You gotta have heard things at Thinwater?'

'Not really...my wife...'

'Yeah?'

Sullivan instinctively pulled a hand up to his coat and rested it against the pocket that held his wife's letters. He slowly shook his head to Turtle, brushing the sentence away. 'It doesn't matter. I do remember things about the old country, when it broke. Some things. But it feels skewed, does that make sense?'

'What about your family?'

'Somehow when I got sent down...those walls...I dunno...'

'Go on...'

'It seemed to suck everything out of me. That place. Maybe I just accepted that I would never get out of there and wilfully shed things. Maybe I knew it would be easier just to let them have me. Who knows? I've stopped questioning it. Fact is everything has changed, nothing makes any sense any more.'

'Only thing that does make sense any more is that nothing makes sense. You think I get this? None of us do. You just play the cards you got stacked in front of you.'

'So, now we're Party men?'

'We're nothing, Sullivan. Don't think that's ever changed. But if the Party hadn't turfed me out of my sentence I would probably have been screwed by the Wash or I would still be there now, rotting slowly away. Party saved me, saved you too. I'm no fanatic man, believe me, but I owe them. What's it to me what they ask me to do?'

'Who the hell were we fighting, Turtle?'

'Shit, you have been out of the loop haven't you?'

Sullivan shrugged and shuffled back against the rock wall, trying to get comfy on the cold floor. 'I can remember what it was like before I got sent down. It was a mess. People were fighting in the streets, rioting, and there were fires everywhere. Yeah, I remember that. I remember the fires. Every night there seemed to be a new building ablaze somewhere in the city. I think back to that place now and everything I see, every memory I can find, all of it is etched in orange or amber. I still dream about that now. Fire. It always seems to be there in my dreams. Those that I can remember and I seem to be remembering a lot more of them just recently. It's weird. What do you think that means?'

'Don't mean anything, man.'

'Don't you think so?'

'I've been dreaming a lot. Been dreaming of falling. Nose diving down from a great height.' Turtle shrugged as his right hand made a swan-diving gesture to reiterate the point. 'Been dreaming of it daily. Well, nightly…you know. But so what? You're born with a fear of that, right? So, just means I haven't grown up yet. I choose to see that as a good thing, way things are now. Dreams don't mean much. Just means you gotta learn to switch your subconscious off. Don't let the fears in. Got enough of them in the waking world, right?'

'You always remember your dreams?'

'Yeah, pretty much. You tend to when you live in a nightmare, I guess.'

'These people that attacked the studios today…back before I got sentenced the anger felt different, at the start it was more chaotic…directionless, don't you think? But this today was…well…'

'Organised? Yeah. They are always evolving. It's always changing. Individuals became groups, groups became gang's…communities, I guess. It became territorial. They're animals Sullivan, feral animals. We'd get word from time to time on our travels that some group had invaded another's turf, that some tin-pot leader's been deposed…disposed…but after a while you realise it doesn't matter any more. You let people off the lead, like we did when we elected that lunatic government that started all this, and sooner or later everyone's going to want to be a king. Course they are. Everyone's going to want their own turn on the throne. No rules, any more? No responsibilities for your actions? Fuck, lets make our own rules! Let's fulfil all our own warped desires. You lose track of who is running the show in each territory, their leaders come and go. It seems like every day they're having themselves a little revolution. It's the main thing in our favour. It's their own thirst for status, for meaning, that stops them growing any further. In time, if we could afford to wait for it, they will probably all kill themselves off fighting power trips out between themselves. Everyone wants to be the king. Nowadays anyone can be.'

'Like Davenport?'

'He's nothing. A mouthpiece. A man of the law with a nice haircut. You must have seen the posters when he took charge? It was image in the old country, it's image in the new. That's never gonna change. Did we learn nothing? Did the leaders not get the message? Plug into the shallow end and all your dreams can come true. The Party changes their figureheads more times than I care to remember. They aren't that much better than the raggedy-end bastards on the streets in that respect.' Turtle quickly lowered his voice and looked back down through the cave, sure that they were being listened to. The others below them hadn't even moved; Bergan was asleep against a large rock, his huge hands closed together over his chest, Davenport and Kendrick were still huddled up together under their coats and Maddox remained on sentry, staring at the tatty canvas door, his right hand still rubbing slowly at the back of his neck. Turtle turned back to Sullivan, his voice staying just above a whisper. 'Don't get me wrong, Davenport's okay for a lawyer, he really is. I mean, in some respects he's the real deal. He's got the good intentions. He was the one who wanted to end the Wash after all. He's a decent man and he's got the heart, but...'

'The Party has got his balls?'

'Yeah. Poetic my man, and on the money.'

'What about Kendrick?'

'He's the Party through and through.' Turtle's voice dropped even lower and Sullivan had to lean forward to hear him. 'I've heard things about Kendrick, his name has travelled. Not sure I care for the man.'

'Not sure I do either, Turtle.'

'They sure got a hard on where you're concerned. Your wife, right?'

'She worked for them. They say she was trying to get me released.'

'Damn, she sure must have made a good cup of tea.' Turtle laughed, then stopped abruptly, aware from Sullivan's accusing look that the question of his wife's involvement with Davenport was still sitting uncomfortably in his mind. On the surface the answer was obvious; for a man like Davenport to care so much for someone of no great importance to himself or to the Party, it could only mean one thing. Sullivan dearly hoped there was more to the gesture than showed itself, because if there wasn't then only the obvious would remain, and that was guilt.

Sullivan coughed and scrunched up his shoulders to the cold, trying to work the thought out of him. 'So where are we going?' he asked Turtle, blatantly trying to change the subject.

'We're going to the hill, man, finally, been on this journey more months than I care to remember.' Turtle's voice had returned to its usual chatty rattle.

'The hill?'

'Bleeker Hill.'

Sullivan fell silent, contemplating a thought that wished to be heard.

'Yeah, you've heard of it, right?'

'Yes. Why? Why do I know that name?'

'It's got a history. Long time back though. Don't mean anything. Every place has got a story to tell.'

'Shit.' The thought in Sullivan's mind was heard and a chill ran through him from heart to head.

'Yeah. I see you know your history.'

'I've read the books. I went to school.'

'Fuck it. There's death everywhere nowadays. No place has got the monopoly on that any more.'

Sullivan leaned back against the cave wall, a hundred old stories flashing through his mind. He shivered again and tightened his coat. 'The Hanging House,' Sullivan mumbled to himself in a distracted whisper.

'What's that?'

'That's what we used to call it. At school.'

Turtle laughed into the collar of his coat and nodded knowingly.

'What is it now?' Sullivan was leaning forward again, shuffling his backside along the cold rock. 'What happened to it after…'

'After we reached enlightened times and stopped executing all the bad people?' Turtle laughed at his own question and the irony wasn't lost on Sullivan who greeted it with his own, half-hearted smile. 'I don't know. Fell to ruin I guess. State sold the land off somewhere down the line and someone made a killing. If you forgive the pun. I don't know how many owners it went through first, but it ended up in the Culp family, one of the Party elders, and he offered it up as soon as things started breaking. Well, you know, I say he offered it up, but its not like he had much choice. Party seized everyone's assets off the bat. What's yours is theirs and all that. They didn't really give him any choice. Be grateful you haven't a pot to piss in. Amazing how the other half live… lived…isn't it? Nothing handed down in my family except a distinct lack of height. Then there's this minted, wrinkly sack able to offer up this massive white elephant for the Party zoo. Party needed somewhere to start again. Somewhere in the arse end of nowhere. Somewhere safe.'

'Define me a safe house nowadays?'

Turtle laughed again. 'Yep, I hear you. It's a warped joke, right? Particularly this place and especially after what happened with the workers, but what do I care? Give me a roof over my head and a kitchen to cook in and I'm a happy man, don't bother me what went on there.'

'Workers?'

'The cons the Party sent down to work on the place.'

'What did go on?'

'Just heard some stories, no big deal. Grennaught would have been the man to ask. If you could. Poor bastard. Stories don't mean anything though. They're just stories, right? You tell a lot of stories living this life.'

'Yeah? Well indulge me then. You really want to talk about the weather?'

'They just had some people go walkabout, that's all. Workers. Party built a shelter in the grounds. A bunker. Wash central it was supposed to be. Somewhere to shove all the shit they were up to.'

'And they deserted the place?'

'Yeah. That.'

'What's Grennaught got to do with it?'

'Kendrick sent him in after they disappeared. He wanted him to oversee the building and keep an eye on things and make sure no one else walked. Maybe have a poke around too, see if he could dig up some answers.'

'And?'

'Well, something rattled him. He was back at HQ after a week, refusing to go anywhere near the place again. Wouldn't speak about it, well not to the rest of us hired hands that is, if he fessed up to the top table they never said.'

'That doesn't bother you?'

Turtle shrugged, his shoulders seeming to catch a shiver as he did. 'Just stories man, don't mean anything.'

'What do you think happened to them, the workers?'

'I dunno. Some people reckon they all killed each other. That they went nuts and started in on one another. But no one ever found any bodies. They say that, but I doubt they ever really looked. With what Schaeffer was doing there, what was a few more stiffs to the Party?'

'I heard that name earlier…'

'Daddy of The Wash. He's the mad, bad, bastard that sold the Party on the idea in the first place. They say he says he could control minds. All I ever saw of the Wash there was no control going on, there was nothing there to control. He emptied their minds. Blasted them till there was nothing left. He was just a butcher, another lunatic just as they were becoming old hat. It don't matter any more anyhow, they pulled the plug on him, that's all done with now. Kendrick sent a team in. This guy Hennessey, top Party plod, he took Schaeffer down. You see there are more of us than just this sorry bunch you've met. There are groups around the country. North, south, east and west. The Party's got them in place and when the time comes, we come together, and…'

'We take back the country?'

'Nah, I doubt that, place isn't worth the fuss and fluster any more. But what we do is we start again. That in itself, being in at the start of that, that's worth it all. It's got to be, right? I love that idea. It's exciting don't you think?'

Sullivan leaned back against the cave wall and stared up at the hole. 'I dunno, Turtle. Who the hell can be bothered to start again?'

2

A feeble light crept in through the hole in the rock wall above them, bringing dawn's announcement in a tired suggestion, the greying sunlight washing Sullivan's eyes and forehead, bringing him awake slowly and gently. Turtle was already up, his hands feeling into the rock wall for places to find purchase. Below them the others were stirring awake, yawning and stretching and wincing with stiffness and discomfort. Maddox remained on watch, unmoving, his eyes never leaving the tatty canvas door until Bergan slapped him hard on the shoulder and moved him on.

Turtle was the first up the wall, scaling it in a series of clumsy fumbles, his stocky frame then squeezing out of the hole above and sending a shower of snow down on to the others, prompting a series of sighs and grunts that echoed out through the cave in a ghostly reverberation. Turtle disappeared briefly, then his face was back at the hole and he was giving the thumbs up. The rest scaled the wall one at a time, Bergan and Maddox following Davenport and Kendrick in turn, pre-empting the two suited men's flailing around on the rock wall and their need for support, which in another world would have been comedy gold. As it was Bergan struggled not to scream at them and try out drop kicking them through the hole with one large toe capped boot.

The hole, as Bergan had predicted, came out about halfway down the opposite side of the valley wall. The skeletal winter forest around Bleeker Hill was below them, bending around their vision on all sides. The trees, stripped and fragile looking, were speckled heavily with snow, the pathways between them chaotically sprinkled white and dotted with fallen branches and brittle foliage. Beyond the forest they could see the break where Bleeker Hill dropped down to the estate, before picking up again just at the tip of the horizon. They were close. But somehow no one seemed to want to say so.

The valley wall was steep and the snow was piled high and solid in the gaps between the rocks, oozing through it like toothpaste. In places the snow was up to their kneecaps – waist in Turtle's case – and moving through it was next to impossible, so they used the scattershot rocks like stepping stones, crawling between each slick grey mound on their hands and knees, before invariably slipping off and thudding into the hard snow cushion and then climbing back on to the nearest rock and repeating the process until the valley wall played out. By the time they reached the forest edge they were exhausted and slumped to the ground, wringing the wetness from their trousers and coat sleeves and shaking with the unforgiving cold, their teeth chattering and limbs pulsing under their wet clothes.

'Well that was fun, Turtle,' Maddox seethed, squeezing his cuffs. 'Remind me to take the scenic route with you again sometime.'

'Shut up,' Bergan said, standing and moving between them. 'Go check ahead, Theo. Find us a route.'

Maddox sauntered off, the rifle swinging loosely in one hand, his free hand reaching into his jacket and plucking out another fat cigar.

'Are you okay, Sullivan?' Davenport was at his side, resting a precious hand on his shoulder and squeezing lightly. 'No bumps or bruises?'

'I'm fine,' Sullivan said, shrugging him off.

Bergan stood a few yards into the forest, staring ahead at some fixed point, his black eyes latched to something. His arms were crossed tightly over his chest, his body rigid and imposing; he looked like a bouncer, an impassable object to stop anything getting in or out of the forest. Davenport approached him from the side, Bergan towering over him like a monument, almost casting shadow over Davenport's neat little body. They said nothing for several minutes, just stared ahead into the forest, eyes squinting to see, and ears straining to hear. The sounds of the forest came to them in short, whispered moments – the snapping, the rustling, and the gentle creaking. It was a tease, and it was beckoning them in. Davenport gazed upward at the tops of the trees and then further up still to the dirty glass sky.

'No birds,' Davenport said a few moments later, half to Bergan, half to himself. 'There are no birds here.'

'No,' Bergan replied, and it sounded like an answer as well as an instruction.

'You've heard about...you know the stories?'

Bergan remained silent. He uncrossed and then re-crossed his arms, his eyes never leaving the point in the forest they had found.

'Frank?' Davenport gazed up at Bergan, trying to read something from his inscrutable expression and his statuesque body. 'Frankie?'

'Yes?' The word came so quietly that Davenport wasn't sure it came from Bergan at all.

'Should we be worried?'

Footsteps crunched through the snow further into the forest and Davenport jumped, his hand instinctively reaching to his side, for a gun that wasn't there. Ahead of them Maddox was coming back, rifle in one hand and a strange object – something that looked like a withered branch – in the other. He stopped still and stared back at Frankie, swinging the object back and forth in his grip.

'Always,' Frankie said quietly to Davenport and then stepped forward, further into the forest. 'Well? he asked Maddox. 'What'd you find?'

'Blood. Patches of blood. Then a trail of it, across the floor and up the trees, all over the place. Something took a hit.'

'An animal?'

'No. Definitely not.'

'Are you sure?'

Maddox tossed the object towards them and it landed with a weak thud at Bergan's feet. It was a man's arm, blue and bloodied and chewed off at the elbow. Davenport recoiled in horror and turned away. The others held firm, gazing down at the ground and the grotesque souvenir Maddox had foraged.

'Pretty sure, Frank,' Maddox replied and turned back into the forest, rifle up in front of him.

One by one the others followed him in.

3

They moved in a line behind Maddox and picked up the blood trail quickly. There were dried splats and blobs here and there along the patches of ground free from snow; others ran up nearby trees, soaked into the bark. Bergan kicked up snow and found yet more, frozen into the mossy ground. At the place Maddox had found the arm there was a larger, darker streak smeared across a felled tree trunk, and beyond it a haphazard series of tracks.

'Human?' Kendrick asked the group, staring down at the tracks and then to each man in turn.

'Possibly,' Bergan replied, flicking away bits of twig and moss with a long stick and squatting down for a closer look. 'There are human footprints here, then something else, been walked through several times.'

'An animal?'

'Possibly.'

'It was an animal took the arm off, right?'

'Possibly. Probably.'

Bergan got up and walked on, joining Maddox at the head of the line and following the vague human prints deeper into the forest. They moved up and down the inclines of the forest floor, the tracks breaking and then starting again, sometimes deep and firm in an obvious human footprint, most times a scattered hotchpotch of scuffed up snow as if someone had been over the tracks half-heartedly trying to cover them and kick them away. Finally, as the trees grew in number around them and the snow became less and less, the tracks faded out into a carpet of fallen branches and browned threadbare moss mounds, before stopping completely at a narrow frozen lake snaking through the forest in front of them. A small derelict bridge straddled it covered in a thick white frosting that made a mockery of the tired, warped wood underneath.

It was Sullivan who saw it first. As the other men wandered one by one to the edge of the lake, stuck in an awkward silence, tapping the ice with shoes and boots and looking beyond it to yet more tangles of branches and trunks, Sullivan hung back and took his rest straddling a tree stump. He watched the men, these strangers he was glued to, and suddenly, for the briefest, most wondrous moment, he felt like he wasn't there, that he was watching the men play their part out through the luxury of great distance, perhaps through a TV screen that he could switch over whenever he chose, and that they couldn't touch him, they couldn't sense him or even see him. It was a glorious emotion, an exquisite con of the mind and he gave himself to it. He pushed himself forward off the stump and on to a soft cushion of moss and then slowly he leant back, tilting his head upwards, his eyes ready to swallow up the calm misery of the sky, to drink it all in and know that, for that moment, it couldn't corrupt him.

He was looking at the body for a good minute before his mind accepted it for what it was. The feeling didn't fade instantly, it was more a gradual trickle as it drained away, falling from his ears and his eyes and out of his imagination, drifting away to become a memory to grab at, unsure it were ever his in the first place. At first he thought how small the man's feet were, then how blue the body was, then he was fascinated by his bare legs, seemingly bent comically into directions in which they shouldn't be able to move, and then finally he wondered where the rest of his right arm was. It was then reality clawed hard at his face and dragged him back to the here and the now and the what's to come.

Sullivan was screaming, jumping up and staggering back, then falling on to the ground again as the others turned to him, and then he was pointing up at the body, stuttering words that meant nothing, trying to escape his body again, just for a minute, but finding himself anchored to the earth.

'Sweet Jesus,' Bergan said, as he walked slowly to Sullivan and stared up at the body.

It was about ten feet from the ground, facing to one side, a snapped branch feeding through the side of its neck and then poking out of its mouth, holding it up in place. It was naked but for a ripped pair of briefs. The corrupted face of a man was frozen on the last sight it ever saw, the eyes bulging from their sockets in horror.

'Get this man down,' Kendrick said quietly, the words stuttering from his trembling mouth.

Maddox jumped at the tree, caught the nearest branch and hauled himself up until level with the man's shoulders. His free hand went to the man's head and started pushing it, wiggling it from side to side, trying to free it from the branch. It wouldn't budge, giving little more than an inch. He pulled at the hair, shoved the body at its back, and then finally, his patience worn through, he let go of the branch, jumped on to the back of the body and brought his weight down hard. The body came free in a horrid snap of branch and bone, and then it was flopping to the ground underneath Maddox, both bodies landing with a thud on the mossy forest floor.

Kendrick bent down to the body, carefully rolled it over and stared deep into its eyes.

'You know him?' Maddox asked, getting to his feet, dusting himself down. 'I'm guessing anyone who wears undercrackers like that comes from your side of the divide. Am I right?'

'His name was Wallace,' Kendrick said into the corpse's face before turning to Maddox. 'He was a good man.'

'Yeah? Well, now he's a dead man, shall we move on?'

'You're a nasty son of a bitch, aren't you, Maddox?'

Maddox smiled to himself and picked up his rifle, smoothed a hand down the butt and then swung it up into his grasp. 'You fucking got that on the money, chief.'

'Enough!' Bergan's voice made them all jump. The deep, booming rasp of his words whenever he was close to shedding his composure was more terrifying a sound than anything the forest had to offer. They looked to him, one at a time, looking up at his giant body and his blank face, waiting for instruction or idea, but Bergan seemed to be searching for words, staring down at Wallace's body and then back to his men, rummaging around for the right thing to say. As it was, he had only one thing: 'That's enough.'

'We move on, yeah, Frank? Nothing to be done here, right?' Maddox was asking through one side of his mouth, planting the stubbed cigar back into the other.

'The man was a friend of mine!' Kendrick snapped, pulling himself up to his feet and steadying himself against the tree. 'Show some respect!'

'Lucky you, having that luxury.'

'I don't need to take this shit from you, Maddox. You have no idea who I am.'

'Best you come here and let me know then, Joey. What you say? Huh?'

Kendrick and Maddox were about to come together, stepping forward to each other like the worst sort of posturing drunk, when a noise – the sharp cracking sound of a breaking branch – echoed out through the forest, bouncing around them between the trees and then coming back in seemingly from all sides. They all turned, each in a different direction, then turned back the other way. A second branch broke and then a small log tumbled down towards the lake and skidded along the icy surface. A figure jumped between the trees beyond it, ducked down and then ran on, bobbing up and then disappearing from sight. Maddox had the rifle trained before anyone even had chance to take in what they had seen, and fired off a blind shot into the trees. Bergan was in front of him quickly, blocking him off and pushing the rifle away.

'Preserve ammunition, damn it. It's all we've got.'

Maddox pushed past Bergan and bounded off towards the lake, crossing it in one stride and then leaping into the trees behind the figure.

'Turtle, with me! Move!' Bergan shoved Turtle on and then the two men were jumping the lake behind Maddox and moving off through the trees, hot on his heels.

4

The trees in front of Bergan shook as Maddox charged on, almost seeming to run through them, the brittle winter branches no match for the fury that was rolling along their path. Turtle was out of breath, wheezing and coughing against the great exertion his little legs were being asked to accept, but he kept to Bergan's side, like a dog on a short lead. They ran left and right, scrambled over felled tree trunks and squelched through ice crusted patches of mud, and then finally Bergan pulled to a stop, one hand thrusting out to his side and knocking Turtle to the ground as if he had just run into a door.

Ahead of them a small one-berth tent was pitched between a small cluster of trees. Empty tin cans of food and drained bottles of drink formed a rubbish path to the partially unzipped door. A charred patch on the ground beyond, a blackened circle, betrayed a recent campfire, and there was still a delicate tang of burnt meat in the air, something slight yet sharp, a keen smell to the hungry. Maddox was stood amongst the rubbish, his rifle up, pointing at the door to the tent. Waiting.

Bergan crouched down and shuffled over to the dazed Turtle, and the two men took position in a small ditch about thirty feet back.

'That arrogant, gung-ho, son of a bitch is completely exposed. I've got to get to him. Stay here, Turtle.'

Turtle didn't need telling twice. Bergan lifted one great arm and started hauling himself up. He crawled for a few yards, his beady oil-well eyes swishing slowly left and right looking for anything approaching, and then, nearing a thick enough tree to hide him, he jumped up and swung behind it. He stretched to his full height and began to move his body around the trunk, those eyes now falling on Maddox and the small tent in front of him, all the while searching, probing, willing the reveal. He began to move out from behind the tree, and then he stopped, suddenly unable to move forward, his legs buckling from under him and his mind unwilling to comprehend what had just happened.

The blow came from above, hard and clean, and Bergan fell back against the tree trunk. The figure jumped down nimbly from the branches above him and swung a fist into Bergan's stomach, winding him and toppling him to his knees. He grabbed wildly at the figure but it was too quick, too lithe and too ready. He tried to speak, to shout a warning to the others but no sooner had he tried than the figure brought a pistol across his face and put him on his back. It approached Maddox from behind, a small figure, comically bound up in oversized army fatigues, trousers and sleeves cut off at the wrists and ankles, tatty trainers on tiny feet picking their way across the ground in light and practised footsteps, the delicate frame seemingly walking on air as it silently drew up behind him and raised its pistol to his large, rock shaped head.

'Drop the weapon and get on your knees.' The voice was calm and assured, the first female voice Maddox had heard in months. 'Slowly lower that rifle and then get on your knees. I won't ask you again.'

Maddox didn't move but the tight tension in his shoulders, the taut muscles that had sprung forth against the butt of the rifle as he approached the tent, relaxed, and as soon as they did a crooked smile broke on his face. 'Sounds like you are a long way from home, darling,'

'You have no idea, now drop that rifle before I put a bullet through your fat neck,' her voice was light but deadly, every word seemed to follow a full stop, every breath was held in each syllable. Had she been speaking to anyone else but Maddox they would probably be on their knees pleading for mercy. As it was Maddox merely turned, held his rifle out to one side and then clamped his mouth over the barrel of her pistol.

'I won't ask you again! Get on your knees!' her voice wavered, betraying her sudden surprise at being caught off guard in such a brazen way, but she held firm, working the toughest expression she had. 'Put that rifle down and get on your knees!'

'Yeah, you said all that,' Maddox mumbled over the pistol barrel, his tongue shooting out briefly and tickling the metal. 'I don't do small talk.'

Turtle was climbing out of the ditch; beyond him Bergan was swaying on his feet like a Friday night drunk on a Saturday morning, walking a few paces then stopping and holding his head, his legs threatening to buckle under him each time he tried to stagger on again. He was spitting out words now, barely formed words that meant nothing without the raw blast of his anger behind them. Turtle ran to him and ducked under one long arm, his head moving up under Bergan's armpit, straightening him up to the scene unfolding just in front of them.

'You're outnumbered here darling, you know that? Why not play nice?' Maddox was sucking the pistol barrel, his blue eyes twinkling at her, smiling at her and patronising her in their cocky assuredness.

Bergan and Turtle were approaching, Bergan's mumbled and indistinct words barking out towards her. "Ear…ear…" he seemed to be shouting. There was enough there for her to recognise, even if she hadn't yet placed the face to the voice, and in that sudden flash of knowing, in the quick dart of her eyes to her side, the drop of her guard, Maddox moved. He grabbed her at the wrist and squeezed; instantly her hand splayed outward against the pain and released the pistol. Maddox batted her arm away and she swayed to her side with the force. He was looking back at her curiously, taking her all in, her pistol still sticking out of his mouth, like the most bizarre type of dummy.

'Mia! Mia!' Bergan was fighting against Turtle's support, pushing him away, desperate to step into the situation, to be heard, and be back in control.

She was turning back to Maddox, her face flaring in rage, and then she was charging at him, hands clenched to attack, and Maddox was standing there ready, arms open wide to receive her. She launched at him, grabbing him around the throat and jumping on to his back. Her fingers dug into his neck, and then they worked up to his face, into his nose and eyes. At first Maddox seemed to enjoy the tussle, writhing and jerking around on the spot like a child being tickled, but as her fingers clamped around the pistol, as they held firm to the butt and managed to resist his attempts to ply them off, his amusement became irritation and his cockiness became anger. He gripped at her hands and fingers, squeezing hard, bringing his full strength to bear on her delicate bones, but she wouldn't shift. He started to spin around on the spot, trying to shake her off but she held firm and wouldn't be moved. He edged a finger behind the trigger, one beefy fingertip just squeezing through to keep it in place, but the pistol was moving in his mouth, withdrawing in wild jerky movements as she yanked, and tugged and wrenched it free, his fingertip twisting and popping out as the finger bone creaked and the knuckle cracked.

'Get her off me! Get this bitch off me!' Maddox was trying to turn the rifle around in his hand, to get the barrel against her body, but she knocked it away and kept on him like a limpet, moving away from it, hiding against his huge body and making any shot impossible. Maddox tried to swing his head back and connect with her face but she seemed to pre-empt each move, ducking away, shifting her head left and right. Maddox dumped the rifle on the floor in front of Turtle and then both his hands went behind his head, trying to grab her hair, her face, anything at all. 'Shoot her!'

Turtle bent down to the rifle on the ground but a giant hand stopped him, grabbed him at the collar and lifted him up again. Bergan was shaking his head.

'Leave it, Turtle. Mia?'

Her pistol barrel jammed hard against the dark stubble under Maddox's jaw line at the sound of her name. 'Mia? It's Frankie. I need you to calm down now. Can you do that for me? Calm down, Mia.'

'You on first name terms with this bitch?' Maddox's face was a strange mix of affront and embarrassment. He glared across at Bergan as she dug her pistol deeper under his jaw, her eyes peeking around his huge head, scrutinising Bergan like he were an antique to be valued.

'Shut up, Theo. Mia? You okay there? You want to tell me what's going on?'

'You came to get me,' her voice trembled, coming through gritted teeth. 'You get me away from this place. You take me home, Mr Bergan.'

'Just calm down. What happened here, Mia?'

'He's dead. He's…'

'I know, Mia. We saw. What happened to Wallace?'

She dug the pistol deeper. 'We should go now.'

'What happened to Wallace? You took his clothes, didn't you? Did you see what happened to him, what happened here?'

She was ghostly white; the dark circles under her eyes were like bruises against the pallid complexion. Her cheeks seemed hollow, her bones as if they would snap on a single breath, yet she had summoned a strength that contradicted what you could see in her. She was scared, terrified, in fear for her life. It was the aggression of one who has faced the end and refused to allow it.

'It sees, you know?' She said the words quietly, her eyes flicking between Bergan and Turtle. 'It sees everything, you, me, this…' she flashed her eyes to the side of Maddox's head, the hand holding the pistol working the cold metal further into the skin like it were a corkscrew.

'What are you talking about?'

'We need to go now.'

'We aren't going anywhere, Mia. Now I need you to calm down and take the gun away from his neck, okay? Will you do that for me?'

'We can't stay here, Mr Bergan, please. It's not safe here. You have to take me out of here.'

'We are here to keep you safe, Mia. Remember? Do

you remember why your father came here? Do you remember, Mia?'

'You can't keep me safe. You can't keep anyone safe. Not here. You want to keep me safe then you take me out of this place. It's tainted. It's wrong here. It's all wrong.'

'Take the gun away, Mia. Trust me. It's okay.' Bergan was walking to her, his hands up in front of his body, cupped for the gun. 'Mia, please.'

'No! We can't be here!' She was screaming, her face haunted and lost.

'Mia put the gun down!'

'NO!' She pulled the gun from Maddox and swung it towards Bergan. It shook in her grasp but her eyes remained still. Bergan stopped and dropped his hands, his eyes never leaving hers. 'Please…'

Maddox seized his chance. His hands thrust up against her slender wrist and jerked it upwards, the pistol firing off a single shot into the sky. Dragging her wrist down sharply and quickly she flew forward, over Maddox's bulky frame, tilting over in the air and landing on the forest floor on her back. Maddox was straight down on his rifle, plucking it up and swinging it back into his grip. Still she wouldn't relent. Pulling herself up she turned to where he now stood, the arrogance back in his face, those blue eyes flashing at her once more, and then she began to charge, her hands up, once more ready to grab, and punch, and kill. Turning the rifle around in his hands Maddox let her come on, and then as she did, as she readied herself to lunge again, he jabbed the butt of the rifle into her face, breaking her nose and sending her flat on to her front in a crumpled heap.

'Friend of yours, Frank?' Maddox asked, staring down at his handiwork, his eyes roaming her frame, her legs and her breasts. He picked up her pistol and handed it to Bergan. 'Spirited little minx. I like that.'

Bergan wasn't listening. He stood apart from Maddox and Turtle, gazing ahead into the forest, alighted on something, watching and waiting.

5

'Let's go.'

'What happened? I heard a shot.'

'Mia? Oh my, that's…'

'Let's go. Now.'

'Is she dead? What happened?'

'Go? Go where? This place is a maze, how do you know where to go?'

'We're on a hill, right?'

'Yeah, so what?'

'So we go down. Dick.'

Sullivan heard the words but couldn't place the voices. They were detached from him and meant nothing. He sat on the tree stump looking down at Wallace's body and he could feel everyone's eyes on him. He had felt, on first meeting them at Bend Lane, like the new boy at school, but now his isolation had gone way beyond that. They were alien to him, all of them, even Turtle. They spoke in their own language that he wasn't allowed to understand, they shared looks and nods and sly little expressions, they were on a different page and he didn't even know the story. Footsteps came across to him. It was Turtle.

'Hey, come on, we're moving out.'

'We're just leaving him?' Sullivan nodded down to Wallace. 'Is that fair?'

Turtle ran a hand over Sullivan's shoulder. 'Let's go.'

They set off in silence. Bergan and Maddox led the way, Mia slung over Maddox's shoulder. Behind them Davenport and Kendrick walked side by side, picking their way daintily across the forest floor, Turtle and Sullivan following some distance back.

'Who's the girl?' Sullivan asked, caring more about the silence that had fallen than the actual answer.

'Mia Hennessey.'

'Hennessey?'

'Yeah, Lucas's daughter. She came out with the point team. Never made it back, I guess.'

'Neither did Wallace.'

'No. No he didn't.'

'And the others?'

Turtle walked on without answering, Sullivan asked it again and again got no reply. Sullivan stopped still.

'Hey! What we walking into, Turtle?'

For the first time since Sullivan had met him, Turtle carried no expression.

'I don't know.'

'Keep up!' Kendrick's voice came at them like a whip. Turtle turned back and carried on. Sullivan took in a deep breath and followed.

As they got further into the forest they started to see balloons in the trees. Just a few at first; red, white and blue shapes caught in the upper branches like fat exotic birds, but as they walked on, the balloons started to grow in number. One tree was all but covered in them. Sullivan gazed up at them in wonderment. No one else seemed to spare them a consideration and Sullivan wanted to ask why, wanted to know what they meant and why no one else seemed to care.

They walked on for another quarter of an hour, each man following the man in front, and then the man in front began moving off to the side, leading the men into a small clearing. The clearing fed off into a track, and then the track opened up into a road, the brilliant white carpet slicing through the gloom of the forest, snaking its way along to a large break in the trees about a hundred yards ahead. In the gap was nothing but sky.

'At last,' Kendrick said into the air, walking to the front of the group and taking the lead. 'Come on.'

They followed him one at a time, starting off in single file but slowly breaking position as the gap in the trees drew nearer. Beyond it looked like a sheer drop, like they were cresting a cliff face, or walking along a water chute that threatened to spit them out into the great unseen, and then slowly a line of dark trees rose up into their eyeline as the other side of the forest grew across the bottom of the horizon. Kendrick and Davenport quickened their pace, encouraging the others to do the same. They grouped together and then moved apart, subconsciously forming a line across the road like they were keeping to lanes in a race.

Ahead of them a black shape lay to the side of the road, at first they thought it a rock, another tumbled down tree perhaps, but slowly, as the light ahead began to work away at the surroundings with a greater purpose, they saw it for what it was and immediately came to a stop, gathering around it like it were a discovery from another world. It was the point teams small, ride-on snowplough. It was upended against a tree, a dent like a blow from a giants fist in its side. A wing mirror hung limply off, tapping away at the side of the plough, keeping time with the sharp, winter wind. A bloody handprint was smeared across the seat. There was more blood on the blade at the front.

'When every sign is telling you to go back and you have nowhere else to go, what then?' Davenport spoke the words to no one in particular, and no one responded.

'Turtle?' Bergan nodded to the snowplough.

The stocky chef tilted the plough back on to the road and straddled the seat, firing it up. It coughed and whined and then failed. Twice more he sparked it and on the third it caught. Bergan turned and brushed a hand in the direction of the gap in the trees and Turtle edged the plough out slowly, chugging along to where the trees stopped and the sky seemed to begin, the others scuttling along in his wake.

They drew up in a line next to the snowplough, standing there at the edge of the forest and gazing down at the estate through a delicate rain of snowflakes, dancing gracefully like sprites on the swirling breeze, cold and sharp and probing. They had arrived.

For several seconds no one said anything. Davenport moved to speak but could do no better than a whine that developed and died in his throat. Bergan was motionless; Turtle the same way next to him, sitting on the snowplough like a sculpture. Maddox sucked on the end of his cigar, staring down the hill along with the others through a cloud of smoke, the fingers on his right hand strumming lightly on Mia's left thigh. Sullivan was the first to move, inching forward and then looking to Turtle, his eyes burrowing into the chef's face, asking questions he couldn't vocalise, but Turtle wasn't meeting his gaze, instead he slowly lowered his head to the handles of the snowplough and his body shivered, still fighting off the cold and now, it seemed, tears too. To the other side of Sullivan, unnoticed by the others, Kendrick had fallen to his knees and was rocking back and forth slowly, his arms wrapped around his chest in a vain grab of comfort.

'Well,' Maddox said, finally breaking the silence and spitting out the end of his cigar into the snow. 'That's not ideal is it?'

The magnificent estate, once sat in opulent splendour in the large bowl of land in the middle of Bleeker Hill, was a charred and blackened mess. Like a burnt meal ripped apart by ravenous animals, the house's carcass was hollow, its heart was ash, and its bones an ugly jet black against the wide expanse of brilliant white all around it. The roof was gone completely, three of the four walls had fallen in on themselves, the fourth, standing bare and lonely, holding up a jagged reminder of the upper floors, looking out over the rest through one blown out window eye. In front of the house were the last reminders of two large trucks, machines sucked into the destruction and spat back out empty shells. Beyond it all a wooden pen sat empty, and next to it a concrete building, one door in its side, poked up out of the snow, untouched and ignored, overseeing all like a judge.

'Turtle?' Bergan called his name and then fell silent again as if he had forgotten what he was going to say. Turtle didn't look up or respond, he didn't even move.

'This isn't...no...no I don't think so, I think...' Davenport was mumbling to himself, looking at the house like it were a mirage, trying to look through it, and then shaking the image in his head, closing his eyes and then turning back and staring into the forest before swinging around again to the house almost as if expecting to see something different.

'Frank?' Maddox was shifting Mia on his shoulder, pushing her up and then clasping a hand back on to her thigh. 'Frankie? Hey!'

One by one they looked across at Bergan, the stoical giant that had led them here. They looked for those dispassionate eyes, the cold assurance in every movement and the confidence in every word, they looked for someone to tell them what to do, and for that moment, for the first time since he had stepped into the role they now needed him to wear so well, the giant was coming up short. His eyes scanned the landscape in front of them, swept across the wide expanse of snow, the pen and the concrete building and then the house again, roaming through the blackness, and then he looked up to his men, to the stupid, dumb looking faces gawping at him hopefully.

'Turtle?'

Turtle nodded.

'Let's go.'

There was nothing else to say and nowhere else to go. Turtle fixed his eyes to the concrete building beyond the black heart of Bleeker Hill and slowly began to edge the plough forward, cutting into the snow carpet and pushing it apart, breaking a path for the others to follow. One by one they did, again falling into their single file, following the man in front.

6

Their path rounded the south side of what remained of the great house. No one could look at it as they passed; catching the black shape in the corners of their eyes they had to look away, look to their feet or to the man before them, anywhere but at the defeated ruins to their left. They could smell the ash on the air, every now and again the wind would blow up and break little clouds, and some of it came down on them with the snowflakes. To a man they focused on the concrete building, or the empty pen at its side, sometimes they would look up at the sky or down at the snow path the plough had cut for them, but no one looked left, no one wanted to look at the house, to acknowledge the warning it represented, or the horror it had seen.

Turtle turned the plough around the last remaining wall of the house and pushed on towards the concrete building, Bergan close behind, his eyes roaming every inch of the building, assessing and searching. From this close distance it looked so much bigger; the angled route they were taking revealing a much longer building than at first sight. Metal casing on the roof twinkled lightly and Bergan could see the top of what looked like a turret poking up from the back wall, a thin metal tube just cresting the top of the roof and running back down into the building. The structure was low and wide and gave the impression that it would go on forever if you carried on around. Each foot forward the plough moved, the more building that fell into sight. But more than being wide, it seemed deep. To Bergan it gave the impression that somehow what they were seeing there in the snow was merely the start, the entrance to something greater than any of them knew. "Man could get lost down there" he had heard Kendrick say many months ago, alluding perhaps to the workers who never completed their job, or to the violence that Schaeffer had perpetuated there, and as Turtle moved the plough along, cutting them a path parallel to the pen, Bergan could quite believe it.

Distracted and dwelling on a hundred thoughts, Bergan was taken by surprise as the snowplough suddenly jittered and rocked underneath Turtle, flipping out of his control momentarily and then thudding into the snow wall it had built up. Turtle was looking around him and then down both sides of the plough and across to the front. It took them all a moment to register what had happened. At first it didn't look real. An arm was flopped over the blade at the front of the plough, and next to it a man's head was squashed between the blade and the built up snow, his legs somewhere underneath the blade and the tyres, blocking the plough from moving on. His face was half sky blue, half a treacly black, the dried blood from a head wound covering one side, running down to his throat and wrapping itself around his neck like a thin scarf.

Turtle screamed and rolled out of the seat, his legs and arms manically moving below and above him like he was a dancing marionette. He landed on the freshly cut path, scrabbling on his backside away from the snowplough, gibbering stupidly and jabbing a finger at the plough in short stabbing motions.

Most of the group came to a stop behind him, looking on in a stunned and repulsed silence, but Bergan didn't even break stride. Walking over Turtle and then gliding to the front of the plough, he bent down to the bloodied face in the snow and then nodded back to Davenport.

'Connor,' Davenport said with a timid shake of the head.

Bergan moved Connor's head to him and cradled his face, gazing down into his eyes, eyes that even in his current condition seemed to carry more life than Bergan's own. With the fingers on the other hand he started smoothing over the head wound, absently picking away at the ice that had built around it. Bergan felt himself back on the valley road, and back in the truck where he had held the dying Kleinman. They had gathered around him then, just as they were doing now, staring at him in mute stupidity. He had wanted to scream at them back then, to rage and to roar at them all and give them out the pain he had been feeling, to let them taste it and to know. Now, looking down at the second corpse from the point team, the over-enthusiastic and once chatty Connor, he could feel nothing but irritation. There was no pity, no grief and no respect to the life lying in frozen death in front of him. Connor wasn't a corpse, not once a human, a colleague or a friend; he was merely one more thing in the way.

'Let's go.'

Bergan dropped Connor's head back to the plough, stood tall, taller than all of them, and started to trudge through the snow towards the building. Each footstep was hard and firm, the snow working its way up to his kneecap, trying its best to shackle him and topple him, but he powered on, and would not allow it. He didn't look back to the others until he reached the door to the building; he didn't need to, he knew they were following, that there was nothing else for them to do but follow, picking their way to him through his own giant footprints.

He slumped down to the snow and leant his weary body against the door to the building, watching the others come to him, stumbling in his wake. The door was a steel wall, a great thick slab of metal, activated by a confusing looking panel built into one side of the building. Bergan had seen such things before; he was used to any official building being impenetrable without codes, or cards, or pressing the right buttons, and it made him feel old. This particular panel had a retina scan underneath its many buttons. He had only ever seen one before and that had been in his last weeks at Party HQ, just before they were overrun. Kendrick had gone to great lengths to explain it to him and assure him of its security values. When they had come, massing in their numbers at the door to the building, they had come with hostages, Party plod that had been patrolling the streets and the alleys. The ones that fought had their eyeballs gouged out, the ones that didn't were simply shot after pressing their eyes to the screen. In the end they got to someone important enough after twenty had been killed before him. They got in eventually, they always did. It didn't matter how many buttons or codes you had, or if you secured your building with a million locks, the fact was, they always got in, in the end. Bergan had lived his life with the gun and the fist and he needed no greater sense of security. Beyond the bullet all you needed was the will to fight longer and harder than the next man.

He saw them gather at the panel on the wall, one by one they came to him and they didn't seem real. They were there but somehow they were many miles away too. The sharp winter wind was against his ankles and his legs, tickling him like long roving fingers, working its way up his body to his face, and then the force was against his head, it was in his nose and his ears and seeping into his eyes. He looked at the others, those corrupted figures, and they seemed to blur in the snowfall; the white flecks growing in definition, as the figures shimmied out to shapes he struggled to place. He saw someone lean down to the panel – Davenport, it was definitely Davenport – and then he heard a loud alarm and saw something flash red on the panel, and then Kendrick was pushing him aside and leaning his own face to the panel. There was another sound, a small beeping, and then the same thing that flashed red, flashed green and then the door was opening behind him. They were all staring at it, looking into the deep blackness beyond and then they were looking at him.

There was screaming from somewhere and then they all looked around at Maddox and Mia. He looked too, narrowing those black eyes against the dancing snowflakes, but he saw nothing but shapes, mounds and lumps in the snow, moving against each other. He heard her voice, recognised her screams, but he couldn't stand, couldn't fight the force that was holding him to the snow.

'No!' she was screaming, over and over. 'No! No! Not there...'

Kendrick was moving Turtle into the blackness ahead of them, and he was signalling to the others. Davenport was following them in. Was it Davenport? He was sure it was.

'Please! Help! Help me!' She was batting at the snow, trying to wedge her hands into the ground to stop him from dragging her and she was failing. 'No! You don't know what you're doing! You don't know what's in there!'

Maddox's shape, unmistakably Maddox, was pulling

her by the legs and then the last figure – Sullivan, it had to be Sullivan – was bending down to her, trying to calm them all and then she was screaming even louder. The three shapes came together, moving and fighting, blurring and blooming in his eyes, and then slowly they broke apart again. Her screams were sobs and he was dragging her to the door now without resistance. Then there was Sullivan and he was standing there in the doorway, the blackness seeming to radiate off him, just watching, looking and waiting.

'Let's go,' Sullivan was saying.

Bergan stood and the force that had held him seemed to fall off his body like thick water, crashing on to his feet and disappearing into the snow. He once more felt the tightness at his throat as he turned to Sullivan and the opening behind him. The blackness there seemed to rush at him like the shadow of an enemy that had been in hiding, waiting to strike, lurching up at him and then wrapping over him, sucking him in and moving him on.

He stood in the doorway of the building, Sullivan to his side, and the door began to close, sliding slowly back into place and then stopping with a clank and a thud. His corpse eyes looked on and the darkness began shifting in front of him. His eyes were adjusting; definition was forming, the way ahead becoming clearer as his eyes started eating up the blackness.

SHELTER

1

At first there was a square landing, a continuation from the metal staircase that led down to their left. To the other side was a cage lift built into a narrow chute adjacent to the landing with two simple buttons built into the top to move the lift back and forth. Beneath the landing was a long corridor, closed doors to unseen rooms on both sides. Some lights worked but most didn't, and this made the shadows creep and hug. It was impossible to see the end of the corridor from the start. There was a smell of damp and decay in the walls and in the floor, infested and immovable. Walking along the corridor, moving into the shadows, the first room they came to was decked out with communications equipment; radios, transmitters, computers and nothing much seemed to work. There were cobwebs everywhere; of course there were cobwebs. A panel was smashed, gauges broken; buttons and switches were rusted into the metal. New technology smothered by an age that had no right to be there. They wandered the room, poking and prodding, flicking switches and tapping buttons. A microphone built into the centre panel emitted a small crackle of noise, a voice came and went from the other end, and then there was nothing. Someone turned on a spotlight above a long panel of equipment. They looked again hoping to see more in the light. No one said anything. They moved out as one, moved on, back into the shadows.

The second room they came to was a meeting room of some sort; chairs positioned around in a semi circle opposite a white board with things written on it that made no sense. There was a musty smell, something emanating from the floor, a thin carpet gave the impression of being wet and there was a light slapping sound as they pressed their boots down. Someone coughed, trying to shift the smell. Next was a bedroom – two low beds were on either side of the room, a small table with a bedside light in the middle. Across one bed were loose straps and on the other bed the straps had been cut free. There were marks just visible in the wall; in the half-light they were thin grooves like scratches from long fingernails. Things crunched underfoot, blessedly out of sight and impossible to place.

Outside the bedroom and beyond, the shadows grew thicker, more impenetrable, and ominous. The floor seemed to have disappeared from underneath them and each step forward was taken on trust. A few more yards along and the floor came out above another staircase, here, barely visible, the staircase ran down to another landing before splitting out into two separate staircases, one leading left and the other right. Kendrick stepped forward, wordlessly breaking from the group, and began to descend the left hand staircase, his footsteps echoing out around the landing, coming back at them from the ceiling and making him sound as if he were twice the size he was. Davenport followed him down, and one at a time the others did the same.

Ahead of them a narrow corridor ran under a curved roof. At the far end a deep orange light shone out from the wall, casting a circular amber patch on the floor. Kendrick led them on, his neat and compact frame bustling, and the scuffed heels of his shoes clicking a steady dull rhythm for the others to follow. He turned at the orange light and they all followed him around a sharp corner, coming out on yet another dimly lit and impossibly long corridor. He walked on with purpose and confidence, striding along a good few yards ahead of the others. At the very end of the corridor a small red light was visible, tiny and bright, it seemed to be floating in the gloom and winking out of the shadows like the bloodied eye of a creature waiting to attack. Kendrick quickened his pace.

Wedged under one of Maddox's huge arms, Mia was shaking nervously, Wallace's cut off fatigues jittering against her narrow body. She tried to dig her heels into the floor and started to wriggle and fight against Maddox's hold but he afforded her no room, tightening at every jerk of her body. Sullivan could hear her shallow breathing as he walked at their backs. He watched her body try and shrink in Maddox's hold, her arms beat against his chest and his back and then, as she turned to the side, refusing to look ahead, not allowing herself to see what was looming out of the shadows in front of them, he caught a delicate tear stained eye, and as he did the eye seemed to glaze over, and then to flare, filling with hatred.

A door rose out of the darkness ahead of them, the red light showing itself to be housed in a small panel built into the side, above a series of buttons. Kendrick came to a stop and for a moment he didn't move. Another corridor was intersecting where they now stood, and as he paused at the door, his hand hovering over the buttons, he glanced slowly left and then slowly right. He seemed to be listening for something, waiting for something to happen, and as he fell into that stance so the others seemed to mimic him, each man gazing along the corridors, looking into the shadows and the darkness, breaching the cradling gloom with their eyes, trying to see beyond it, second guessing what it would reveal. To Sullivan both ends of the corridor felt like nests, as if something lived and breathed just beyond them out of sight, and that to enter the darkness would be like invading someone's home, and that whatever lived there in those shadows would surely attack. They were weak and defenceless against whatever was there, and whatever was there knew it, revelled in it, and would tease them, play with them, and then swallow them whole.

Kendrick coughed loudly, sharply, and then began punching away at the buttons on the door panel. The thought quickly clattered out of Sullivan's mind like a barely remembered dream and he laughed to himself, at himself, at his stupidity and paranoia and fitful imagination.

The door in front of them clanked and then pushed forward slightly before swinging out on its hinges. They gathered together as Kendrick stepped in and a few seconds later threw the light switch, bathing the room in a brilliantly bright, and clinical whiteness that made spots break across their vision.

At first Sullivan thought the blood was more shadows. It streaked up the wall in long tentacles and across the floor in a wide circle, so prominent against the harsh light. His first instinct was to question what object could cast such grotesque shadows and shapes, and that it surely couldn't be anything human, and then, as his eyes readjusted to the truth, the sight crept up and oozed over him and he felt goose bumps break on his arms. The room looked like an operating theatre; there were two long beds and a gurney visible through the door. A row of medical equipment, knives and scalpels and other dangerous looking implements that he couldn't name, were positioned on a small metal trolley next to the gurney. There was a machine against the back wall, more switches and buttons, and unlike the neglected technology rotting away in the first room they had entered these looked clean and new. Kendrick was standing in the blood circle in the middle of the room, his eyes ahead at a sight unseen. Davenport was following him in, his delicate footsteps almost tiptoes as he crossed the bloody pool to join his second in command.

Mia was starting to claw at Maddox, her body writhing and thrashing against him as he tried to edge her into the doorway. Her eyes were scrunched up so as not to look into the room, her legs pulled up from the ground, as if touching the floor would hurt her. She wedged her feet either side of the doorframe, pushing against it, leaning back into Maddox, not allowing him to force her into the room. He started hitting at her legs playfully, laughing into the back of her head and jigging her body in his grip like she was a toddler needing amusing. But the amusement was Maddox's alone.

'You're a sorry son of a bitch aren't you, Maddox?' Sullivan was at his side, a hand grabbing one of Maddox's beefy forearms. 'Why don't you leave the girl alone?'

'This isn't your business, killer. How about you take your limp mitt off me before I snap it off and bitch slap you with it?'

'Can't do that, let her go.'

Maddox turned to Sullivan, bringing Mia with him. 'What's that you say, killer? Sure you can, you just turn around and walk away. That's how you do it.'

'Would you be so good as to bring Mia in here,

please?' Kendrick's disembodied voice was low and controlled, magnified by the room; he sounded like a headmaster summoning a pupil to his study.

'You're wanted, nice to be wanted isn't it, darling?' Maddox said into her face, lightly licking her neck.

'Let her go, Maddox.'

'We got an impasse here, killer, because you are going to have to make me if you want that. How much do you want it?'

'Bring Mia to me, now!' Kendrick's voice was faltering, losing its composure.

Turtle was approaching Sullivan, a friendly hand up ready to move him away, but Sullivan beat it back instantly. Mia was frantic in Maddox's grip, her legs kicking out wildly, sweeping past Sullivan.

'Don't get involved, Sullivan.' Turtle was trying to move between them but Sullivan wouldn't let him.

'He's already involved, isn't that so killer?'

'Let her go.'

'Look at you, standing up to the big, bad bully. Your little letter-writing bitch would be positively gooey eyed right now wouldn't she? Think she going to think her husband's a hero, do you?'

'Don't push me, Maddox.'

'There are no heroes left, killer.'

'I'm no hero. I'm just pissed off.'

'You think she's at home counting the days until you return, I bet you think that don't you?'

'Don't…'

'Or perhaps you think she's dead? Because I think she is. Because you know what? When we are done here, when I've put you on your arse, I think I might go search her out. Send her your love. What do you think?'

The rage was instant and over powering, Sullivan felt it submerge him, soak him, and he seemed to be on Maddox before he even realised it himself. A fist slammed into the side of Maddox's skull as a knee jerked up into his groin, and as Maddox recoiled, Mia took her chance and swung her head back into his face. The burly brute staggered back into the wall, one hand shooting to the pain breaking over his face, the other grabbing at the side, probing at Sullivan's neck. Mia fell to the floor, landing gracefully on her haunches, and then she was up quickly, pushing off and running at speed down the right hand corridor, disappearing into a gloom that seemed to be pulsing out around them all.

Turtle was at Sullivan, pulling his arms, trying to prise him off. Maddox was gaining hold now, bringing his huge size to bear, roughly grabbing at Sullivan, one hand at his neck as the other clubbed clumsily at his body. The rain of blows were hard and quick, and even after Turtle had wrestled Sullivan away, Maddox had one last parting shot to offer, a giant fist swooping through the air and landing just under Sullivan's ribs. Sullivan fell as a horrid rasping wheeze escaped his throat, and as he fell he took Turtle with him, the stocky chef landing flat on top of him; the cherry on that particularly squashed cake. A few seconds later and Maddox was leaping over them both and beating a path after Mia, chasing her down, his loud and heavy footfall pounding through the corridor like a twenty-one-gun salute.

Turtle and Sullivan clambered up and slumped against the wall.

'You okay?'

'Define okay, Turtle.'

'Yeah, I know, I hear you.'

There was a sharp clicking sound coming from the other corridor – once, twice – and then it stopped. They looked up quickly, their laboured breathing catching momentarily in their chests, and it was almost with surprise that Sullivan found they were looking across at Bergan. He was checking the bullets in Mia's pistol, slamming the chamber closed then easing it out again, spinning it and then pushing it shut once more. It was him, unmistakably Bergan, but somehow what Sullivan saw there felt like an impression of the man. A gunslinger waiting down a duel on the barroom steps, that's what he looked like to Sullivan, and with his great hands swamping the pistol, it seemed almost comical, as if he were playing with a child's toy. It was his face that betrayed the image. Half turned to them, and just resting on the edge of the shadows in the left hand corridor, it was not just devoid of expression, but it seemed, of anything human at all. It was as if those corpse eyes had finally sucked the last signs of life from him. He looked grey, ashen, and his skin appeared to have creased and sagged, and as he looked across to them he seemed to be looking through them, choosing not to see them, and even as he spoke, the words seemed to be an offer, detached syllables put out there, waiting for someone to stumble by.

'With me. Come on.'

Turtle peeled away from the wall, breathing deeply and gently tapping his chest. 'Yeah, Frank, it's just...I've gotta...'

'With me. Now. We have to secure this place.' Bergan turned from them and began to wander slowly down the left hand side of the corridor, his words trailing behind him, waiting to be caught. 'Don't you want to be safe? We all want to be safe.'

Turtle scrunched his face up to Sullivan who replied with a shrug.

'That seem normal to you?' Turtle whispered, nodding to Bergan who was now barely visible in the gloomy corridor. It took Turtle a moment to respond to Sullivan's slowly developing smile. 'Define normal, right? I hear 'ya. I hear 'ya.' Turtle scuttled away, following Bergan into the corridor and then slowly disappearing from sight. 'Hold up, Frank, I'm coming.'

The pain from Maddox's punch was stuck like indigestion just under his heart and Sullivan's slow breathing was doing nothing to shift it. He straightened and stretched, his bones clicking and throbbing, their wailing articulating in his skull and a delicately blooming headache. He shuffled over to the doorway and then pulled up short. Kendrick was there again, leaning across the shaft of light, his body angled in the doorframe and he was flexing his small, and improbably neat hands, his garish watch poking out from under a sleeve and catching and reflecting the unforgiving glare of the room.

'Sorry,' Sullivan said looking over Kendrick's shoulder, one blood streak just visible on the cold, white wall behind him. 'What's the matter?' Stepping to the side he could just make out Davenport under Kendrick's outstretched arm, he was sitting on the gurney, his legs swinging back and forth like a child waiting for his supper. His face was expressionless, staring absently at something across the room.

'You let her escape. Why would you allow that?'

'Maddox was roughing her up. Terrifying her. Why would you allow that?'

Kendrick was stepping forward, his hand smoothing down the doorframe before dropping to his side, the watch sucked back under his sleeve. 'Are you questioning me?'

'She's just a kid.'

'Don't ever question me.'

'I wasn't aware I was. I just got a line I don't cross.'

'No you don't. You don't have that luxury any more.'

'I won't see her hurt.'

Kendrick leaned forward and spoke into Sullivan's face. 'Then don't look.' He stepped aside and shoved Sullivan into the room.

Sitting in the blood pool, slumped in one corner, was an old man. In the palm of one hand was a scalpel, and along one exposed arm what appeared to be roughly scrawled letters. Beneath the letters the man's wrist had been slashed.

'Ellis Schaeffer,' Kendrick said to Sullivan, extending an arm to the bloodied heap as if it were a formal introduction. 'I would say Mia has one or two things to explain. Would you not agree, Mr Sullivan? Perhaps you'd be so good as to go help find her?'

Sullivan tilted his head and slowly read the word scratched into Schaeffer's arm, whispering it to himself before saying it again to the room.

'Leave.' He turned to the others, furrowing his brow. 'Leave?'

'Now,' Kendrick cut in, holding an arm to the open doorway.

Sullivan took his cue and slowly ambled from the room, Kendrick following to the doorway, watching him disappear, and then turning to Davenport and the expectant gaze he could feel at his back.

'Not a word, Eddie,' Kendrick said. 'Don't say a fucking word.'

2

Somehow it was easier for Sullivan in the oppressive gloom of the shelter. It was like a dream; a deep sunken unreality where he could hide from the horrors the waking day presented. His memories came with definition in the darkness. She was there in the darkness, they both were – his wife and his daughter – and they walked with him, sat with him and breathed with him. Moving through coffin like corridors, wading through the hanging, thick gloom, searching for that frightened girl, Mia, he suddenly felt a cool otherworldly calm hug around his body. It was an empty dream that he could populate as he saw fit. It was skewed and shifting, but he held it for as long as he could, fighting away the thoughts of where they had been, and what he had seen.

"Leave the light on," she would say. "It's not that I'm a baby any more, it's just that there are things in the darkness. Bad things. It's where they feel safe." She had meant it. Believed it. That was always the dangerous thing…belief. Maybe it was just the young that had it nowadays. "I saw something in my cupboard. It spoke to me…"

There was something off about where they now were –

Bleeker Hill, that old story that held the stench of death from the crumpled pages of a history – it didn't take a genius or a madman to finger the sensation. "It was where the bad people went," his teacher at school had said. It was a scare story, a monument to the blurred line between good and evil. The line that was now impossible to see. He remembered old sepia photos in big old battered books, of convicts lined up before a self-appointed court in the great house that now lay in ruins. He was sure he could remember photos of them tied to the trees too. But perhaps, he tried to convince himself, that was merely his imagination, the corruption of a memory, blackened and bent by where he now stood. Whatever it was, whatever it had been and whatever explained the dream-like calm that now caressed him, there was definitely something wrong with this place, and Sullivan knew it. He had felt it as soon as they crested the hill and stood there looking down at the burnt carcass of the house. He knew the others had as well. Turtle, certainly, and surely Bergan too; the great expressionless giant had looked lost. He remembered what Turtle had said to him: "Stories, that's all, just stories," and the image of Schaeffer's bloodied body swam up into his vision as if he were floating through his eyes. Then there was the naked blue body pinned to the tree with the look of frozen horror on his face, and also the body in the snow with the wound at its head. For the briefest moment the darkness in front of him seemed to turn, to mould over a shape, and then it broke away, hanging at the walls like blackened cobwebs.

"Stories, that's all, just stories."

He felt a chill run through him as he turned the next corner.

It was all in the mind, that was how these things worked, that was what he told himself; the power of suggestion, the fear of the dark, the terror of the unknown. You could create horror from anything if you attached a history, a story. And what had he been told anyway? Nothing. Yes, they had killed people on Bleeker Hill in the dark old corners of time, but so what? With all that had happened in the most recent pages of history did such things even carry an echo any more? Then there were some missing workers, and was that so strange? People had died here in the past and the Wash had killed and maimed and destroyed people in the present, but did any of that really matter? There was hardly anywhere people hadn't died these days. He remembered the first dead body he had seen, that had been a horrible sight; a maimed torso in the back of an old van, slumped over, the bloody pulp of a face squashed against the glass, looking out at the world beyond through wide, surprised eyes. There was a period after that where he would see them daily. He would see them on the news when that was still broadcasting, and in the blurred masses of the lawless that swept through the streets consuming all. He would see them in the flames of the buildings, and the fire of his dreams. Everywhere. He couldn't remember the point where he became desensitized to the sight. Perhaps everyone had. Maybe that was the tipping point where everyone realised all hope was lost. At that understanding he fell back once more to the memory of that young kid in his house and in that moment everything connected, the images painted bright and brilliant and unavoidable, even if he closed his eyes – especially if he closed his eyes.

He was coming in from the garden, through the kitchen, along the corridor adjoining the living room, and his wife was screaming upstairs. His daughter was huddled in one corner of the living room, crying, her face buried in her hands.

"Why is Mummy screaming? Who is that man upstairs? Is it the man from the cupboard? Please tell me it's not him! I didn't mean to speak to him, I promise I didn't!"

Sullivan had gone straight for the gun. That wretched gun that his wife had bought. Bought? She said, "bought" but he had never believed her. She had found it, maybe plucked it straight from the hands of a corpse, she never said and he never pushed. She had been the one that demanded it. He had never wanted it, refused to allow it, was fearful of it, of what it meant to them. Was it giving in? Or maybe letting go? But at that moment he went straight to it like it were the most natural thing in the world. She had placed it on the bookshelf in the living room, high out of reach of their daughter. He found it immediately. No searching, there it was, falling straight into his sweaty grip. The living room door clattered open at that moment and there was his wife stumbling in. The kid was behind her, his pockets bulging with possessions; necklaces around his neck, at least five, and watches on his wrist. The kid was lunging towards him, pushing his wife away, his arms were out before him, reaching for Sullivan and his face was contorted by an effort he seemed to never have used before. But there was fear there too. He saw the gun, he reacted to the gun, and he tried to shove it away. They tilted over a chair; Sullivan cracked a knee against a table, there was more screaming, wailing, and then there was the gunshot. The full stop. The start of the next chapter. It was the loudest sound Sullivan had ever heard. He was staring down at the kid's chest, the gaping bullet wound, and then he had fired again, then twice more. He had fired the gun empty and then slumped to his knees next to the kid's body, next to that harsh, unforgiving stench of death. He had convinced himself that the gunshot was still echoing through the wound. He had, in one brief thought, imagined that the initial wound at the kid's chest was like one of those seashells that when you hold them to your ear you can hear the sea. He told himself that if he were to hold his ear to that first wound he would hear the echo of the gunshot again. His wife was at his side now, holding on to his wrist above the gun, and he could feel the perfect smoothness of her hands and then her slender, toned arms as she hugged him and wouldn't let go.

I pulled her head away. I wasn't going to let her see the blood and understand death. I refused to let her be lost to me.

He heard his name whispered quietly in his ear. It pushed through his mind then disappeared. He was half in a dream, but reality was pulling at his body, picking up his thoughts like driftwood and washing them away.

Sullivan was yanked out of his self-indulgent dream. He was swaying on his feet and shaking his head, standing in the centre of a half-lit corridor and looking at a great black shape in the middle of the floor, just up ahead of him. Around him he heard music, a gentle tinkling of notes, light and airy and played with the most wondrous heart. He turned a full circle in the corridor, looked up and down, but could not place the source of the noise. He moved to the wall to his right and pressed an ear close and then did the same to the left. The music neither grew in volume nor faded away. It was constant and it was everywhere, yet it was also just quiet enough to convince him it wasn't there at all. Almost at that thought the music stopped and a chill ran down his back as if ice were falling from the nape of his neck.

He walked forward a few more paces and the black

shape in the middle of the corridor revealed itself to be a large chair, much like a dentist's chair, with long armrests and a high back, supporting raised sections for the legs. At each armrest were metal cuffs bolted on at the ends and at the back of the chair there was another to be fastened around the neck. The chair looked unsteady, the metal base rusted and dented. He approached it, ran a hand over the armrests and the back and his hand came away sticky. He passed it and moved on, and then something stopped him, a sound, a small creaking. Then something else, some instinct or suspicion, made him look back. The chair had turned itself around, swivelled on the fragile looking base, and was now facing him again. He hadn't noticed the writing on the wall when he first entered the corridor, his attention had been at the chair and at the beautiful music, but now he saw the words and they seemed as big as he did, and he couldn't believe they had been there before. Written in a deep, crimson colour, the colour of dried blood, THE PARTY LOVES YOU was scrawled along the left hand wall.

3

Maddox pounded along corridors and down staircases. He passed empty rooms, emptied rooms, his rifle up in front of him, his eyes growing accustomed to the drabness, seeing just enough, seeing what he wanted to see. From time to time he caught Mia's footsteps up ahead and quickened his pace, then they would stop and silence would return. But not quite silence. There was something there, something underneath it. The lower he got in the building, the further into its core, a low rumbling noise seemed to grow from the floor, reverberating in patches up the walls. The building's power source, its generator, he was sure of it, yet it sounded off, different, at once like a purring engine and then as ugly as the struggling death throes of breaking machinery.

Stopping at the head of yet another staircase, Maddox plucked out a cigar, clamped it into his mouth and sparked it up, sucking the smoke in through quick puffs. He listened, and he waited. Turning first to the left hand side of the stairs he slowly craned over and looked down, then he did the same on the right and then returned to his stationary position at the top and swung the rifle into both hands and popped the magazine out. Three bullets were counted into a palm and then fed back. He sighed over the fat cigar, his breath breaking the smoke cloud, and rammed the magazine home.

'You think you can hide from me sweetheart?' he said into the darkness beneath him. 'You think you can sneak away into the shadows and I'm not going to find you? You really have no idea who I am do you?' He listened again for a moment, for a movement, but there was nothing. 'One time, few years back, in the north of the old country, I stalked this girl for three days. Three whole days on her tail. Yeah. Three days without sleep. I tracked her across the whole city. She thought she could beat me, you see? She thought she could outdo me, her and her bastard of a husband.' He laughed to himself as he leant on the recollection. 'We did this job you see? A diamond haul it was, my biggest score, a big fat win for everyone. But what I didn't know was they had no moral code. My partners had no code, Mia, neither of them. She started playing whore with me as we divided the haul, brazen little slut. Hands everywhere. Got her pinkies between my zip, got me ready, and got me thinking things I shouldn't have been thinking. But it was a scam you see? A diversion. Her old man sneaks up on us whilst she's doing her thing and he shoves a knife in my back. They left me for dead, Mia. How unfair, wouldn't you say? They took the stash and left me on the floor with a knife between my shoulder blades and a raging hard on between my legs. No way for a man to go out, Mia.'

Maddox started to descend the stairs, the tugs on the cigar getting stronger, the smoke thicker. 'I caught up with him the next morning and ripped his neck open with my bare hands. Then I killed his sister and her boyfriend. I burnt his house down and stole his car. Then for three days I stalked his wife. When I found her she was in bed with another man. No moral code, you see, Mia? She begged for forgiveness of course, offered me her mouth and her snatch in return for her life. She blamed everyone else, of course she did, she blamed her husband, she blamed the injustices of life, she would have blamed the weather if I had let her carry on. As it was I dumped her out of the window in the all together. Bitch landed in the bins.'

He reached the base of the stairs and moved out to the right, the low throbbing at the floor stopping for him as he set his path, then starting again in a grotesque rumble as he walked on. 'Why does this matter to you, Mia? Right? Why do you care? If you've any sense you know that you can't escape me, you can't hide in here forever, sure, you know that. You know that, right? You aren't stupid. Right? You push me and I don't relent, you see? I don't relent, Mia, I bite. Maybe the rest of them give a damn about you and care that you aren't harmed, but I don't. You make this any harder than it needs to be and I might just lose my temper. I got no compunction about paining you Mia, and if it came to it I'd put a bullet in you in a heartbeat. Perhaps you want to think on and decide how long you want to draw this out?'

Three amber lights were set into the right hand wall just beneath the ceiling, housed in cages thick with flies and insects. In the orange wash at the walls he could see more scattered blood patches. There was a smell of disease and decay, a pungent aroma somehow trapped in the corridor, ebbing back and forth between the walls and the open doors. He pulled down to a squat, the rifle rested in the crook of a shoulder and with his free hand he thumbed the walkie-talkie attached to his jacket.

'Frank? You hear me?' He dropped his voice to a whisper and was met with silence. 'Frankie? You out there?' He raised his voice and said the words again. The walkie-talkie crackled briefly, indecisively, and then cut out. Maddox released the button and stubbed out the cigar, pocketing the end. 'Party loves you too, baby,' he chuckled and pulled himself back up, yanking his jacket up over his nose against the eye-watering smell that was washing up and down the corridor.

There were three doors positioned along the left hand wall, three small squares of piss-yellow light coming from the inside as light bulbs gave their last squeeze of life. He turned into the first doorway, walking through blood and brittle shards of bone on the floor like they were water and fag ends. A man's body lay on a trolley in the centre of the room, stripped bare and bluer than the ocean in a child's painting. Something was attached to his head, a strap, something holding him down tight. The man's eyes were two blackened, crusted eye patches staring up at the ceiling. On his chest was a bloodied tool, something metal and medical, and something Maddox afforded only a token glance before sauntering out of the room. Nothing to see here.

The next room was all but empty, again there was the bloodied floor, the suspicious looking lumps and splats underfoot, and in the middle of the room another trolley, but this one was empty, the holding straps ripped off and lying like dead snakes on the floor. He swept the room once, took in the opened cupboards and the spilt drawers, the medical implements on the floor and the insects dive-bombing the light bulb, but there was nothing there to hold him. He backed out into the corridor and turned off towards the third room.

He knew she was there. He could feel her. He thought he saw a faint shadow dance across the yellow light spill, convinced himself he heard a noise coming from beyond the doorway, but more than either of those things he could sense her in the room. He pulled up by the doorjamb and dropped the rifle to his side, listening, breathing in his own odour from underneath his jacket, patiently waiting for her to reveal herself, playing with her from his position of strength.

'You're not seriously going to make me come in there are you?' He brought the words out with a nasty laugh. 'You got nowhere else to run to sweetheart, only choice you got left is doing this the easy way or the hard way. I'm good either way. I'm easy.'

There was a small tinkling sound like glass shards scattering to the floor, then the room settled again. The low thrumming underfoot was growing in a steady pulse and he could feel it vibrating through his boots. Another fleeting shape etched over the light spill as something passed across the room.

'I will make you a deal, Mia, how about that? You come out here now and I promise I won't hurt you.' He began to tap the rifle barrel against the wall, slow methodical taps like a metronome, counting her out. 'You don't want me to come in there, because that would make you stupid, that would make you seem belligerent and foolish and then that's going to make me angry.'

A thin metal chair leg slowly rolled out of the doorway, past his boots and then across the light patch into the shadows, coming to a stop against the wall with a delicate clunk. Maddox buried the rifle butt against his right shoulder and looked back to the side of the doorway.

'You wanna play? I can play, Mia.'

He was about to step forward when a loud blast of noise shot from the walkie-talkie and made him jump. He fumbled a huge fist on to the tiny unit and lowered the volume. Turtle was shouting through the other end like it was a can on a string.

'Maddox? You there? Come in. Over.'

'Don't shout in my fucking ear!'

'Is Frankie there? Did he come by your way? I can't find him. Came down this corridor and found the walkie-talkie and the gun but he's not here. Anything?'

'What do I care, Turtle? Deal with it. I got me a little hunt of my own.'

'Hennessey's kid? Nah that's all sorted, you can get back to the others.'

'Huh?'

'What the hell you do to her, man? She looks scared to death.'

'What? When did you see her?'

'I'm looking at her now,' Turtle lowered his voice to a whisper. 'Shit Maddox, girl looks like she's seen a ghost.'

Maddox quickly pushed off the wall and swung around into the room preparing to fire. It was larger than the previous two, but as before it was a solitary trolley set in the middle of the floor that caught the eye. Another body, another man, some nameless stranger, lay strapped to the trolley, his naked body a revolting mix of blue and red. There was shattered glass on the floor, a small bank of medical equipment against the back wall and a broken and legless chair toppled on to its side in one corner. Beyond that there was nothing else in the room. Maddox stood alone.

4

Turtle remained several steps behind Bergan as they walked their side of the building. At the start he had tried to make conversation with him, his natural chatty impulses heightened by his unease at the surroundings and the unrelenting nervousness he had been feeling since ploughing into the frozen body of Connor, but Bergan wasn't biting. The great giant merely wandered on, checking doors and empty rooms, feeling out the lay of the building. He never once turned back to Turtle, that horrid warped impression of Bergan's impassive, blank face remaining blessedly out of sight, soaking up the drabness ahead and not the shit-scared chef behind.

He could hear Bergan talking to himself, mumbling into the air, not quite words but sounds, expressive utterances sighing out of his mouth, articulated in some unseen place and escaping out of him in every breath, every heartbeat. He seemed to be walking differently too; there was something off about his usual, casual stride. He had always walked like a man who knew he held total control over everyone he spoke to – because he did – but now his walk seemed to stutter and falter every other step, like a limp; his great big army boots scuffing at the floor. Still he fiddled with the pistol, spinning the chamber, pocketing the weapon and then pulling it out again several steps on as if he had forgotten he had it. For Turtle, more than the ghostly face, the faltering walk and the random, alien words, it was Frankie Bergan's measure of seeming indecisiveness that really scared him.

They arrived at a giant pair of double doors at the end of a corridor and Bergan led them through into a huge arched room. Even in the half-light, Turtle could see how grand and imposing it was, with its wide walls and an unnecessarily high ceiling. Bergan flicked on a switch at the door and a long line of lights flickered and popped high above them like muzzle flashes at the ceiling, blasting the room with an ethereal brightness that made Turtle blink in discomfort. The room stretched a long way back and along each wall were a line of symmetrical beds with upright lockers separating each. At the far end of the room an empty doorway led to a toilet block and a line of sinks. It reminded Turtle of an army barracks and a hundred war films he had seen as a boy. Each bed was made; the duvet turned back, the pillows plumped, the ordered clinical nature of it all wildly out of step with the neglected rot that they had encountered so far. Moving closer he started to run his hands across the metal bed supports and they came away smeared with a light stickiness. A tap was dripping further on in the toilet block, the steady plop-plop of water magnified against the wide emptiness that seemed to pull out all around them. The room was a veritable palace compared to everything else they had lived and breathed for the last countless days.

'Y'know, for the first time in I don't-know-how-long, I don't actually feel I'd catch a disease if I touched something. Things looking up, Frank!'

Bergan stopped halfway down the room then turned away, retreating back to the corridor again.

'Frank? Hey, Frankie, I gotta take a piss. You mind?'

Bergan made no response, merely stopped in the doorway, his back to Turtle. Turtle crossed between the beds and wandered into the toilet block. The tiled walls seemed to shine for a single, split-second as he entered, the grouting between each as clean as freshly fallen snow. The floor, whilst not quite buffed like the walls, was still slick underfoot and he felt as if he were ice-skating as he crossed it to the urinals. To one side, next to the sinks, was a small row of shower cubicles and Turtle couldn't help but smile as he unzipped his flies.

'Damn, they got showers too. Man, what heaven that is. These clothes are beginning to feel like they've been painted on. Frank? You hear me?'

Turtle craned a look back through the open doorway and saw that Bergan hadn't moved, his giant frame was still there, gazing ahead into the corridor they had just left. Turtle shook his head, turned back to the matter in hand and began to whistle a happy tune, a tune that soon rose in pitch perceptively. Finishing up with a shiver and a satisfied sigh he moved across to the sinks and tried to tighten the dripping tap. It wouldn't budge, not even a fraction. Swivelling it around the other way the handle suddenly came off in his hand and the tap gurgled and burped and then released a torrent of scalding water into the sink, a huge cloud of steam blooming and building and eventually blowing up in front of Turtle's face. He could feel the sharp slash of the heat on his hands instantly as the water hit the sink and spat up on to him and he stumbled back, clasping them together at his chest. The steam grew, billowed upwards and started to fill the room. Turtle rubbed his hands together trying to soothe out the pain and then shook them down at his sides, combing at the cool air with his frantically dancing digits. He crossed to a sink further along and spun the cold-water tap, letting the water splash and soak his hands and the pain slowly numb out.

The mirrors above the sinks were now thick with condensation and he rubbed at the nearest one with a clenched fist. He gazed back at the stranger before him – the tired and haggard face, the greying and unkempt beard, and the greasy tangle of hair, blacker than it should have been. He looked like one of the bums that used to scavenge in the bins outside his restaurant in the capital, all those years ago. He used to chase them from the place with a kitchen knife. Disgusting tramps. This guy looked hungry, you could see it in the eyes, ravenous eyes, and the hollowness in the cheeks. Poor bastard.

Turtle watched him disappear in the steam cloud, the condensation creeping back, smearing over him, blocking him out. He felt something shift inside him as his heart tried to switch places with his stomach.

He turned back to the first tap, pulled his sleeve down over his right hand, then took up the handle and wedged it back on, turning it quickly back to its original position, the water plop-plopping away again in small drips as if nothing had ever happened. He wafted a hand at the last of the steam and as it parted his eyes instinctively went to the mirror above the sink, preparing to greet the unkempt stranger once more. At first he thought he was seeing things, but as the steam thinned and he blinked and looked again he realised what he had thought he had seen was not in his mind but directly in front of him. Or rather just behind him. The stranger was there, but he wasn't alone. There was a black shape under the condensation at the left hand edge of the mirror; a figure, impossibly tall and shrouded in clothes as black as the night sky. A hand was out before it, long twigs of fingers reaching for the back of Turtle's head.

Turtle spun around, his boots slipping on the slick ground as his backside slammed into the edge of the sink. There was no one behind him. He jumped forward and yanked open the curtains on each shower cubicle. He found no one. Nothing. Back at the mirror he saw only the terrified tramp-like stranger, the warped, mimic of a face he barely recognised.

'Hey, Frank! Frank?' Turtle seemed to fall into himself, his distracted mind yanked back as if tethered. 'Frankie?'

Turtle backed out of the room and turned into the sleeping quarters, his right knee banging instantly into the metal support of the first bed. He looked up quickly to the doorway and was about to call for Bergan again, when he noticed the doorway was empty. Bergan was gone. Stumbling forward and shoving the bed out of his way he hobbled to the door, the pain now in his knee not being heard past the overwhelming panic consuming the rest of him.

He looked up and down the corridor and then back into the room almost as if expecting to have found that he had walked past him, but Bergan was nowhere to be seen.

'Frank?' He whispered his name, then said it louder, and then finally called it, first down one side of the corridor, then down the other. There was no reply, not even a sound; there was nothing except the steady plop-plop of the dripping tap and the pounding of his heartbeat.

He didn't see the pistol and the walkie-talkie until he stepped out of the doorway, the toe of his left boot making contact with the walkie-talkie and skittling it across the floor. He could hear Maddox's voice on the other end briefly and then even that fell silent. For a moment he just stood there stupidly, not knowing what to do, then he gathered up the pistol and the walkie-talkie and regained his position, looking up and down the corridor, a pupil waiting for instruction, a frightened man looking for answers.

When the footsteps came they were so light at first that they didn't register. A small delicate shuffle, they seemed unable to find purchase on the ground, undecided and unsure, they didn't sound like footsteps at all, they sounded like someone sweeping the ground. Then, slowly, along the left hand side of the corridor a shape arose as if dragged from the cast shadows on the floor and moulded into something vaguely human. At first it was a silhouette, nothing more, and then as it drew nearer it began to be coloured in by the light of the room. Turtle stood there watching, his mouth hanging open at one side, the pistol in one shaking hand, the walkie-talkie bunched up in the other, and he didn't think to use either. He was incapable of anything logical, nothing seemed to make sense except standing there like an idiot, and in that he excelled.

Mia was in front of him, standing at the edge of the light from the room, staring back at Turtle from a face as bright as the moon. Her eyes burrowed into him, pleaded with him, but she said nothing. She just looked.

'Mia?'

There was no reply, but she seemed to smile, fleetingly.

'Are you okay, Mia?'

Turtle fumbled at the walkie-talkie, the puny little unit felt wrong in his hands, like it would break. 'Did you see Frankie? He was just…never mind.' He took the walkie-talkie to his mouth, almost swallowed it and spoke loudly, firmly, his purposefully loud bluster shattering the unnerving silence. 'Maddox? You there? Come in. Over.' Mia lowered her head, the dark curtains of hair falling over her luminous skin. 'Is Frankie there. Did he come by your way? I can't find him. Came down this corridor and found the walkie-talkie and the gun but he's not here. Anything?' He stared back into the room, across to the sinks and the showers and the brightness seemed to wink at him with a mischievous malevolence. 'Hennessey's kid? Nah, that's all sorted, you can get back to the others.' Turtle lowered his voice. 'What the hell you do to her man? She looks scared to death.' He glanced back at Mia and saw her hands clenching at the air, her body tightening. 'I'm looking at her now. Shit Maddox, girl looks like she's seen a ghost.'

There were more footsteps in the corridor, this time just beyond him, heavy and firm and coming closer. He looked up expectantly, the walkie-talkie slipping out of his hand and on to the floor with a delicate thud.

'Frank?'

Behind him Mia was raising her head, looking to the source of the sound, the figure approaching, growing out of the shadows.

'Will you help me?' Mia asked in a soft and gentle voice, so quiet that it passed Turtle without registering.

'Frank?' Turtle said again to the shape in the corridor,

his eyes squinting to see. 'That you Frank?'

'Turtle? It's Sullivan. You okay?'

Sullivan drew up to them, reading their expressions instantly. 'What's the matter?' He saw the fear and the confusion, and wondered if they saw it too.

'You pass Frankie that way?'

'No. Didn't see him.'

'Shit.'

'Everything okay?'

Turtle turned back the other way and started to half walk, half jog down the other side of the corridor. 'Define okay, man,' he shouted over his shoulder, and then he was gone, leaving Sullivan and Mia alone.

5

'Please,' Mia whispered, now fixing Sullivan with planet sized eyes. 'Please don't hurt me.'

'I'm not going to hurt you.'

'I need you to help me. Please, will you help me?' Her voice was wavering; the whisper was cracked, like a broken phone line.

He couldn't place her with the angered, snarling woman that had fought so hard with Maddox just a matter of moments ago. A helpless young girl seemed to have stepped out of that hardened female form and in that moment, from that image, Sullivan's heart leapt out to her, leaving the rotten void in his soul, left open and exposed by the last touch of his daughters skin.

Sullivan found himself nodding.

Mia turned into the light of the doorway and led him by the hand into the room. She perched on the edge of a bed, her hands falling into her lap, the toes of her battered trainers moving together, forming a V shape. She looked so young under that ghostly face, barely a teenager. Her nose was now a reddened lump, raw and angry against the calmed coolness of the rest of the skin but she seemed to pay it no attention. She nodded to the space on the bed next to her and Sullivan sat. For a moment neither of them spoke. Sullivan looked around the room, pushed a palm on to the bed to test its bounce and then offered a glance to the dripping tap further back.

'Your name is Sullivan?' Her voice was low and gentle, belying what her face showed. 'My name is Mia.'

'I know. Hello, Mia.'

'You have a first name?'

'Call me Sullivan.'

'Sullivan it is.'

'How's your nose? Looks sore, you okay?'

Mia looked confused, quizzical and then absently took a hand to her face and ran an index finger along the crusted blood that sat under her nostrils, as if she had forgotten all about the break at the end of Maddox's rifle. She dropped her hand back and delicately shook her head.

'He's a bastard, Mia. That man. I'm sorry.'

Mia shook her head again and started flashing quick, darting looks past Sullivan, over his shoulders and then down to her side. Agitated, apprehensive, she shuffled closer to him on the bed, slender fingers gripping lightly at his nearest sleeve. 'I need you to help me. Will you do that?'

'If I can, of course.'

'Why "of course" you don't even know me?'

'I have outdated sensibilities of what is right.'

'You do?'

Sullivan shrugged. 'I hope so. If I can help people, I like to think I would.'

'You clearly don't belong here.'

'Been thinking much the same thing, Mia,' Sullivan replied through a slow, wistful smile.

'The Good Samaritan?'

'I wouldn't go that far.'

'I've heard stories about you, Mr Good Samaritan.'

'Stories don't mean anything.'

'I could tell you stories.'

'I bet you could.'

Mia gripped his sleeve more tightly, turning her fingers against the cuff of his jacket, squeezing his wrist. Sullivan could see she was desperate to talk to him, to share something and take him into her confidence, but something was holding her back.

'What is it, Mia? Talk to me.'

'You've got a sad face, Sullivan. What made you so sad?'

'I thought we were talking about you, Mia?'

She dropped her face and let her greasy hair fall down against her cheeks. She started to nod slowly and Sullivan could see the rise and fall of her chest as she summoned up the words she wanted to say. 'I need to get out of here. We all need to get out of here. I need you to help me.'

'I think you're talking to the wrong man.'

'You're a Party man though?'

'I'm nothing.'

'What do you mean?'

'I'm a hired hand, Mia. A convict taking the longer of the two roads offered me. Sorry.'

Mia raised her head and took in a long and lingering breath. 'What did you do?'

'Killed someone.'

'How?'

'With a gun.'

'Did you enjoy it?'

'No.'

'Why did you do it?'

'It was self-defence.'

'Was it?'

'My wife and daughter were in danger. Yes. I had to protect them.'

'Do you regret it?'

'I regret what it cost.'

'A life?'

'Several lives.' Sullivan bowed his head this time and felt the familiar sting in his eyes. 'I regret a lot of things, Mia.'

'Do you consider yourself an honourable man?'

'Why all the questions?'

'I need to know who I'm trusting with my life.'

'Why would you want to do that?'

'You're the Good Samaritan.'

'More likely a great disappointment. You wouldn't

want to do that. I'm nothing, Mia. Nothing.'

'Where are your family now?'

'I don't know.'

'So you didn't protect them after all? That's why you have a sad face.'

Sullivan was taken aback by the coldness of her words, the economy of interest. He felt like he was in a business transaction. The hardened fighter he had first encountered was bubbling back at the surface; the little girl lost was back home, out of sight. He could sense her trying to soften her words, as if she were aware of his unease at the line of questioning.

'I'm sorry, Sullivan.'

'Don't be.'

'I've lost people too. My parents. I understand.'

'What happened to you here?'

She glazed over, seemed distracted and her hand dropped from his sleeve and thudded gently to the bed.

'You came with your father, right?'

Mia gazed at her trainers and jumped as Sullivan touched her, his left hand on her shoulder, squeezing lightly.

'How long were you in the forest?'

She froze, her tiny body seeming to fill with cement, her muscles tightening, eyes widening. Sullivan withdrew his hand and let it flop into his lap. They said nothing for the longest of minutes. Sullivan could see the little girl struggling to the surface, being fought away.

'I'm sorry, Mia.'

'I had never seen a dead body before, not before coming to this place. Even with the way things are in the country, I was always protected from things like that. My father did all he could to make sure we never saw the things that were happening. I heard things. I knew things. I knew what was outside the door whenever he wouldn't let us out. I'm not stupid. My friends all talked about it. They had all seen corpses. They all said they had anyway. It was like a rite of passage for them. My friend Alice saw five in one day once. Not me. Not any. Not until I came in here. Alice reckoned she saw a transporter van overturned one night. Five people taken for the Wash all covered in hoods. Tied up. Burning up in this van. I think she was lying.'

'You know about the Wash?'

'I never believed it, you know? What people had said about the Wash. I didn't believe it. Not until my father… not until we came here.'

She seemed in a trance, the words tumbling out of her as if someone had dynamited her subconscious. She kept her eyes at the ground, at the space between her turned in trainers.

'My father thought there was nothing more evil.' She laughed. 'But there is.'

'Depends on the company you keep, I suppose,' Sullivan offered with a light chuckle. Mia seemed oblivious to his words, to him, and ploughed on.

'He said he couldn't think of anything worse than robbing people of their memories. He said it was memories that got us through. He said if we didn't have our memories then nowadays we wouldn't have anything worth anything. Memories are all we've got, he said. As long as we've got them then this doesn't have to be a reality. Not if we've got memories.'

Her hands were clenching into fists, the veins an impossible blue under the snowy white skin, the knuckles looking like they would tear through. He thought of resting a hand on her shoulder again but the crazy emptiness in her face unnerved him. He struggled to think of the right thing to say, fearful that the wrong words would bring that fighter back to the fore, so said nothing and for several minutes she didn't either. Above them the air conditioner whirred like static wasps, a sharp gust seething through the vents. Behind them the tap dripped away. Beneath them the low thrum of machinery continued to send vibrations up through the floor.

'I wish they had taken my memories. I wish I couldn't remember.'

'No you don't.'

'They say…well, my father said, at least I heard him say, he never said these things to me of course…he said that the Wash was all about trying to implant new memories in people. Hypnosis I think. Brainwashing. Something like that. No one really knew. But I heard him say that when they got people here they would wipe their minds. A blank slate, you know? I'd go for that, Sullivan. Really I would. Wouldn't you?' She looked to Sullivan and he could feel his heart tear at the utter hopelessness in her wet eyes. 'Maybe you could choose who you could be? Wouldn't that be nice, to be someone new?'

'Would it?'

'That doesn't sound like a question.'

It wasn't. Sullivan knew he was betraying his true feelings and he knew she could see it, could see herself in the sadness at his eyes, but he refused to acknowledge it. "Acknowledgment is death around these parts" Wiggs used to say. Damn right.

'Mia?'

'Yes?' Her voice was suddenly light and child-like; the little girl back on the bed next to him, the scared innocence, the pleading eyes, the hand back at his sleeve.

'What are you so scared of?'

She looked momentarily incredulous, her pale skin creasing at the forehead, as she seemed to catch on a memory and then let it go.

'You have felt it too. I know you have.'

'What?'

'I saw your face when we arrived here. You could sense it, Sullivan. I know you could.'

'Sense what?'

'This place. There is something wrong with this place.'

His spine seemed to flush with ice water and his head went numb. *"Stories, just stories…"* He fought to hide the fear on his face, clumsily nodding, stupidly smiling and as he spoke he laughed a broken laugh that sounded as false as it was. 'Well, I could think of other places I would rather be!'

'Yeah. You can feel it too,' Mia stated matter-of-factly. 'You know about this place? You know what they used to do here? You know what they used to do to people out there in the forest?'

'They hung people.'

'They judged people.'

'We're good at that.'

'Men, women and children too, did you know that?'

Sullivan nodded. 'I've read the history books. I've heard the stories.'

'Stories don't mean anything though do they, Sullivan?'

'Not nowadays they don't.'

'It doesn't bother you what went on here?'

'History is full of the self-appointed good deciding the fate of the rest of us. This was all a long time ago. This place, what happened, it was all so long ago.'

'Why does that matter?'

Sullivan had no answer. Mia hadn't wanted one.

'Sometimes, so people say, the convicts necks wouldn't break straight away and they would take an age choking to death. My father said that they would often leave them on the trees for days after for people to see. Then they would bury them in unmarked shallow graves. You know that they let people come up here to watch? They would bring their families. Their children…'

Her words drifted away, her lips moving over sounds that didn't form.

'Look Mia, I know that there are stories about this place.'

'Stories?'

'But that's all they are, stories, there's nothing to be scared of in stories.'

'I'm not scared of stories. I'm scared of what I've seen.'

Sullivan felt the coldness hug him, icy fingers tickling, digging into his flesh.

'And what is that, Mia?'

She looked away, slowly shaking her head. 'We can't get out through the main door. But there is another way out. The lowest floor has a hatch in the ceiling.'

'Mia, please…'

'It leads up the turret. Did you see the turret? I think it's a turret, I don't know what else to call it. It's a shaft that runs through the building and comes out on the roof. A shaft? Perhaps I should call it a shaft. Maybe that's the term for it? We can get out that way, but I checked, the hatch is closed. I can't open it by myself. I need you to help me.'

'Mia…'

'You can help me do that.'

'I don't think I can do that, Mia.'

'Scared what they might do to you are you, Sullivan?'

'More concerned about what being out there will do to you, Mia.'

'I can't be here. None of us can. Don't you understand?'

'No. No, I don't.'

'We have to get out of this building.'

'So you said.'

'So listen to me then!'

'And where do we go? There's nothing outside these walls, Mia. There is nowhere else. Have you any idea what it's like out there?'

Mia looked up at him with her huge eyes. 'It's not what's out there that worries me, it's what's in here.'

'What does that mean?'

Her hands fell on his and she started to squeeze.

'If we leave, if we go now…'

'What are you talking about?'

'Please, you convince the others before it's too late. You can do that, Sullivan. You can get us out of here…'

'What are you going on about, Mia?'

'Please! You have to help me get out of here! Please! Help me!' She was shouting, her hands gripping his, squeezing with an unnatural strength.

'And go where? There is nothing for miles. There is no transport, no food, we are down to the last of the ammo…' Sullivan's voice began to rise, breaking as he barked the words at her, instantly regretting the force of them, the fear they seemed to cause her. 'There is nothing else out there! Don't you understand that? There is nothing else!'

'It's not good manners to walk out on someone, you know?'

They recognised the cocky drawl instantly and at the realisation they found the pungent cigar smoke at their nostrils. Neither wanted to look up to see him. Mia seemed to shrink on the bed, her hands moving from Sullivan's own and climbing back into her lap. Sullivan bowed his head once more and could see the great big boots walking into the room, drawing up to the bed. He could see the rifle at his side, moving upwards, swinging across his vision and then a hand was at Mia's hair, gripping tight, pulling her to her feet.

6

Sullivan, the rifle firmly against the small of his back, led them through the maze of corridors, back to Kendrick and Davenport. Maddox's left hand was wrapped tightly in Mia's hair and she stumbled along beside him. Sullivan and Mia said nothing as they walked, smothered by the grim inevitability of Maddox and separated by the words Mia had just spoken. Sullivan could feel the truth in her paranoia and fear. "There is something wrong with this place," she had said, and he knew she was right. The building somehow felt shifted, as if it had been moved just outside the line of reality. The feeling of suffocation, of being trapped, was brimming over the edges of Sullivan's mind, threatening to breach his imagination and drown it.

As they approached the room where Sullivan had left Kendrick and Davenport, Turtle came into view from the opposing corridor, scuttling forward with the pistol in hand, looking at them keenly, eyebrows raised, looking for answers he knew they didn't have.

'Anything?'

'What?' Maddox's voice was a loud crack in the corridor.

'You find Frankie?'

'Wasn't looking, Turtle.'

The chef glanced from Maddox to Sullivan and caught the troubled expression on his newfound friend.

'You okay, Sullivan? What is all this?'

'Killer here was getting a little too cosy with my date for the end of the world. What's a man to do?' Maddox cackled and pulled Mia's face to his, planting a slobbering kiss on her cheek. 'I thought you only had eyes for me, darling?'

'Get your damn hands off her!' Sullivan shouted, turning and then drawing up in front of them.

Maddox didn't break stride for him, merely raised the rifle until the barrel was plum in Sullivan's face, and then jabbed it against his forehead. 'Seems we've been here before. You didn't come out of that too well, you sure you want to try again? Just give me an excuse, killer, just give me an excuse.'

'Enough of this bullshit. Get in here!' Kendrick was back in the doorway, glaring at them like a teacher admonishing unruly pupils. He turned beady, angry little eyes on to Mia and then ducked back into the room. One by one the others followed him in.

'Hello, Mia,' Davenport was on the gurney, his neat hands gripping the edge as if he might tumble off at any moment. 'Nice to have you back with us.' Davenport's velvety voice was like that of a kindly, gin-soaked uncle. It was an impossible attempt at reassurance. Sullivan was struck by the smell of Davenport as he approached and took position at the wall alongside him; even with the overwhelmingly unwelcome stench of unwashed male bodies that had been their own personal scent from the start, Davenport still carried a delicate tang of aftershave on his skin. Clearly, Sullivan mused, Davenport still had the politician's skill of wading through shit and letting others carry the smell.

Mia caught sight of the bloodied mess that used to be Ellis Schaeffer and quickly turned away, her hand rising to trembling lips. Kendrick jumped in front of her, gripping her at the arms, moving her to him.

'Not nice is it? Why don't you take a seat dear, this may take a while.'

'Joe…for heavens sake, go easy on the girl…' Davenport's voice was now rich and smooth, a pontificating actor chewing on an old master's well-worn words.

'This is easy!'

'She's not going anywhere, take a breath.'

'Oh that's true. That's so true,' Kendrick spat, his eyes flaring momentarily. 'You're going nowhere, Mia. You know that don't you? You can't leave this place. You understand that? You do, yes? I hope you do.'

She pulled away and turned to the gurney. Davenport was gently tapping the space next to him, his warm and caring demeanour slightly undone by the politician's smile.

'Come, Mia. Sit with me. It's okay.'

She turned to Sullivan just beyond him and seemed to be searching for his opinion. Again Sullivan felt his heart shift at the sight of that lost little face, the doleful eyes looking up at him like a child asking if it were all going to be okay in the end. He had seen that look on his daughter. He had told her it was all going to be alright in the end, he had stolen the smile she gave him at that and now, being asked again, lying to Mia was just as easy. Sullivan found himself nodding to her, and that seemed to be all it took.

Mia jumped up on to the gurney next to Davenport and stared out across the room, past the smears of blood and the statuesque figures of Turtle and Maddox and to the body of Schaeffer; impassive eyes soaking up the scene, capturing the image, developing it under each slow blink of the eye.

'Turtle?' Kendrick was moving into the centre of the room, drawing their eyes to him, taking control. 'Find something to cover Schaeffer with.'

'Why?'

'Because even bastards deserve dignity.'

'They do?'

'It's the new way, Turtle. It's how we're going to save the country. Now get on with it.'

'I'm a chef, not a skivvy.'

'You're whatever I tell you to be. It's an ever-changing world, Turtle. Man needs to be able to multi-task.' Kendrick snapped his fingers and then jabbed a thumb in Schaeffer's direction. 'And where's Frankie?'

'I dunno, up and went. Disappeared.'

'Don't be ridiculous.'

'Left his pistol and the walkie-talkie,' Turtle plucked the pistol out and handed it to Kendrick, his free hand searching for the walkie-talkie and landing on an empty pocket instead. 'Shit.'

'Frankie Bergan doesn't just disappear.'

'Well, it is an ever-changing world, isn't it?'

'Don't be facetious with me, Turtle. It's not in your job description.'

Turtle turned to the mound of blood and rags that used to be Ellis Schaeffer and let out a long sigh. 'So this really is the daddy of the Wash? We used to tell stories about this guy to the new lags in the nick, spook 'em up a bit. Don't seem so scary now.'

'Get on with it Turtle, no one cares about your opinion. Then when you've done it, get something to clean down these walls.'

Turtle wandered from the room as Kendrick swept around and turned his attention back to Mia, one hand rising to a hip making him look like a low-end catalogue model.

'Well? Mia?' he snapped, making no effort to conceal his impatience. Every word was short and sharp, a probing weapon. He slid the pistol into his jacket pocket, and gently pulled his clothes straight. He coughed. Then coughed again. 'You have something you want to say?

What happened, Mia? What happened to my safe house?'

'Calm down, Joe.'

'I'm perfectly calm, Eddie. Wouldn't you say I was, Mia? I mean, considering all the corpses and the burnt out safe house, I would say I'm the model of calmness. I'm calmness per –fucking –sonifed, wouldn't you say, Mia? I mean an irrational man would probably be pounding your head into the wall to get some sort of answers from you right about now, wouldn't you think? But not me, oh no, not me, because I'm a calm man, Mia. Really. Right now I'm really fucking calm, so, you know, take advantage of that, that's what I suggest.'

'Hey, how about you treat her with a bit of respect?' Sullivan hadn't meant the edge to the words he gave, but once there he went with it, moving away from the wall and walking around the other side of the gurney, next to Mia.

'What was that, convict?' Kendrick spat.

'You heard me.'

'Your point?'

'She's just a kid.'

'Oh but don't kids grow up so quickly these days, Mr Sullivan? They have to, you see, because whilst you were rotting away in your six by nine that we saved you from, the country moved on. The country decided to declare war on its own. Perhaps the last couple of days have highlighted the urgency of our situation, or perhaps you are just ignorant enough to think it a passing fad? Of course if you really wanted to know about our predicament you should have spoken to her father...' Kendrick moved closer to Mia, leaning in. 'Good old Lucas knew how far we had fallen didn't he, Mia? What a straight arrow he was. Party through and through. The only man I could entrust such a delicate assignment to. The only one who could secure this place for us. So you see, Mia...Sullivan, when I see the results of what happened here it concerns me. Perturbs me. Confuses me. And I don't like that. I don't need that. Dear old Lucas. What happened to dear old Lucas, Mia? What happened here?'

Sullivan could see she wanted to speak but something was stopping her again; ashamed, confused, scared, every conceivable emotion seemed to be working through her, shaking her, consuming that delicate frame. Sullivan wanted to hold her, comfort her and tell her fatherly lies. He wanted to make it all better for her; he wanted that impossible task and that unwelcome power, yet he had no idea why. The girl was a stranger. They were all strangers. Yet he was the biggest stranger of all, the outsider and the gatecrasher, tethered to someone else's nightmare.

'What happened here, Mia? Talk to me. Who killed these people? Who burnt down my safe house? What the hell went on here?'

She turned away from Kendrick and gazed up at Sullivan, some sort of corrupted love behind her watering eyes, and he could see the question in her face again, the seeking of permission, and at that moment he couldn't give it. He could hear the words before she said them, could hear the reaction from Kendrick and Davenport, and worse still – Maddox, and for that moment he silently pleaded with her not to say what was at her lips. To not put him in the position of defending her against the disbelieving aggression that would pounce on her like a trapped animal. Tell them a story, he found himself thinking; lie, bullshit, tell them something they could believe. Stories, they are just stories...

'There is something here,' she said to the room.

Sullivan pulled away and shut his eyes as Kendrick stepped forward once more, moving within biting distance of her.

'I beg your pardon?'

'You heard me. There is evil here. In this building.'

As conversation stoppers go it was hard to beat. It seemed to knock the venom out of Kendrick momentarily, his irritation and anger replaced by incredulity and a thin break of a smile. Davenport started picking at his nails, one set of fingers at work on the other and then changing places. His face dropped for a second and then he regained it only to screw it up in an ugly show of bafflement. Sullivan turned and faced the wall, fearful that she would be looking to him again. He could feel the icy sensation returning, running through his spine, that horrid feeling that what she said made sense, belief in unbelievable words. He thought back to that chair in the middle of the corridor, the one he had brushed past, turning it around. At the time he thought it had turned around of its own volition, but surely…

It was Davenport that responded first, his fingers finishing their probe at their neighbour's nails and then locking together as he clasped his hands as if in worship.

'Evil?' His voice was low and empty, as flat and dry as scorched wasteland. 'What does that mean?'

'What do you think it means? There is something wrong with this place. It does things to you. It has a… presence. I don't know, I don't know what the word is Mr Davenport. But there is something in here.'

Davenport stiffened and then looked to Kendrick, something in his eyes, an old memory, a half articulated thought yanked forward, but Kendrick wasn't watching, wasn't interested in helping Davenport bring it to the surface.

'Wow really, Mia? Really? You really want to do this?' Kendrick was struggling to keep the laughter out of his voice. 'You've had all this time to think up a decent story to explain all this and what do we get…what…monsters and ghoulies? Is that what you're saying?'

'You wanted the truth. I'm giving you the truth.'

'Don't try my patience, Mia. Please don't do that. I'm a tolerant man, and I know you must have been under some…stress, recently. I understand that, really I do. I'm trying to be reasonable here, honestly I am. But don't try and play me for a fool girl. Don't do that.'

There was pleading in her eyes, raw fear, utterly wasted on the coldness Kendrick carried. 'Please let me out of here. I don't want to be here.'

'Want has nothing to do with it any more. You are here and you are staying here. You are Party property now and believe me, when they get here you are going to want a friend. You are going to want me onside, Mia. So I ask you again, what happened to my safe house? What happened to the point team?'

'They're dead.'

'All of them?'

The tears came again and she rubbed at them viciously, refusing to allow them, not willing to give into them in front of Kendrick.

'Yes,' she said, swallowing hard.

'What happened?'

'I told you...'

'No, you told me nothing.'

'Joe...' Davenport was slipping off the gurney, moving closer.

'I want to know why you, Mia, are the only person to walk away from a pile of stiffs and that little itty-bitty charred piece of what used to be our safe house. Someone went nuts here, right? Was it Schaeffer? Lucas? Was he protecting you? We all know he had a temper. Is that it?'

'No!'

'Joe!'

'Listen, Mia. Just tell me the truth. If I'm putting two and two together and coming up with a tutu then tell me, but the way I see it, it seems pretty damn obvious. Who was it? Who did this?'

'That'll do, Joe. That's enough,' Davenport said, moving between them, his hands up to Kendrick trying to placate him, but Kendrick seemed to be looking straight through him. 'She's one of us, they both are. Party looks after its own. Remember?'

Mia, renewed with hope by Davenport's intervention tugged at his jacket and fixed him with the same pleading eyes. 'Please, Mr Davenport. Please let me leave.'

'It's not safe out there, Mia, surely you know that?'

'It's not safe in here.'

'Tell me what happened here!' Kendrick was flexing his hands again, coiled in frustration and fit to explode. 'What happened to my fucking safe house?' Kendrick screamed the words, his fists up in front of him like he was about to shadow box.

'That's enough, Joe! Stop it!' Davenport replied in kind.

'It was Finn…' she said it so quietly that it took both men a moment to register that she had said anything at all. 'He burnt the safe house down.'

A deep silence dropped on the room, seemed to penetrate through the space, like a light going off in a cage, and through that quiet they instantly heard the whispering, whispering that had been there for several minutes hiding under the shouting and the bluster. It was Sullivan that first found its source, and as he turned slowly to the other side of the room, Kendrick and Davenport followed, pivoting around like figures on a board game, slowly manipulated by an unseen hand.

Maddox was standing in the doorway, his back to them, speaking in secretive whispers, one hand cupped over his mouth. The slither of doorway visible beyond his giant bulk revealed nothing else. He was, it seemed, talking to empty space.

'Hey!' Kendrick said and clapped his hands together. 'Hey, Maddox!'

'Is that Turtle? Who's he talking to?'

Sullivan could feel Mia drawing herself down, pulling her arms up around her body as if for protection. The chill at his spine was spreading out across his shoulders now and the hairs on the back of his neck were standing up, each a tiny little pin and as sensitive as exposed nerves.

'Maddox!'

'Theo! Hey, Theo! Who are you talking to?'

Maddox fell silent and dropped his hand; he raised his head and then cocked it to one side and seemed to nod. He brought his other hand up and held it across the back of his neck, squeezing it slowly. For several seconds he didn't move, frozen in the empty doorway, and then in one swift motion he spun around and faced them, confusion sprinkled across the blue eyes.

'Huh?'

'What were you doing?'

Maddox looked genuinely perplexed by the question. 'Wasn't doing anything, just standing here, why, what were you doing?'

He seemed paranoid, affronted, vaguely embarrassed, as if he had just been caught with his hand where it shouldn't be.

'Everyone's rocking their nuts off these glorious days, it would seem,' Kendrick said, shrugging the incident off as if it were happening in a different world. 'Right, so, Finn? You were telling us what Finn did, Mia. Tell me what happened and don't miss anything out.'

Davenport was still staring at Maddox in a stupefied amazement. To the other side of the gurney Sullivan was gazing at the empty doorway, at the congealing shadows outside, marvelling at the way they bent in on themselves and then seemed to bloom out at will, edging around the light spill like storm clouds around a brilliant sun.

7

Her words came slowly to start with, a stuttering jumble of recollections and thoughts, but soon she picked them up and put them together, concluding that she had gone far enough into disbelief already, and if it were to break it would be better to be done from pushing on rather than pulling back.

She had jumped as Turtle returned to the room carrying what looked like an old dustsheet. He had draped it gently over Schaeffer and silently returned to the doorway where he stood as if on guard. The room gave her quiet as she tried to explain the unexplainable, only the air conditioning outside stirred against her, breathing and whispering its deep unearthly chill.

Schaeffer's left arm poked from under the sheet, the bloody letters printed in the congealed blood on his skin still evident, and it was here Mia let her eyes rest. She rubbed gently at the right sleeve of her fatigues and then she nodded across the room, as if there sat the answer to all their questions.

'It's a warning.' Mia gently pulled up her right sleeve and one by one they took in the same letters scratched along her arm as were scratched along Schaeffer's. 'It didn't want me here.' She let the sleeve fall back and then gazed up at Kendrick with a stony set expression. 'Yet you brought me back.'

Kendrick backed off momentarily as if the word on Mia's arm were a threat, a weapon that was coming for him. He turned back to Schaeffer and then to each man in turn and was met by the same gormless, confused expression on each. Only Sullivan seemed to carry any light or understanding. The sight of the lettered scars on Mia's arm, as frightening a sight as it was, had only made Sullivan want to her hug her, to hold her close and protect her from this macabre circus. He waited for her to turn back to him and offer that hopeless, searching face again, but Mia didn't seem to need reassuring anymore. She was picking up her story and the threads of her memory and pushing on, as her audience remained caught in their silent stupidity.

'I don't know what happened to Wallace or Connor,' Mia said. 'I don't remember arriving here. I was unwell with a fever.'

'You took Wallace's clothes. He had already died when you found him?' Kendrick's words seemed to catch in his throat and they came out in jumbled beats. He started to pace the room, from Davenport to the door and then back again, his suspicious eyes flicking intermittent looks to Mia's right sleeve every time he passed the gurney.

'Of course.' Mia looked momentarily insulted. 'I found him like I assume you found him. Why shouldn't I have taken his clothes?'

Kendrick shrugged.

'Did you see his limbs?' she asked. 'You really think a human could do that?'

Kendrick gave no reply, merely waved his hand around in the air, pushing her on again. He stopped at Schaeffer's body and then bent down and tugged the sheet back over the exposed arm.

'He knew, you know? Wallace. He knew.'

'Knew what?'

'Wallace knew what was going to happen to him. I heard them talking. He dreamt it. At least that's what he said. He told my father that he dreamed how he was going to die.' She took a hand to her neck and tapped it lightly. 'Somehow he seemed to know. He knew...he knew that he shouldn't be here.'

Sullivan caught a look from across the room, Turtle was staring at him, his eyes questioning, looking for understanding in Sullivan's own. Their conversation in the cave came back to Sullivan in quick gobbles of fractured sentences and then Sullivan's own dreams, those stains in his mind, flared once before dying out again, waiting for him to acknowledge them. To Turtle's side, Maddox was rubbing at the back of his neck, and he looked as if he were about to speak, to take up Mia's story and pull it his own way, but Kendrick cut him off, turning in front of Mia and then raising his hands to his hips once more.

'Just how big a fool do you take me for? Need I remind

you that you're talking about a friend of mine? You calling my friend a crackpot, is that it? Is that what you're doing?'

'I'm telling you what I know.'

'I think you're trying to feed me a pack of lies to cover up whatever you've done here. That's what I think. You know what else? If I find out that you had a hand in what happened to my friend then I will see that the same thing happens to you. Because you know what, Mia, we haven't yet lost our way, not completely. We can still make people pay for the bad that they do.'

'Stop it…let her talk.' Davenport's voice was faltering, frightened and weak. He was looking at Mia yet somehow looking through her. 'Mia, please, please continue. You took Wallace's clothes, right?'

'I was trapped in that damn forest and I wasn't going to freeze to death. Yeah, I took his clothes. Of course I did.'

'And you got away on the snowplough?'

'I took it as far as I could. It bucked from under me and hit a tree. I tried to get off the hill. Get out of the forest. I went a little further each day, I got to the edge of the valley eventually, but I knew people were on their way. If I could just wait, stay hidden…'

'You thought they would come and rescue you?' Kendrick returned with a sneer. 'Is that what you thought, Mia?'

'I thought they would take me out of here. Yes. I hoped…'

'That they would believe in ghosts?'

She looked away from him, gazing absently into the room, shaking her head. 'You really have no idea, Mr Kendrick. None of you do.'

'Well I'm all ears, dear. Tell me. Tell us all. I'm sure we will all be riveted.' Kendrick waved his hand around again in front of her face, the vulgar watch waggling on his wrist and turning itself around. 'Go on then, get on with it.'

'The first thing I remember I was lying across the front seats of the truck and someone had come in. I felt them leaning over me, pressing into me. I thought it was...' she had meant to mention her father but instead just flicked a hand out, hoping that would do. 'I could feel them breathing in my ear. We lay there for a while. I don't know how long. Time didn't seem to stick. Didn't seem to work. I was in and out of sleep, I couldn't move, I felt like I was made of lead. You know...then, well...' She reached for her sleeve again and tugged at it once before shrugging. 'You don't want to hear any of this...'

Kendrick leant forward again, delivering curt words on stinking breath. 'I'm fascinated, Mia. Truly.'

Davenport, his professional façade tentatively regained, puffed his chest out and then gently ran a hand through Mia's hair. 'Carry on, Mia. Tell us what happened.' He smiled his well-rehearsed smile and then wiped his hand slowly down one trouser leg.

'I was jolted awake. The front cab of the truck was

bouncing, rocking, getting colder. I felt like I was in the middle of a block of ice. I could feel that breath in my ear, at my mouth, all over me. Then my arm...it pulled my sleeve up and then...' she looked to Kendrick, waited for him to jump in, to pounce on her words but Davenport was moving in front of her, blocking Kendrick off, encouraging her on.

'It's okay, Mia,' Davenport said gently.

She took a breath and held it, and then as she released it there came a small laugh, like an old memory, trapped inside her. 'There was no one else in the cab. I was alone. The doors were locked from the inside. The tailgate was up. There was nothing. There was no one there.'

'A dream,' Kendrick said blandly, shrugging his shoulders.

'No!' Mia snapped. 'No, it wasn't.'

'Go on.'

'I couldn't open the doors in the cab. They seemed to be...the locks seemed to be frozen. Maybe the cold had...I don't know...I climbed into the back and got out over the tailgate. It was so cold. It was horrible. The front door to the house was open but I couldn't find anyone there. I called. I shouted. No one came. I called for my father but...' Mia's words tailed off to a whisper and she seemed to be lost in a thought, turning something over in her mind. 'You know, it was the weirdest thing...there were these two paraffin lamps either side of the front door and I swear they lit themselves as I walked in.' She paused, waiting for more sneers or laughter, but nothing came. She went on: 'Then…it was strange…time seemed to…it seemed to stop. That is the only way I can explain it. I wandered that whole house, went in every room from the kitchen to the attic and yet somehow I didn't leave the entrance hall. It was like…'

'A dream.'

'Like my mind was in someone else. My body stayed still but my mind took off, carried away in a separate person, walking the halls and wandering from room to room. I could smell everything, the damp in the hallway to the musty staleness in the attic, yet I didn't move. Not an inch. Finally, I went into the kitchen. I remember doing that. I know I did. A meal was prepared and set out on the table. I was so hungry, famished, I hadn't eaten in days.'

She kept her head bowed, staring down at her battered trainers dangling above the floor, turning them inwards and delicately bouncing the ends together. She waited. She was convinced that someone, perhaps Kendrick, or more likely Maddox, would suddenly erupt into peels of uncontrollable hysterics, but for a minute or two no one said anything. Were it not for the delicate whispered breath of the air conditioner, she would have sworn that she had actually slipped into a dream.

'What of the food? Were any supplies ever brought in? Food, ammo, anything?'

'I don't see how they could have been. I didn't see any. I don't know. When I escaped I took what I could. Just one pack, just what Finn gave me. There wasn't much. Ammo I don't know about. I had the pistol. I didn't even want that.'

'We have no food?' Turtle suddenly shouted from the other side of the room, but no one was listening to him, he was merely articulating the question they were all asking in their minds, the one question no one else felt the need to vocalise. 'No food or ammo? Are you kidding me?'

She looked up and took in each man's identical expression. Far from laughing, they looked horrified. Davenport was playing nervously with his fingers again, looking away, staring at the wall. Maddox's eyes were flaring, the piercing blue diluting. Kendrick's face seemed to have drained of colour, yet he hadn't lost the anger, it was just there under the surface. His waving hand came again, this time a little slower, a little unsure.

'Go on.'

'I kept calling for someone, I kept shouting but no one came. I went out of the back of the house and shouted across the grounds. Nothing. Then I saw…the door here was open.' She shrugged. 'I didn't know. I didn't know anything. I saw blood in the snow. Then I saw Connor. I don't know what happened to him, I swear I don't.'

'It's okay.'

'There were bodies in the pen too. Lots of them all in a heap…' A hand went to her mouth, the index finger rubbing along the lips, the teeth chewing on the skin next to the nail. 'I had never seen a dead body before coming here. I honestly hadn't. They looked so peaceful. I remember thinking they looked happy. Is that weird?'

No response. Vacant looks. Scared eyes.

'They were from the Wash, right? Experiments. Your guinea pigs?'

Davenport gave Kendrick and Sullivan a sideways glance before confirming it with a slow nod.

'Well, it was a massacre, Mr Davenport. One body was missing a leg, another one an arm. There was a woman that had got caught on the barbed wire, trying to escape. She was riddled with bullet holes. Torn through with them. Yet she looked so pretty, so peaceful. What's going to happen to them, Mr Davenport? What will you do about them?'

'The Party will see to it. I promise they will. They will receive a proper burial.' Davenport seemed to retch and held a steadying hand out to the wall. 'When the Party arrive it will all be okay.'

'The Party loves everyone,' she said mockingly, biting off a bit of skin from her finger and spitting it to the floor.

'That's right, Mia.'

'And they loved those poor people too?'

'You are tasked with saving this country, what would

you do, Mia?' Kendrick asked. 'You have no idea the challenges we have faced trying to create a new world. No idea.'

'Cure violence with violence? Doesn't sound much like a new world to me.'

'Sometimes it takes a lunatic to change the world, Mia,' Kendrick said as if it were the most obvious thing in the world.

'Or to break it,' Mia returned.

'Semantics.'

'What about your father, Mia?' Davenport asked. 'What about Lucas?'

Mia fell silent and dropped her head, hiding behind her greasy hair. Her trainers banged together once and then were still. A sound escaped her throat, a squeak, and then she was quiet again, her body hunching over as her arms hugged against her chest. Sullivan walked behind her and then jumped up on the gurney, shuffling over to her side. She didn't jump, didn't move, and didn't even seem to notice him.

'So you came in here, what then?' Sullivan's words were gentle and calm. Fatherly. In front of her Kendrick was snapping his fingers, jigging about on the spot like a petulant teen having a tantrum. Sullivan reached down and moved Mia's face up to him, leaving the hand long enough for the coldness at her skin to cool his fingers. 'What then, Mia?'

'You have such a sad face, Sullivan.'

'Mia, tell me what happened.'

'Don't be sad, Sullivan. Please don't be sad.'

'You came in here, what then?'

'No. I don't believe I did come in here. It was like before, it was like it was in the house. I never left the door. Yet somehow I went everywhere. Every room and every corridor, like I was searching the building for something, but yet I also never left where I started.'

'Sleepwalking. It was a dream, dear,' Kendrick said, cutting in.

'No, Mr Kendrick, no it wasn't. There was music. I remember the music, such beautiful music. I seemed to carry with the music, float with it…'

Kendrick mumbled a steady stream of expletives and turned away.

'I know the complete layout of this place yet I swear I've never set foot in here before. But I've felt it. All of it.' She lost herself in Sullivan's face and the words started to come easier, quicker, with confidence. 'I was calling for my father. Shouting. I could hear noises further down. Like people talking. So I carried on. I ran to the noise, shouting his name at every landing and every turn in every corridor. I could feel that breath again, it was at my neck like someone was behind me panting. I couldn't get away from it. It was like…like when you run through a spider's web, and no matter how much you scrub yourself you can't shake the feeling that it is still on you. Yeah, that's what it felt like. You know that feeling?'

Sullivan nodded.

'I was looking for something but I didn't know what. Then there were those noises again. People talking, I swear it was people talking. I came down here,' she pointed outside, motioning to the corridor. 'The light... this room...' A shiver passed through her and into Sullivan. 'It smelt funny.'

'Did you see Schaeffer?'

She looked across to the covered mound just behind Turtle. 'I saw them both. He...' she stopped. Froze. Her face emptied, emotion and expression lost again, scared away. Her arms began to stretch out to her sides momentarily and then they stopped too, flopping back to the gurney. 'He was on the wall.'

'What?'

'Hanging there. Just hanging there. But there was nothing holding him. He was just...just there. Off the ground. Looking at me, not looking at me, looking through me. He didn't see me. He didn't know. He was dead. Blood. There was blood at his chest. A wound.' She began rubbing at her right arm, fingers reaching under the sleeve, scratching, nails digging at the skin, pinching and breaking small blood streaks. Sullivan reached across and held the arm away and she let him. She seemed oblivious to it and to him. 'He always said he would look after me and keep me safe. He promised me.'

'You're talking about your father?'

'I swear he was there.' Mia gazed absently up at the wall above where Davenport now stood and Davenport quickly backed away into the centre of the room, gawping up at it with horrified eyes. Kendrick looked at him with a barely concealed contempt. 'It was what I was supposed to be searching for. It was what I had to see. It was another warning.'

'The levitating corpse?' Kendrick said, laughing. 'That's a good one, now let me guess, at this point you turned into a chicken, is that right, Mia?'

She didn't hear him, the words drifted past her, she was deep in a memory, lost to them. 'I ran. I screamed. No, I tried to scream, but I couldn't scream. I ran. Yet I wasn't there. Not really. Somehow I knew that, yet I was still frightened.' Her eyes moved up to the ceiling and began tracing a path from one end to the other. 'I didn't see him. No wonder I suppose. I heard him but I didn't see him. I got to the turret. I think it's a turret. Is that what you call it? I don't know. The hatch was down. Open. I saw the ladder. A long ladder going on for miles it seemed. The hatch at the other end…a small white circle, miles away, like the moon. Years ago people thought they could build a ladder to the moon. People tried. Did you know that? But we know now that you can't.'

'Mia?' Sullivan could feel the light hairs on her arm, erect like she was receiving a static shock. Still she looked to the ceiling, seeing something no one else could.

'What's the matter with her?' Kendrick demanded.

'Mia?'

'I think…' she said quietly and then stopped, nodding to herself, to a question she hadn't asked. 'Yes, I think he was on the ceiling. He was following me on the ceiling. Yes. I couldn't see him but I could feel him. I could feel his breath on me. He was number thirteen and he was chasing me out of here. He said I didn't belong here.'

'For fucks sake,' Kendrick seethed and turned away, throwing his hands in the air in a dramatic show of exasperation.

'Who, Mia? Who are you talking about?'

'Him.'

'Who?'

'Them. Everyone. They walk through him. Number thirteen.'

'Mia…'

'There is so much anger,' Mia said flatly. 'There is so much anger here.'

Sullivan moved down her arm and lifted up her hand. It felt lifeless and cold; a delicate squeeze would surely shatter her bones. He looked to the others, waited for someone else to take the initiative but no one did. He pulled her to him and she came easily, flopping into his hold like a much loved rag doll.

'What about Finn?' Sullivan asked, gently stroking her hair.

'He got me away from here and took me back to the

house. He was alive. I think he was alive. But his face was bleeding. Something had attacked him. He was frantic. He was terrified. Finn never got scared. Finn never knew how to feel fear. He just didn't. He got a pack from the truck and told me to take it. He threw the pistol at me. He was screaming. Shouting. Finn knew. I could see it in his eyes. He could feel it too. He looked so scared. He looked so old.'

No one heard the first crackle from the walkie-talkie. Maddox heard the second a few moments later.

'What happened to Finn? What was it?'

'He started reloading his machine gun and was running back to the house, firing at something, chasing something I couldn't see. He fell at the door. Though he didn't really fall. He was pushed. It was as if his legs were taken out from under him. His legs were bleeding when he got back up, I could see the blood through his trousers. They were slashed and ripped and…'

'And?'

'He took up the paraffin lamps from either side of the door and threw them into the house. Then he fired his gun through the door. Just kept on firing. Firing through the flames. Then he was down again and I never saw him get up. I ran then. Ran to the snowplough. I ran. But I didn't scream. Honestly, I didn't.'

'Hello?' The voice from the walkie-talkie was low and quiet, hiding under the crackle, looking for a way through, but it was unmistakably the voice of Frankie

Bergan. Beyond the voice was the faint echo of footsteps and then, one by one they all froze as if playing a game of musical statues.

8

'Frank?'

'Frank, it's Theo, where are you?'

'Hello?' The voice at the walkie-talkie was hollow and distorted, but there nonetheless, infesting the room.

'Come in, Frank. Where are you?'

Maddox stepped out into the corridor and Turtle followed. Davenport took their place in the doorway, his neat and tidy hands playing nervously with the collar of his shirt.

'Hello…Hello?'

Kendrick remained rooted to the same position, his body twitching and jittering in his suit as his narrowed and angry eyes roamed the crumpled body tucked under Sullivan's supportive hold. Sullivan could see he wanted to shout, to rant and to rave and drag an answer from her that he could understand, but even Kendrick could see that Mia was lost to them at that moment, and that any logic had shut down with her.

'I just want you to know, Mia, that whatever you think you've seen, whatever you think you know, you are not leaving this place. Can you hear me?'

She turned her face into Sullivan's side and said nothing.

'Until the Party gets here it is for me to decide what happens to you. I just wanted you to know that. I need you to understand that.' Kendrick turned on his heels and swept from the room.

Sullivan could feel her shaking again, one cold and clammy hand holding his own. He wanted to comfort her, to tell her it would all be okay in the end, but he couldn't. Somehow it would be a betrayal, not just to the man he thought he was, but also to the man she needed him to be. At that moment he was neither, he was a spirit floating somewhere between them both, disorientated and trying to escape. It felt that if she were to release her hold on him at that moment, he would float away. At that point, in that room, he wouldn't have fought it if he had. She wasn't close to letting go though; instead she tightened her grip even more.

'We have to leave this place,' she mumbled. 'You believe me, don't you?'

He said nothing, only squeezed her hand once, hoping that would fill in the great cavernous gaps in what he understood. Their hands remained closed over each other, fingers resting against fingers, sweat mixing with sweat, staying together in their flimsy connection.

They stood in the corridor outside the room. Maddox had the walkie-talkie to his mouth and was shouting into the silence. Again and again he bellowed; Bergan's name echoing out along the corridors, bouncing and breaking and then dying in the air as it wafted back to them.

Turtle took a few steps to the left, convinced he'd heard something.

'Frankie? It's Maddox, where are you? What the hell happened to you? Talk to me!' Maddox released the button and listened. The familiar crackle returned, and again, just under it, there came echoes of footsteps; heavy thuds of boot on metal, feet ascending a staircase, coming back to them like a corrupted heartbeat. 'Frankie? Come in. Frank?'

Standing at the crossroads of corridors, they each stared off in a different direction. A light in the main corridor, the one they had walked to get here, gave a weak bloom of orange at the ceiling; the bulb seemed to be spinning, the light patch moving against its distorted wash. Then, as quick as the light grew, it faded out, and back in the darkness there was a delicate shatter of glass as if the bulb had suddenly broken.

From the left hand corridor there was another noise, a shuffling sound and this time they all heard it. They turned to it, Maddox's rifle out in front of the three men, ready to fire. It sounded for a moment as if something was being dragged, a body, many bodies perhaps.

'Frank?'

Kendrick took a step back, involuntarily moving in behind Maddox's bulk.

'What is that?'

There was a voice from the walkie-talkie, yet not quite a voice; a sound, a growl, words pushed together by the cry of something inhuman. Again it came and the noise seemed to fill the corridor and each man's mind in turn. Turtle held his hands to his ears, pulling his neck into his collar as if trying to escape it. Even Maddox seemed to waver in his rock steady position.

There were suddenly sounds all around them; a light scraping like fingers at the wall, a crude snapping like fingernails breaking, footsteps starting and then stopping, a cry, the delicate whimper of something unknown, and then out of the shadows in the left hand corridor, Frankie Bergan slowly limped forward, stumbled and then fell flat on his face before them. The sounds rose up and then dropped down on them, echoing through the three corridors and dying to silence where they stood.

NIGHT

1

Time had become a contradiction. For so long it had been the most valuable of commodities, it had been their greatest weapon and their biggest desire – the time to escape, to rebuild or just to think and to plan – but now, prompted by Turtle simply asking the room what the time was, it soon became obvious that not only did no one know, but that no one saw the need to know either, not any more, not where they now stood. This far underground, in windowless rooms feeding off corridors with broken lights and steadily growing shadows, somehow knowing the time seemed utterly irrelevant. Kendrick rolled up his right sleeve, wiggling the flashy timepiece on his wrist and realised it was broken, the hands frozen and the glass cracked. The only other member of the group to own a watch had been Bergan and that had long since given up the ghost.

Kendrick shrugged at Turtle's question, no one else even acknowledged it. 'Night time? I don't know. Does it matter?'

They had decamped to the sleeping quarters that Turtle and Bergan had found earlier, Maddox roughly depositing Bergan on to the nearest bed and staring down at him like he were about to perform the last rites. The others were gathered around like concerned family members, gazing at the ashen face and the oil black eyes in reverential silence. Only Mia hung back, standing away from the group, just behind Sullivan, her head lowered against his back.

Turtle pulled off Bergan's boots, placing them neatly at the head of the bed and then tucked the giant man's legs under the sheets, yanking the bedspread over his body and up to his neck. Bergan's head sunk into the pillow, his eyes roaming the ceiling and the lights before disappearing under slowly closing lids.

They all just stared.

Gently he breathed, his large chest rising and falling, occasionally catching and stuttering before finding the rhythm again and carrying on. The giant hands turned and rested palms down on the bed covers, and his mouth broke delicately into what seemed to be a smile. Their fallen leader slept, and for several minutes no one knew what to say, let alone what to do.

Kendrick didn't need to look up from Bergan to realise that eyes were now on him. He could sense it. Turtle and Davenport were staring, that he was sure of, Maddox too, he thought, and he took a moment to enjoy it before speaking, and when he did the words were calm and assured, an order not allowing any room for doubt or question.

'We rest. Now. Turtle and Maddox, I want you with Frankie,' he said, placing Bergan's walkie-talkie into the breast pocket of his jacket. 'He says anything, he moves, he so much as gets a hard on, I want to know. It would do neither of you any harm to have a shower either.'

'What you saying there, Joe?' Maddox's words were light and jovial, the tone utterly unsuitable.

'I'm saying you stink.'

Maddox laughed and ripped open his jacket.

'I'm not staying in here,' Mia said towards the floor, moving further into the protective wall of Sullivan's back, putting him between herself and Bergan.

'No, no you're not. I want you near me,' Kendrick said, pulling out the pistol and waving it casually around like it were a sparkler, lest anyone be in any doubt who was now in charge. 'You think I'm leaving you alone? You need to be kept in check. You want to do that for me?' He was looking at Sullivan. It wasn't a question and he made no attempt to convince Sullivan that he had any choice.

'And where are you going, Joe?' Maddox asked accusingly, pulling off his jacket and shirt and sniffing his armpits in turn. 'Mia, sweetheart, you wanna stay and do my back?'

Mia kept her head down, shuffling even closer to Sullivan.

'Communications, Theo, we need to try and make contact with the Party and the next group. Let them know our…situation. Have to see what's left worth a damn. Something must still work.'

'Good luck with that.'

'Excuse me?'

'Good luck trying to raise the dead.' Maddox blew the group a kiss and then stripped down and swaggered off towards the showers. 'Be seeing 'ya, killer,' he shouted over his shoulder to Sullivan. 'Be sure to keep our girl warm for me.'

Kendrick swiftly moved the others on, leaving Turtle alone, sitting perched on the bed opposite Bergan. For a second or two he couldn't help but nod in synch with the rise and fall of Bergan's chest, it was hypnotic, almost calming, and then, as water began to spurt from a shower cubicle at the back of the room and Maddox started to merrily whistle a tune he couldn't quite place, Turtle turned to the line of sinks and mirrors just at the edge of his sight. He had seen something there earlier. Someone. At the time he could have conned himself, the rational mind could have answered the question a thousand ways, but now, much like time, rationality seemed just out of reach, blessedly hidden somewhere outside, unable to breach the walls. Not wanting to. Turtle felt an icy grip at his neck, and as the sensation travelled through him the squat chef started to shiver.

2

Kendrick led them back through the safe house, reversing the path they had taken when they arrived. He stopped at certain open doorways and peered in, trying the light switches, going no further into the rooms that gave no reveal. He walked in short, direct steps, his body a twitching bag of nerves, yet he tried so hard to cast an air of authority as he spoke. His words were direct, teacher-like proclamations, delivered, it felt to Sullivan, with the rhythm of the waving gun he couldn't seem to holster. As ridiculous as he knew the emotion to be, as dangerous even, Sullivan couldn't help but find Kendrick's demeanour ever so slightly sad. Was he so very different from Hudson, the feared jailer of Thinwater prison? Indeed, was anyone who sought power in a hopeless world any different?

Then there was Davenport, the weak man that held the title of power as if it were aflame, chaotically juggling it, dropping it or passing it on. Davenport walked along behind them, and Sullivan didn't need to see him to make the contrast between the two men. Davenport gave away his position in every weak utterance, more so in everything he didn't say, or didn't do. Sullivan remembered seeing posters of him plastered all over

Thinwater; the smug look, the impossibly clean and unblemished face. A man more suited to selling shaving cream than politics, yet was that not the point? Davenport was supposed to be a salesman. Sullivan had vague recollections of that time rattling around his mind like memories of a childhood film watched a thousand times, and he could recall the accusations, the jokes, the pen moustaches drawn on to the posters. Davenport was, in some respects, every bit as lost as Sullivan was himself. Had Wiggs called him a patsy, or was it he who had said it? He couldn't remember. He didn't really care. He was merely painting pictures over great, gaping holes in his mind. Nothing mattered except the answers that would fill those voids and connect up the empty galaxy of dots. She was holding his hand, the girl, Mia, the haunted looking child that claimed the most incredible things. He gripped her hand tightly and she gripped back. He wasn't ready to float away. Not just yet.

They arrived back at the first floor, the great metal doorway standing atop the staircase just in front and above them. Davenport, his head bowed, entered the communications room at the base of the stairs. Kendrick was blocking Sullivan and Mia's path, an arm out again, the pistol tapping at one leg. They were at the door to the small bedroom on the opposite side of the corridor. Sullivan gave no argument, merely turned into the room and made for the nearest bed. Mia broke their hands apart and remained in the doorway, drawing up to Kendrick.

'I want you both to rest,' Kendrick started. 'It's been a long day. They aren't likely to get shorter anytime soon either. Perhaps when you have slept, you may be more… coherent. Yes? We can talk some more later.'

'You're optimistic,' Mia said, pulling back her greasy black hair into a ponytail and tying it with an elastic band plucked from deep within Wallace's old trouser pockets.

'It's my job. Optimism.'

'Coming up short, Mr Kendrick. If you don't mind me saying.'

Sullivan read those big, pained eyes again, knowing what was at her lips and what she was going to say before she said it. Kendrick clearly did too and jumped in before he could hear it. 'You're Party property now. Both of you. The Party will decide what to do with you. The Party looks after its own.' Kendrick pocketed the pistol in a wildly elaborate manoeuvre. 'One way or another.'

Kendrick slowly pulled the door to and left them.

For a while they just stood in the middle of the room, looking at each other, looking away, unsure, awkward, like it were a first date.

'Sleep,' Sullivan said quietly and motioned to one of the beds. Mia looked ready to protest, to ask things of him that he wasn't ready or able to do, so he said it again, louder and firmer, stopping her before she had chance to begin again. 'Sleep, Mia. Please.' He slumped down to the other bed and fell back with a weary sigh.

'They're going to kill me.' She said it as if it were the most obvious statement she could have ever uttered. 'You know that, don't you?'

He raised a hand up before him and slowly closed his eyes. 'I wont let them,' he replied, unaware at that moment of the weight of the words. Tiredness washed him, drenched every fibre of his being. It was a heaviness pushing on to his body and he had little choice but to let it take him. Drifting away he could sense her crossing the room, could hear the other bed squeaking lightly as she sat.

'Don't sleep. Please don't leave me alone.'

'It's okay. Really, it's all okay.' He didn't know what he was saying, just that he needed her to stop talking and let him succumb to the sudden aching exhaustion. 'Just sleep, Mia. Please. Sleep.'

'Tell me about your daughter.' It was a ploy; a ruse to stir him awake again, to keep him with her and Sullivan knew it.

'Please, Mia.'

'Where is she?'

Sullivan shook his head and scrunched his eyes. There was a dream waiting for him just beyond the door of his subconscious. He could feel it watching him. He opened his eyes slowly and felt the definition in the room softening. "A padded cell" he said to himself. "Good." He rolled into the dream and her voice fell away, calling to him from a great distance and an impossible height.

'Please don't leave me.'

'Have you tidied your room?'

'What?'

'You have to look after your mother. Will you do that? Will you do that for me? You know I love you, don't you?'

He was in the dream and his daughter was there on the bed next to him. He expected her to start reading him a bedtime story, something about monsters and castles and heroic knights. The dream started to wrap itself around him.

"Don't leave me alone."

The dream ate him alive.

His wife was there as she always was – her home, the place she crawled from his heart so as to speak to him – and she was touching him, reaching out and taking him in. He looked for his daughter again but couldn't find her. His wife held something in her arms, something that wouldn't show itself. She was leading him down endless corridors and through doors that led back to where they started. The maze never ended. She turned as she walked and spoke words he couldn't quite hear. He could smell her; still she carried that delicate aroma that he knew so well and as she touched him his skin flared with a coldness that caught his breath and made his heart falter. It wasn't love, it was fear, "and how tightly those two things are tied together" he could hear Wiggs saying in his ear, and then Wiggs was there in front of him, his body bent and broken under Hudson's rage, and then the body was Ellis Schaeffer and it was carving things into its skin with a scalpel, gently and methodically, like a child that had just learnt to spell.

He parted the blackness with a flat hand, like cutlery running through treacle; it moved, but only briefly, oozing back again slowly to where it began. She was there and he was falling behind. He pushed on, but it hurt, the muscles in his legs now nothing more than balloons with the air slowly being released from them, and then as he fell through the blackness, red and white and blue shapes started to fill the corridor, belching out of nowhere like a probing tongue. The balloons came towards him, hundreds, thousands, bobbing and drifting, bouncing together and floating past. His wife stood in the middle of the steady flow, hands reaching out to them, jumping to catch them, playfully beating others away, and laughing like a child. He called her name but she didn't hear, he shouted it, but she didn't seem to understand. She looked to the sound and stared straight through him. Lost eyes, he thought. Not dead, just lost. Much worse.

There are things worse than death.

Blood in her eyes. She was crying blood.

He ran to her and forced her into a hug. Her arms

flapped at her side and her head lolled around. She gibbered things at him as a small trickle of saliva escaped one corner of her mouth.

The hug became a slow dance.

A white balloon wafted up between them and she caught it, holding it up in front of her, caressing it, laughing at it and then taking it to her face and pressing it close. He could see her hands gripping it, the veins like brilliant blue lakes washing up to her arms under the snowy skin and then, in one quick moment, the balloon popped with an unearthly bang.

He awoke with a start and sat up, his face seeming to break through a large cobweb above his bed, yet he knew the cobweb wasn't there and that it was in fact the air itself that was breaking apart and sticking to him. There she was again, hiding from him at the foot of his bed, giggling childishly and then running to the door as soon as he caught her. She swung it open and jumped out and he was following. The girl was lying in the other bed stroking a finger along the grooves cut into the wall beside the bed. Blood in the grooves. A fingernail embedded in the wall. Then, as he passed her, she rolled into the wall and then started to fall up it. Her nimble, frail body tumbling over and over, until she was at the ceiling, squatting into it and staring down at him with bloody eyes blasted through a face as luminous as the moon. She growled, just once, like a cornered animal and then started to reach for him with a hand that seemed to be extending; impossibly long fingers, like spiders legs, rising and falling as they combed the air before him.

He turned away and lunged for the door, out he went and instantly he was standing in a wide room opposite a chair bolted into the floor. His wife, or at least what he had known as his wife, was sitting on the chair before him, her arms and legs secured by unforgiving metal. Again she was looking past him, through him. Flames were sprouting from the floor, fiery arms growing out and stroking the walls, beckoning him in. A man in white surgical scrubs entered from somewhere, just to his side, and approached the chair. In his hand an implement, something long and thin, and sharp at the end. Sullivan called to the man but it did no good. The implement was at his wife's head and he was leaning in, starting to apply pressure and then the man was turning to Sullivan just as the sharp end of the implement broke his wife's skin, and Sullivan could see his face. It was bright in the darkness. He was looking at himself.

"Please don't leave me alone."

Sullivan awoke drenched in sweat and short of breath, one hand at his chest whilst the other scrabbled at the wall. The dream held in fractured thoughts inside him and he could feel it trying to work itself together. He focused on the ceiling, the dreary nothingness there like cool water over the heat of his imagination. Slowly his breathing became steady and the sharp cold of the room began to poke and jab him back. He came readily.

He turned to his side, turned to the girl, suddenly needing to see her, wanting to hold her and steal comfort for himself whilst he tried to give it, but as he looked he saw nothing but an empty bed. Mia was gone.

3

As Kendrick pulled the door to on Sullivan and Mia, Davenport turned out into the corridor to meet him, rubbing his hands slowly together as if cleaning them on the air.

'Nothing works.'

'The mic?'

'Just noise, I can't make them hear me. They won't answer. Everything is broken.'

'Welcome to the world, Eddie.'

They entered the room together, gazing at the control panels and the displays like it were the mothership.

'You know what any of this does?'

'Nope.'

'We're in a lot of trouble, Joe.'

'You've just worked that out have you?'

Davenport bent over the main control panel and ran his hands across the dials and the buttons, flicking switches back and forth and rapping gauges with his knuckles.

'Nothing works, there's nothing, nothing's happening.'

Kendrick pressed a button beneath the main microphone in the panel and spoke: 'Hill to control, hill to control. Is there anybody out there?' His words were met with a light intermittent crackle. 'Hill to Party. Location secured. Come in. Who's out there? Hello?' Silence. Kendrick pulled off his jacket, swung it over the back of a chair and then slumped down to join it, readjusting a large cushion that had been crudely taped to the seat. Rolling forward he blew a cloud of dust from the main panel and prodded a monitor with a finger. 'There's rust on here. Dials have rusted to the panel.'

'What the hell happened here?'

Kendrick leant forward and shoved a loose cable back into place in the main control board. Next to it he pressed a button on a small monitor centre place above the panel and suddenly a picture popped up, a fuzzy white image that took Davenport a moment to place.

'Outside?'

'There's a camera built into the frame. At least something works.'

'Great, if we get some holy rollers door-stepping us we will know not to answer the door.'

Kendrick looked more closely at the picture and with one extended finger, wiped a layer of grime from the monitor screen. Their footprints and tracks to the door were now gone, a brilliantly white snow carpet lain over them under a steady shower of snowflakes. 'It's still daylight.' Kendrick smiled to himself then stopped, confused as to why he even started.

'This is wrong Joe, this is all wrong. Room looks like it's been rolled over in water, how the hell could this happen?' Davenport tapped a knuckle against a glass-fronted display and it shattered at his touch. 'Joe?'

Kendrick was gazing at the monitor, not really listening. 'Hmm?'

'The things she said…Mia…'

Kendrick slowly turned around on the chair, crossed his legs and waited silently for Davenport to continue.

'She was terrified.'

'Yes. Yes, she was, wasn't she?'

'You don't care?'

'I don't care because I don't believe her.' He squinted his beady little eyes, scrutinising Davenport's face, reading his concerns and doubts.

'Her arm?'

'She did it to herself. Why would you even doubt it?'

'You think she's lying? Seemed a pretty convincing liar to me.'

'Perhaps we should sign her up then.'

'Hilarious.'

'She's lost her mind, that's all. It happens. She saw something here, sure, I believe that. She saw her father and the point team. Left alone in a strange place with a bunch of stiffs, well, that's going to mess up a young girl isn't it? Takes a hard heart not to be changed by something like that. Encouraging actually, I would say, don't you think? In this day and age it's rare to find someone with enough humanity left to be worth saving.'

'Simple as that?'

'Maybe. Maybe she's just been hitting the glass cabinet too hard. Lot of drugs in this place, Eddie. All sorts.'

'Don't be ridiculous.'

'Easier for you to believe in ghosts is it?'

'What about Grennaught?'

Kendrick's face suddenly drained of colour and he shifted and straightened on the cushioned seat. 'What about Grennaught?'

'He came here. Right? When the workers…'

'I sent him to investigate. Yes. How do you know this? That was before your time.'

'People talk. Lot of stories round here, Joe.'

'No. There are a lot of storytellers. There's a difference.'

'There's something wrong with this place. You feel it too, you must do. Grennaught knew. First time I ever met him I knew there was something troubling him. Then there were things he said…'

'What did he say, Eddie?'

'Well nothing much, nothing specific, nothing… just…whenever anyone mentioned this place…'

'Man always did have a wandering vocabulary. You'd have hoped for a better code of silence from a copper.'

'Well, he'll not be saying anything any more. I shouldn't worry.'

'Who's worrying?' Kendrick's tone was accusing and confrontational. 'Am I worrying? Should I be worrying? Why would I worry?'

The two men stared each other down in silence, a creeping, horrid thought working into Davenport's mind then being pushed away. He broke the tension with an unconvincing laugh and a shrug of the shoulders and then returned to his hands, fingers working on fingers, nails rubbing at nails.

'And you don't believe it? Any of it?'

'I'm having trouble enough believing in the living. I live in the real world, Eddie.'

'Yes, but...'

'And that's bad enough.'

'So that's it? That's how you dismiss this? Madness?'

'Don't talk to me like I'm the unreasonable one here, not believing in magic.'

'You mean ghosts?'

'Don't tell me what I mean. Magic. Ghosts. The Loch Ness mother-lovin' monster, whatever. I deal in facts. I deal with what's in my face. I'm not irrational and I don't deal in make believe. I'm trying to keep us alive. I'm trying to keep us safe. I deal with the walking scum out there running amok through our country, those people that would see us dead and not even think twice about it. Them. That's my gig. That's my job. I'm very sorry if my remit doesn't stretch to walking through walls.'

'Those workers that disappeared here, how did Grennaught explain that?'

Again Kendrick shifted on the cushion awkwardly. 'He didn't.'

'How do you explain it?'

'I don't. I don't have to. They were lags. All of them. Saw a chance to skittle out and took it. That's all. They did a runner.'

Davenport straightened his clothes and crossed the room, perching on the edge of a small filing cabinet. 'What do we do with them? Sullivan and Mia?'

'Leave it to the Party to decide.'

'They will want them killed. You know they will.'

'The girl certainly, if she doesn't curb her fantastical ramblings.' He fixed Davenport with a firm stare, looking deep, making sure his words sunk in. 'Party doesn't deal in the fantastical. The stories or the storytellers.'

Davenport dropped his head and nodded, unconvincingly. 'We owe them.'

'No we don't.'

'I do.'

'What?'

'His wife?'

'Ah, the guilt complex, of course. Though how you stretch that guilt to Mia Hennessey, I really don't know.'

'We sent her father here.'

'It was his job. Lucas was doing his job, a job, lest we forget, that he really rather enjoyed.'

'His job was clearing up a mess we made. Let's not forget that either.'

'One man's mess is another's work of art.'

'What? Are you trying to defend what went on here?'

'The Wash was working. You know it was.'

'Dear God, man. What are you saying?'

'You know I thought you were being hasty closing it down.'

'You would have let him continue?' Davenport's voice raised and then wavered. 'Do you know what you have done to all those poor bastards that ended up here? How many of them are actually still alive? How many were you prepared to butcher for your experiment before you realised it was a waste of time?'

'Me?'

'Us, then. Us. Them. Christ, Joe. This place was a slaughterhouse.'

'Some people kill with science, some with a gun, and you kill with a pen. What's the real difference?'

'I never killed anyone!'

'All those incursions you signed off on, those little food raids, intelligence gathering? They didn't come without cost you know? Those places we have holed up in since leaving the capital, they had to be cleared first. You understand what that means?'

'At times you repulse me, Joe.'

'You're in good company, Eddie. One day they will make badges.'

Once again they stared each other down, neither wanting to give to the other. Davenport's' chest puffed out briefly, but he couldn't hold the pose.

'We're all killers. One way or another. There's not one of us clean enough to look down and judge. Party was built on force. This wasn't given to us. Lucas knew that better than most, you know? Lucas was a killer. You think that because he did it for us that he is absolved from sin? It was what he did.'

'We still owe him. We owe his family.'

'Four armed men against one scientist and a bunch of vegetables? You gave him pretty good odds.'

'You really think that was all they faced here?'

Kendrick gave a long sigh and swivelled around in his chair.

'Hate to think you're giving concession to craziness, Eddie. Think on.'

'We owe them. Both of them. Though quite how you balance that debt, I really don't know.'

'We owe them nothing. Lucas knew the mission was dangerous. He knew the risks. His daughter should have known the risks too. Sullivan's wife as well. She walked into the lion's den knowing full well that she may as well have just painted targets on her tits.'

'She did it for her husband. She did it to save him. Get him out of that place.'

'More fool her then.' Kendrick flapped his hands dismissively and returned to gazing at the small monitor.

'At the very least we owe it to Mia to listen to her. To take her seriously.'

'Sounds awfully like you might believe her, Prime Minister? Is that what I have to tell the Party when they arrive? Is that where we are?'

Davenport eased himself off the filing cabinet and wandered past Kendrick to the doorway, staring absently out into the corridor and then looking back in at the room, at the lines of switches and dials, and at Kendrick sitting before them and he despised everything he saw. There was a sound over Davenport's shoulder and he turned quickly and caught something in the corner of his eye. Mia was standing in the corridor looking at him, gently closing the door to the bedroom behind her. She paused, waiting for his response, readying herself to run when he made his move. Slowly, delicately, and unseen by Kendrick, Davenport pushed the communications room door to.

'Where's Baxter when you need him?' Davenport said, waving a hand absently at the confusing control panel.

'Dead.' The word came colder than it had any need to and Kendrick tried to dampen it with another casual shrug. 'And you're not, Eddie. That's how it works now, right?' Kendrick pulled the pistol out and rested it gently in front of him, wedged between two dials. 'It's them and us.'

'I think you've a slightly inflated sense of the importance we hold.'

'Party is everything, Prime Minister; I'd hoped you knew that. There is nothing else. This is the Party's country. It is ours to shape and define. From your tone one might suggest you don't fully appreciate your great fortune.'

Davenport gave a small snort of disdain.

'Ok, get it out of your system. Do it now, go on Eddie.'

'Meaning what?'

'You are unhappy, questioning, you have concerns, best you talk to a friend now than a committee later when the Party arrive. What troubles you?'

'What apart from being sealed off in this hell hole, with no food, no ammo, no communications and you?'

'Yes, Eddie, apart from that.'

'It wasn't lost on me, you know?'

'What's that, old chap?'

'The retina scan. You always taught me it was the little things that said the most.'

'Don't fancy making it say it a bit louder do you?'

'I didn't have clearance. You did, but I didn't.'

'I see.'

'Still, I'm just a mouthpiece, aren't I? I suppose I shouldn't be so surprised. Was it ever any different? I'm a face, an interchangeable dartboard, somewhere to direct anger. That's all. We are all just disposable to you, aren't we? Get on the page or get out the way.'

'The Party is everything.'

'So what of a man that stands against the Party's wishes? A man like Grennaught, say? That sort of man would have to be removed wouldn't he?' Davenport puffed his chest out, high and proud. 'He warned you not to come here, didn't he? What did he see here?'

'Has it really come to this?' Kendrick asked slowly, quietly, with a small shake of the head. 'Am I really the only sane person here?'

'Don't worry about us madmen, Joe. We are but easily ignored and quickly replaced.'

Kendrick moved so fast, so nimbly, that Davenport was caught off guard. He heard the rip of the tape holding the cushion and saw Kendrick lunge forward, and in that one brief moment he had the bizarre idea that Kendrick was coming in for a hug.

Their bodies slammed together and they stumbled back to the closed door, Kendrick bringing his weight down on to Davenport's weaker frame as the cushion pressed into his face. As Davenport crumpled, Kendrick buried the pistol deep into the centre of the cushion and yanked back on the trigger, turning his head from the small blast of blood and feathers that came and went and left its memory on the back of the door.

Kendrick returned to the chair and slumped on to the firm, un-cushioned, seat. Slowly he leaned back and rested his feet on the large panel of meaningless buttons and switches before him. He gazed at his battered shoes, a curdled look of disappointment on his face.

4

He knew he still had one foot and half a mind in the dream. He couldn't let her go, and like the heartbroken pathetic male he held the fiction just as tightly as the facts, willingly corrupting himself and refusing to see the edges of its limits. She walked at his side, visible just at the very corner of his eyes. He could feel her lightness next to him, the delicate breath. At times she would move across him, through him, and take position on his opposite side. His walk was too light to be fully real, like a spaceman treading air without the pull of gravity he felt anchored down by little more than a frayed cord. He was one of the balloons in his dream, drifting aimlessly along, lost and trapped yet too scared to float away. Time and again he seemed to turn corners he had already turned and walked corridors he had already walked, but still she moved him on. The girl. He had to find the girl. Had to find something. The dank and dirty smell that had suggested itself from the moment they had arrived was, the further he went into the bowels of the building, moving beyond suggestion and becoming a statement. He would put an arm to his nose, turn his face away, rub at his watering eyes, yet still the smell washed over him, seeped into him, proved inescapable. Beneath him there were noises, rumbles and thuds and other sounds that seemed to have no source, and the walls, those thick, impenetrable, suffocating walls, seemed to billow and vibrate, as if a mighty, ungodly wind was blooming just beyond.

He was into the building's black heart and now she had left him, stuck somewhere in the darkness, caught like a butterfly in a spider's web.

Before him was a set of white doors. They came to him slowly, whilst at the same time tried to pull away. He fumbled at the handles and as he pushed them open a thousand detached images flew around his mind like objects on a child's mobile. His hand found a light switch and a dull, sickly yellow colour grew at the ceiling, then all that he held in his mind scattered, blown away like the seeds from a dandelion. He said his name once, in his mind, then let the name fall off his tongue.

'Sullivan.'

Fastened to the floor in the middle of a wide and empty room was the same large chair he had seen earlier and seen again in his dream. The long arm rests and high back, the metal cuffs bolted on and opened out ready for the next visitor. Hanging over the back of the chair were a set of headphones and before the chair was a film screen pulled down from the wall. At the back of the room a film projector was placed clumsily on a stack of books, pointing toward it, dusty and rusted. There was little else to be seen except another door at the back of the room, partially open and leading to a small office beyond. He crossed to it. Beneath his unsteady feet discarded syringes shattered at the pressure of his thick boots and further down, deep below, machinery seemed to scream on its last turn of life.

The office was small and cramped, the walls lined with intersected shelves piled high with large dusty tomes and dog-eared folders. A small corner desk to his left held a chaotic field of paper and a cluster of photos in frames. He could see Schaeffer staring back from some, a tall, dark haired woman in several others, and a slight, smiling girl in all. The sheer joyful normality that emanated from each trapped image held no place in this building and it threw Sullivan off balance. He held one of the photos close to him, turning it to the meagre light, looking wistfully at the young girl that stared back, and at once – with the same sheer heart-tearing predictability it always came with – he was seeing nothing but his daughter.

Sullivan replaced the photo and the memory and turned to the shelves, thumbing the spines of the books, and flipping over the covers of various folders. The books felt as dry and heavy as the air around him. He pulled a couple of medical journals from the shelves, casting a confused eye over words he didn't understand, and then discarding them to the table in a small cloud of dust. More books were dragged out and dumped to the table, cursory glances showed words and phrases he had heard of but had no care to rediscover; electroconvulsive, anger, suppression, retrograde, amnesia, hypnosis, therapy…there were books on dream interpretations, brain function and hallucinogens, papers and case studies, so much information, so many facts and figures, and each one started to feel like different edges to the same picture. He looked back to the chair in the other room and felt a lump swell in his throat. "Memories are all we've got," he could hear Mia saying to him. "As long as we've got them then this doesn't have to be a reality. Not if we've got memories." How many? How many had there been? He pulled a case study file from the desk and it seemed to perish in his hands, papers and photos spilling from its useless skin and on to the floor. He bent down and gathered up the photos, his eyes stinging at each nameless face he took in, each in varying stages of whatever collective horror had been taking place here. From the photos in his hand he turned back to the photos on the table, Schaeffer and the tall woman and the smiling girl. How much time and space separated what he held and what he saw?

'What the hell happened to us?' He found himself asking the air around him. As if in response to his question a book fell from a shelf, and with it the shelf seemed to tilt and rock and tip over. A small shower of papers and files landed on him, breaking open around him, spilling their secrets before him. His hands went to the ground, pushing through photos and papers, moving them to the side, searching out something else, searching for…

It was a small, grey Dictaphone sat on its end under the corner table. His hands shot to it and pulled it out across the floor and into his lap. His fingers played along the buttons. He popped it open and saw a tape inside, and then pushed it shut and thumbed the rewind button. It was Schaeffer's voice that came to him when finally he played back the tape, lost and lonely, from another world, just out of reach.

BH13 fascinates and repels. I feel torn between wanting to study him and being terrified of even being in the same room. The things the other workers would say about him and I never listened. My work consumed me. I cared only for what I was creating. I was blind to him. It is only now that he chooses to make the truth unavoidable that I can see him for what he is. We shouldn't be here. He keeps saying we shouldn't be here. Yet somehow our arrival seems unavoidable. Preordained. This place must be buried. It is not a place for life. I question the life now within him. It is no longer a soul but a force. It is a vessel for the dead. He wants to be heard but I am fearful that if he is he will then kill us all.

A pause. Laughter. The lighting of a cigarette and the slow deliberate exhales of the smoke. Somewhere in the background, music is playing. The recording clicks off.

Silence. A few moments later a different sounding Schaeffer returns. Distracted. Nervous.

It is my belief that BH13 is somehow feeding on the energy here. Somehow, in ways I am not qualified to even try and explain, he is tethered to this shelter. He was always meant to be here. Maybe, in some way, we all were. It was BH13's fate that he should end up here. Maybe we all share that same fate. This place seems to need him. It calls to him. It judges him. It judges us all. Was that not what always happened here? Can the dead not judge as well as the living? Whether BH13's gift is genuine or just an elaborate ruse to play up to a persona, I cannot say, but I catch him on the odd moments talking to himself, turning to some unseen person next to him and opening a full and frank exchange. It is a deeply unnerving thing to witness. What does he see? Is it just a con? The story of this area is well documented, so I have no need to doubt that BH13 would be as fully versed in its dark history as most others. Though if it is a con, he's the greatest I have ever seen.

I have so much I want to ask him yet I find myself increasingly frightened to approach. He is displaying occasional bouts of uncontrollable rage at the other workers and for the most part he works alone. I have assigned him to the chamber, deep below at the core of this terrible place. He looks as if he is not sleeping and has hardly eaten much over the last few days. He is distracted and distant. My instinct is that he should be removed immediately for both his own good and that of his fellow workers, and yet I can't bring myself to seek approval for it. He is grotesquely fascinating. I think he is the only person who truly understands this place. What price knowledge?

Click off. Silence. Click on. Whispered voice.

An extraordinary and troubling night. I worked late preparing to receive the next batch of test subjects for the Wash and was returning to my room gone midnight. Something drew me to the workers sleeping quarters, a sixth sense, a notion, a vision; I don't know what I should call it. Something. There was something there. I took the slightly longer route back so as to pass where they slept and it was with little surprise that upon arriving I found BH13 to be the only one awake. More than that though, he was sat up in bed and staring out across the room. He looked so pale. So very haunted. He was rocking back and forth in bed, his arms tight around his chest. A catatonic state for want of a better description, yet a description that does not do it justice. He seemed…consumed. He was fixed at a point before him, his eyes unflinching, widening, he glowed in the darkness like a diamond in the deepest mine. Then, as if struck, he fell back on to the bed and seemed to be choking, his hands went to his throat, scrabbling for purchase on something that wasn't there, long fingers trying to prise something from him, gripping, tugging, and digging into his flesh. I stood

*watching. I couldn't move, couldn't step forward to help him.
Now, safe in the company of single malt I ask myself what I
could have done to help him and can find no answer. If I
approached would those hard hands not turn on to me? I find
no shame in my cowardice.*

Schaeffer's words seemed lost for a moment, they came
but they came quiet, as if he were speaking from inside a
sealed box. Sullivan raised the Dictaphone to his ear.
Something else was there; a growl, a snarl, something…
when Schaeffer's words returned, they were so loud
Sullivan almost dropped the Dictaphone.

*…flung upwards above the bed! His body bending back on
itself in a huge, impossible arch, and then with one sudden
jerk, like he were a wet towel being flicked out by an invisible
hand, his body whipped itself straight and tumbled back to
the bed like a pile of rags. I have been in my room ever since,
afraid to go outside. A foolish coward. I have tried to make
contact with the night watch above but no through line is
active. I must wait until morning. I have a childish dream
that all will be well in the morning. I do not believe in
weaponry, my distaste for guns is, I hope, well documented,
but I have taken the gun that the Party supplied me with
from inside the cabinet. I am disgusted by how it makes me
feel safe.*

Click. There was nothing but silence for several minutes.

Sullivan wound the tape on and then flipped play. Schaeffer returned.

I have blood on my hands, both metaphorically and literally. There is a fine line between the unseen and fear and I sit astride it now. As a man of science I watch him in awe, the things he does, the personalities he seems to create, marvelling and dreaming of what he can do, yet the compassionate man I hoped to be is torn in two by the madness he seems to be enduring and I cannot let this progress. I ask myself about compassion, convince myself that I was ever worthy of that trait and then I see what I am doing here. I strive to create something incredible and whilst I do, I am but merely a butcher. The carnage is a path to cure. That is the line. That is the line I straddle. Last night I fired the gun at the wall in my room and I have no idea why.

He is now fully removed from the others.

Click. Fast forward. Play.

He is awake again. At least something is. I have heard at least five different voices within him. I can hear them calling at me from deep below in the chamber. It would seem even the very bowels of this dreadful building is not a deep enough place for this man. I confess that now, when the bodies are sent down to the chamber, we don't even look at him. The patients stir each time he awakens as if they sense something.

Whilst this recognition in the subjects shows how far we have progressed with the Wash, my joy is tempered by the rage in that corrupted soul's voice.

Kendrick has sent someone out here to investigate the disappearance of the workers. He had no interest in my concerns as I suspected he wouldn't. He does not believe me. He patronises me. Kendrick cares only for the Wash. He is delighted at the progress and chooses to hear nothing else. I hear they are changing leader again so I put his blinkered attitude down to him being too busy with Party affairs to be concerned about our trivial little horrors. The very notion that the Party would choose this place for the country's rebirth seems too thick an irony to swallow.

He is a killer. I am sure of it. The watch won't even come near him now. Even with him sedated and chained they will not breath the same air. We are into the last days of building and that we ever got this far is a miracle. Grennaught watches him like only a policeman can. BH13 is all but gone from within the thing I see. He talks but it is with the tongue of others. Many others. At times I believe I can hear him. There are moments when I recognise his voice but in that time he says only one thing. He speaks only a warning. Grennaught believes he can question him like a normal suspect. I warned him. I warned Kendrick, but neither believed me. They believe the missing have run away, somehow escaping the watch's rifles up above, to hotfoot it through the snow and into the forest. They say they will search, but they won't. I wish I could believe them. I hope they have escaped. I hope what I dreamed last night was just a dream.

A long silence. Sullivan wound the tape on. When the voice returned it was not Schaeffer. Not at first. It was a deep, scratching growl that seemed to come not from the Dictaphone, but from the walls. When Schaeffer finally started talking again he sounded tearful and scared, a horrid resignation weaving through the words he quietly spoke.

There are things worse than death. In the weeks...maybe even months...I don't know...time...time seems...I don't know...since we rid ourselves of him, things have started to fall apart. Something has awoken with the death of BH13. Things are...strange...things I can't...strange, yes, very strange things. I can still feel him. In my dreams I can hear him. Sometimes I swear he walks through me.

I am sure that this place is the ultimate answer. This place is the end and the beginning, and what is playing out before me is a bastard of both. I ask myself if I felt it when I arrived. Did I feel it in the house or in the grounds? I believe there was something. There was a force. An energy. An unremitting negativity covering us all like the thickest of shrouds. But the shelter is the heart; it is the rotten core that ties it all together. It is his black heart and he is its vessel. I can feel him talking to me, screaming the pain of those that lay here. We came here to build but all we did was break down doors that had never meant to be opened again. We burrowed into land, which should have lain untouched. BH13 talked of an evil here and if that is such then it is us that must take responsibility for it. It is us that released it. Such lunacy. How do I even say these things? I am not a man of words. I am a man of science. At this time I find my beliefs as stretched as my ability to fully articulate what I have seen. But I have seen. I have felt. He feels for me. At night he tries to get inside my head. I fear that when I dream I somehow grant him permission. In my dreams I keep seeing his face. I am forever reminded of how he looked as we killed him. The look of humour, of release and of knowing. He had been waiting for Greenaught and I to do it. Now I fear he is too powerful to stop. A memory you can't wash away.

'There's a lot of it about, it seems, this madness. Seems to be catching. Turn that shit off and get on your feet.' Kendrick was leaning across the doorway, staring in at Sullivan as though he'd been caught in his wife's knicker drawer. Plucking the walkie-talkie from his jacket, Kendrick took it to his lips. 'Maddox? She's gone walkabout again. Go find her, will you?'

He stepped into the room and kicked the Dictaphone from Sullivan's hand, bringing a heel down on to it as it fell to the floor, shattering the frail plastic and booting what snapped off across the room. The pistol was in his right hand, a pointing finger from a clenched fist, ramming his words home.

'I seem to remember asking you to keep an eye on her, Sullivan. I distinctly remember that. Imagine my surprise to find that bedroom empty. Not cutting out on the Party are you?'

'You knew,' Sullivan said accusingly, looking down at the smashed plastic as if that was all the explanation needed. 'You knew what went on here. Yet still you led us here.'

'Nothing went on here.'

'Nothing?'

'One guy lost the plot. Went mad. That's all. It happens.'

'And Mia?'

'As I said, this madness…'

'How many madmen is it going to take?'

Kendrick crossed the room and perched on the edge of the desk, staring off at the broken bookshelf. As he sat his suit jacket flopped open and Sullivan could see an ugly blood splat down one side of his shirt. Between the two men a small feather gracefully rocked back and forth on the air before resting amongst the papers on the floor.

'What did you do to him?' Sullivan asked quietly.

'What?'

'You had Grennaught kill him?'

'I didn't kill anyone!' Kendrick snapped.

'Of course you didn't.'

'He was a lunatic. A lag. A man with no point. Much like you.' Kendrick was beginning to snarl, fighting the corner Sullivan was trying to back him into. 'He was a killer!' He picked absently at the cut on his cheek, a thick crusty scab now peeling off under his fingers.

'I'm a killer. Maddox and Turtle too. Shall we all line up against the wall?'

Kendrick's lip curled and he bared his teeth in a crazed half-smile. 'You want to be careful how much you ask, Sullivan. Eventually you might just get an answer. That would put me in a difficult situation.'

'Would it? Why? You're going to shoot me either way.'

'True.'

'Where's Mr Davenport?'

'Why do you care?'

'I don't care.'

'You've an awful lot to say for a man who doesn't care.'

'You've blood on you.'

Kendrick pulled his jacket closed and turned the pistol towards the floor just in front of Sullivan. 'Don't you worry about that. Don't you worry about anything.'

Sullivan slowly started to stand, the pain in his muscles flaring like a warning as his legs straightened. Before him the pistol followed him up and then Kendrick came too.

'You don't believe in what we are trying to do here do you, Sullivan? You cling to an outdated, timid notion of right and wrong and think that we blur the line. Good old Sullivan, the man who swore he'd never hold a gun again. The last man with any morality. Am I right?'

Sullivan shrugged. 'I don't give a fuck about you or your Party. You took all that mattered to me.'

'We did?'

'Yeah. You did.'

'However did we do that, old chap?'

'Did she suffer?'

Again Kendrick's ugly smile flashed and with it seemed to come a begrudging admiration.

'How'd you know? Who told you?'

'I asked if she suffered.'

'I understand the process can be quite painful. At the start. Once they are drooling and dribbling I guess they don't feel so much. Or that's what Schaeffer used to say, though I'd always thought that perhaps it was just that our conscience didn't feel it. It's easier if they don't have…it all there, if you know what I mean. Course you know what I mean. Now I asked you who told you?'

The knowing did little to assuage the grief or the anger, merely blew at the flame in his heart. The dream was still there, it always had been, but she was no longer within him, it was just the wreckage she had left.

'She did.'

Kendrick laughed. 'You poor sad soul.'

'Did she have a choice?'

'Who would willingly volunteer for such a thing? Of course she didn't. I had to move her out of the way. Having a stranger with such power over the command? No. That could never be allowed. Davenport was getting weak with infatuation, taking his eye off the enemy. When we were overrun…well, it was easy for her to just disappear. It was beneficial to have him think that she had been killed. Guilt can empower a weak man. I don't think she ever loved him, if its any comfort.'

Sullivan held a hand to his mouth to steady trembling lips, and then pushed the palm to his forehead, hitting it clean and hard, trying to push new images out.

'We had it, Sullivan. It worked. We were doing great things here. But then of course our esteemed leader convinced people to pull the plug. All that work. All that time and effort. Davenport killed her, really, don't you see? It was all his fault. His love drove her here and his misguided sense of what is right killed her.'

'I really am here because of guilt then?'

'His guilt complex was always going to take him down in the end.' The pistol was raised into Sullivan's face, the hammer slowly pulled back. 'Morals are great, in an ideal world, and we're working on that. Really we are. But we've got a long way to go yet. You and him, you're just men in the wrong time. That's all.'

'Who's judging?'

'Oh, you might be interested, since you did ask; I

should have said…the madman you seemed so concerned about? You wanted to know what happened to him?' Kendrick nodded down to Sullivan's boots and the heavy concrete floor beneath them. 'You're standing on him.'

Sullivan didn't look down to the floor, his eyes were fixed ahead just over the pistol barrel and were firm and unblinking, looking deep into the flared corruption of the man before him.

'Sorry, Sullivan. Really. You won't come back and haunt me will you?'

Kendrick laughed loudly and wildly and then squeezed the trigger.

5

Turtle stepped out of the shower and stood naked in the centre of the floor, the water trickling off him, cresting his body's ridges and curves. He closed his eyes and savoured the moment, the feeling of being clean, the dirt and grime scrubbed off, the cuts and bruises standing out sharply, proudly on his body. He felt his beard and then ran the hand through his hair, pushing the fringe back, smoothing his fingers through it. He opened his eyes and looked at himself in the mirror on the opposite wall, the same mirror he had convinced himself he had seen someone else in, standing behind him, just a short time ago. He managed a wry smile at the memory. "Trick of the mind," his mind told him, reassured him. "I conned you, baby, that's all." It was the place, the place messed you up. That's what the stories said, and heck, he'd heard so many stories about Bleeker Hill that law of averages must suggest that some of them might be true. He could see how the place played you – the lack of light, the thick walls – it was a tomb, yeah, a glorified tomb, why wouldn't such a place freak you out and make you see things? Somehow, in his current state all answers seemed obvious.

A gentle push of cold air licked at his legs and moved

up his body. He shivered, one quick all-over body shiver, and then reached over for the bed sheet, the makeshift towel he had hung over the curtain rail of the next shower, and quickly whipped it around his waist before padding back into the sleeping quarters. Maddox was dressed and lying in the bed next to Bergan, one hand under the back of his neck, gently rubbing at it, the rifle at his side, a maniac's teddy bear.

'You feel that?' Turtle asked, crossing to the opposite bed.

'Feel what? Your dick?'

'Never mind. How's he doing?' He nodded to the great giant in the next bed, still in the same position as they had placed him.

Maddox casually looked over to Bergan and shrugged.

'Man, I need some sleep.' Turtle slipped his T-shirt back on and perched on the bed, staring at Bergan solemnly. 'He looks dead.'

'Always did, how'd you tell the difference?'

'His face, Maddox. Look at his face.'

'Face like a dead man's scrotum. There you go, he was never winning any beauty awards anyway. Take the weight off, Turtle and get some sleep. Don't feel like you need to talk to me.'

For a while neither spoke. Maddox stared off dreamily at the ceiling, cuddling into the rifle, shifting his head on the pillow, looking for a cool spot. Turtle dried himself down and pulled on his trousers, raising one knee to his nose and sniffing at them in disgust. He pushed himself back on the bed, sitting up and staring off at Bergan again, once more watching his chest rise and fall against long stuttering breaths. He could feel coldness tickling his arms, gently blowing under his shirt, and then it was all over him, his body breaking out in goose bumps seemingly from forehead to foot.

'You feel that?'

Maddox ignored him.

'Did it just get cold in here?'

'Huh?'

'It just got really cold, you felt that, right?'

The tinny tones of Joe Kendrick suddenly sounded from Maddox's walkie-talkie, resting on his great, bulky chest. 'Maddox? She's gone walkabout again. Go find her, will you?' Maddox made no attempt to hide the glee in his face as he swung off the bed and barked his compliance, a small light of craziness cracking through his blue eyes.

'Got me a date, Turtle. You okay to stay and look after dad?'

Turtle could see Maddox's breath in the air, blooming out of his mouth as he spoke. He looked across to Bergan and saw the same; little puffs of breath coming from his nose and breaking over his face. The sight chilled him even further.

'Hey, Turtle! I'm talking to you!'

'Why don't I go?' Turtle suddenly said, the light tone suggesting he were doing a great favour for a good friend. 'I'll go, you stay here.' Turtle leaned over and reached for his boots.

'You trying to cut in on my girl there, short arse?'

'I just think that…'

'What sort of man would I be if I didn't go help find a young girl who's gone lost her way out there?' He swung the rifle up over his shoulder and rearranged the front of his trousers. 'I'd be a bastard wouldn't I?'

'Why don't we both go? Yeah, I'll come help you.'

Maddox was moving out to the door, a huge cloud of breath blasting forward as he offered Turtle a maniacal laugh as a response. 'The fuck you will.' He was gone even before Turtle had time to slip into his boots.

Instantly the temperature in the room seemed to plummet even further, the cold becoming sharp and unforgiving. Turtle looked up at the ceiling and then back across to the open door to the showers. The walls seemed to have lost all colour and definition. He held his hands before him and the skin looked blue, impossibly smooth, unreal and inhuman. Suddenly it felt like he was sitting in a deep freeze and the coldness started to hurt. His breath was an angry cloud of smoke, moving, finding shapes as it danced mockingly before him, and he followed its form as it drifted across the room, bending and curling over itself in the air, slowly finding its way towards Frankie Bergan's bed.

Turtle's heart suddenly froze in his chest.

The great giant was sitting up in bed and staring back across at him, his dead eyes rolled high in their sockets, two pale moons where the darkness used to be. His huge hands were reaching out before him, his legs moving from under the covers, as slowly he started to get out of bed.

ATTACK

1

There was a pressure at his arms, a strong grip holding him to the bed. He could feel the force climb on, could feel the heavy weight grow at his chest as it slowly started squeezing the air from him. He lay on his back trying to crane up to the sounds coming from his boss' bed but he could lift his head no more than a few inches, the grip tightening at every move he attempted, like a snake coiling around its prey. He looked to the ceiling and tried to piece together the moving shadows with the sounds he could hear but it was a chaotic jumble that made no sense. His mind was telling him it was all a dream, that it was playing him again and he found comfort in the absurdity of it. For one brief moment he found himself laughing through the terror welling up inside his body, and then, as if what held him had also seeped into his mind, demanding his attention, a long, deep gash opened down one arm as something slashed across him, and with it Turtle was back in the room, drowning in fear.

'Frankie! Please! Get this thing off me!' He sounded like a child, his usual sharp rattle, the voice that would bark and swear and challenge all day long in his kitchen back home, diluted to a weedy whine.

He could hear Bergan's soft footsteps padding back and forth across the floor, and then a bed being shoved roughly to one side, the metal legs scraping across the smoothness like fingers down a blackboard. He tried once more to look up, to turn his head, to find Bergan, but each jerk and movement only served to tighten the force that covered him. There were ripping sounds from across the room; loud, long tears of the bed sheets and then the bed was tumbled over on to its side and next to it, near it, somewhere, a locker was shoved to the floor with a loud thud.

'Frankie? Frankie please...' Turtle whimpered. 'Frankie, please help me...'

To his right he could hear noises coming from the showers; the ugly gurgle of water, the straining of pipes as if someone were trying to bend them out of shape. The steady plop-plop of the dripping tap was louder than it had ever been. Each drop of water was a stone in a puddle, heavy and angry.

Across from him he could feel Bergan pass his bed, a black shape with human form, yet surely not the man he once knew so well, this was his shadow given life. He heard Bergan's bed moving again and then a loud clanking sound as the metal headboard hit the floor.

'Frank...' his name came quietly now, no more than a whisper, an echo of a previous thought. 'Frank...please.'

He heard the upturned bed strain, the metal scratching the floor and the wall, and then he could hear what sounded like light footsteps on another locker. At the ceiling a shadow grew like spilt ink on old parchment; it found form, slowly, and the shape became human, tall and imposing, great long arms and mighty hands reaching up above its head, working away at the ceiling.

The pressure at his arms suddenly abated, and Turtle yanked them up above his body and struck out at whatever held him firm, sweeping through the impossible coldness and the ash clouds of breath, yet striking nothing. The wound at his arm flared and he saw the blood streams running down to the crook of his elbow like hideous talons, the red brilliant and deep, the only rich colour in a room drained of definition. Still he fought against what was at his chest but he couldn't shift it, his legs now waggling at the base of the bed, trying to buck the heaviness off him. He pulled at his shirt, rubbed his hands against the pressure but there was no soothing it. He dug fingers in, one breaking through the material to the skin, and clawed at himself, trying to scour himself free.

Suddenly, and with a heavy, impossibly loud thud, a locker hit the floor just at the base of his bed and its cold, unwelcoming echo reverberated across the room, through Turtle's body, and seemed to shatter the force at his chest. He pulled himself up immediately, coughing and hacking, doubling up as he cleared his chest and throat through a shower of mucus and spit on to his bed sheets. It hurt, he felt raw and brittle, his heart like flint and his bones the most fragile of glass.

As he looked up, his watering eyes blinked wildly at the sight before him, slowly taking in the image, seeming confused, squinting and then widening, moving up and down it, swallowing up the impossible information. His mind couldn't, wouldn't, process it: "You're on your own, baby," it told him and jumped ship. Before him the body of Frankie Bergan seemed to hover in mid air, those eye whites shining dully in the corpse face, matching the off-white noose of bedsheets that was roughly and tightly wrapped around his neck. Above him the bedsheets ran to the metal chain that held the first light in place, where they were tied in one small bunched knot. Turtle had just enough time to question if the smile on Bergan's face was real and then he was knocked roughly off the bed and on to the floor, landing with a thud on his back.

The bed he had just left jumped off the ground, flipped over in the air and then came down on top of him. One by one the other beds down his side of the room did the same, rising up in sequence, spinning over, and then crashing to the floor. He was screaming in his own head, his hands at his face, his body scrunching up into a protective ball. As the last bed crashed down he was dragged forward from under his own and shoved crudely into the fallen locker. He moved again, this time on his front, pushed across the ground like an icy hockey puck. In front of him a series of loud bangs sounded as each showerhead exploded in turn and jets of water shot up and across the room, raining down on him. Turtle staggered up and again was knocked aside, lifted off the ground and then hurled across the room into the wall. The lights above him shattered one after the other in tiny little explosions of glass and sparks. He batted his arms around him, screaming an angry garble of words, and then he was on his feet, swaying back and forth, feeling the walls come out to him and then push away, the ceiling fall and then disappear completely.

He was turning to the door, moving his little legs like he were trying to run through treacle, pushing past Bergan dangling in front of him. His fingers were losing all sensation, the unforgiving cold shooting up through his hands, into his arms and gathering at his head. His bare feet slipped and skidded on the cold ground and he was unable to get a hold; for every foot forward he went he seemed to fall back even more. Something blew against his face. Something touched his arm, then yanked at his shoulder, and then just as he reached the door it slammed shut on him. A pressure started against his eyes, the force was on him again, long fingers probing at his cheeks and mouth and then as he was shoved back into the wall he could feel blood seeping from his nose, down to his mouth.

'Please, please stop!' He could taste the blood, could feel it flying from his mouth with congealed saliva, and mucus as he spoke. 'Please…'

His feet went from under him and then he was on

his back once more looking up at the ceiling, and the low hanging clouds of breath that held their form like suspended cobwebs. He could feel vibrations under his back as something far below thrummed and shook, dancing its ugly dance. As if in reply to what played out beneath him, the ceiling suddenly gave its own stuttering wail as the air conditioner in the room argued its last, gave to a weary sigh and then fell to silence. He fought what held him, frenetically writhing and thrashing, imbued with an adrenaline soaked fear. He moved to his knees, shuffled forward and then turned back to the door. He saw it instantly; bright and red and inked from his own blood, a crudely drawn arrow was in the middle of the door pointing upwards, directing him out.

'Yes!' he suddenly screamed, unsure why. 'I'm leaving. I want to leave! I don't want to be here. Let me leave!'

He got to his feet, stumbling forward.

'I want to leave! I want to leave this place. Let me leave!' He roared the words up to the ceiling, through the clouds of breath, the shattered lights and into the broken air conditioner. 'I don't want to be here! Let me out!'

There was a gentle click and a weary moan. In front of him the door was slowly opening. He pushed through into the outside corridor and began to hobble, jog and then run. Somewhere ahead of him, further on through the building, there was a gunshot, but Turtle paid it no attention.

2

Mia heard it all from where she was hiding; the screaming, the crashing of beds and lockers, and then above her the loud clunk as the air conditioning stopped working. She had felt it as soon as it happened and the images she saw as she closed her eyes were monstrous. Yet for all that was playing out around her and despite the encroaching threat she could feel creeping through the empty corridors, she found herself relieved and just for the merest of moments, smiling. For now she wasn't a crackpot or a liar any more. Even if the screams belonged to just one person, she knew she was no longer alone.

She turned on her side and looked out from under the bed. The higgledy-piggeldy stand she had made from a small chair and a low standing bedside table looked back at her from the corridor, just underneath the hatch to the shaft. The holding strap that she had prised off the bed and fastened to the small circular hatch handle dangled down like a fat light flex. She had been sure it would be all the extra help she needed to turn the handle, that several hard tugs on that strap would loosen it just enough for her to swing it around until the lock released, but it had ripped in two and she had fallen off the makeshift stand, shouting reproaches to her own wishful thinking. She had come back into the bedroom to tear off the second holding strap when she heard the footsteps. They were heavy and confident and she had heard them before. She knew who it was.

Giving no time to remove the stand she had tucked herself under the bed, pushing back against the wall, as far into the shadows as she could get. Waiting. Hoping he would turn away or pass the room by. The footsteps came and went. He was walking from room to room, looking in and walking back out. But the cigar smoke was constant and getting thicker. She tried to remember how many of those small, cramped bedrooms she had passed on this level, working over in her mind how long she might have before he pulled up in her doorway. *Bedrooms!* She suddenly shouted in her mind. *Did I really think they were bedrooms?* She could smell the hopelessness in the room. The decay. She wondered who had been held there, had it been one of those she had seen up above in the pen? Maybe it had been that beautiful woman, slain trying to escape over the barbed wire? How many had been here? How many lost souls?

The footsteps came again, much closer, and she could see his shadow along the wall, that great, bulky rock on legs, and up before the shadow of his body was the shadow of the rifle, long and thin like an antenna. A small cloud of cigar smoke wafted past the open door, heralding his arrival, and then the shadow stopped moving, hanging on the wall before sinking down to the floor as he drew up in the doorway and stood looking at the stand like it were a piece modern art he just couldn't grasp. He tilted his head at it, walked around it as if expecting to see something different on the other side of the corridor and then in one quick action, kicked it over and turned into the room.

She was flat against the wall now; yet still she tried to squeeze herself back further. Her arms were up above her, stretched out with her body and she felt her hands breaching a thick spider's web, the fingers tearing through the carefully crafted home, as they pushed against the wall. She could feel a spider walk on to her wrist, the legs tickling against the light hairs of her arm as it began to wander under the loose cuff of her outsized fatigues and pass under the sleeve.

She watched his great, heavy boots walking across the room; saw the rifle drop down and the barrel begin to scratch against the floor as it was slowly pushed under the bed. She closed her eyes, allowing the con of the darkness to make her feel she were even further away. Slowly she held her breath. The barrel rubbed at the ground and began to probe the space around her.

The spider was under her upper arm, feeling its way to her armpit and then it was up to her shoulder, then her neck, scuttling out from under her clothes and climbing on to her chin. The legs seemed to swamp her and she imagined how it looked, how big its jet-black body would be, how freakishly long those legs were. She could sense one touch her lips, as it felt its way forward across its foreign terrain, and then in one quick, jerky movement the spider was sitting across her mouth, the legs stretching from chin to nostril.

The barrel skimmed in front of her and brushed her trousers, lightly enough for her to feel and he to ignore. He gave the rifle a long shove and the barrel hit the wall just above her waist. He moved it along and did the same again, this time connecting with the wall just above her ribs. She could hear a small creak of joints and knew he was starting to crouch down so as to look under the bed. She could feel her held breath ready to escape, wondered if the spider would move away or fall into her mouth when she finally gasped, and as the thought occurred to her she found herself opening her eyes, ready to meet the piercing blue of his own, deciding that if he were to take her he would first have to see the hatred she felt, and not the fear.

A gunshot suddenly sounded above them, the echo pulsing through the corridor, and then Maddox was back on his feet instantly, the same creaking joints giving small, angry snaps. She pulled her eyes open in time to see his boots pounding across the floor and turning out sharply into the corridor. One small wisp of smoke slowly breaking in the space where he had just been.

The spider scuttled quickly from her mouth, moved across a cheek and found a path to a new home on the cold wall of the room.

3

The blast of the pistol exploded at the right side of Sullivan's head and the sound blew through him, the heat scorching his ear and some of his hair. He had jerked to the side as he lunged forward, his eyes closing and his hands reaching out for Kendrick, scrabbling for the pistol, never believing he would reach it, the action no more than a token last stand, a refusal to bow to a bastard's desire. They fell together in a clumsy cuddle, toppling against the shelves. The pistol fired again, this time into the ceiling, and the shot was flat and hollow, coming to Sullivan like a cannon fired underwater. Everything was muffled, shorn of its edges. He gave a moment to tell himself that he was deaf, shouting the conclusion into his numbed mind before regaining his position and his hold on the enemy.

He reached down to one of the framed photos, Schaeffer and his wife, and smashed it across Kendrick's face, shattering the glass. He jumped on to him as the pistol fell to the floor amongst the debris of books and papers, and shoved him back into the bookshelves. Kendrick's hands were at Sullivan's face, fingers pressing into his cheeks as his thumbs searched out and squeezed down into his eyes. Again Sullivan pushed him back, then again, then once more and three bookshelves broke to the pressure showering them in a dusty paper cloud. Sullivan brought a knee up between Kendrick's legs as he pulled his head away from his grip and the two men closed around each other, falling to the floor.

Kendrick was raining wild, scattershot thumps to his body as Sullivan let his right hand scrabble blindly to his side, rummaging through the mess looking for the pistol. His left hand went up to Kendrick's throat and tried to find purchase, tried to squeeze and force him back but still Kendrick came at him, the small and neat fists making contact with Sullivan's nose and chin and one clean swipe landing at the right side of his head, making the pain rage again.

Sullivan's right hand pushed fingers through glass shards, over bent folders and torn paper, sweeping around in a wide arc, brushing aside all that it found. He tilted to his side to try and cast an eye to the floor, letting Kendrick take his rage out across the left side of his body. He felt a rib blaze under a blow, his arm sting as an old wound was opened and then finally, as Kendrick swung a fist across his left cheek, and Sullivan's pained right hand side thudded into the floor, he saw it; the pistol was there, just in front of his searching fingers. He jerked for it, summoning all the energy he had left, his body tipping Kendrick back, knocking him off balance. His fingers were on the pistol butt, clamping around it, dragging it closer. He felt Kendrick turn around, his body weight shifting, lifting, and he knew that finally he had seen it too. Kendrick lunged, his red raw fists giving out to childish, grabbing hands and greedy interfering fingers, but he was too slow. The pistol was already in Sullivan's hand.

The pistol jerked up, hard and fast, and it struck Kendrick plum across the nose. Sullivan swung his hand back and then brought the pistol to Kendrick's face again, this time reopening the cut along his cheek. He writhed and wriggled under him and then finally Sullivan was free of his hold, and getting to his feet, a hundred old pains reprimanding him, trying to make him stop. The pistol, a lead weight in his hand, was turning to its target on instinct, free of thought or consideration. It was aimed at Kendrick before he even realised.

'You bastard, Sullivan! You've cut my face!' Kendrick spat the words as he sunk to the ground, flopping against the desk.

Sullivan felt the rage coursing through him, could feel the thrill of the situation and in one blessedly brief glimpse he saw himself feeding a bullet through Kendrick's skull and watching in wonderment at the blood explosion that would blast from the back of his head. It went as soon as it came and it left only the sharp taste of revulsion. He stared back over the pistol in a stupefied grip of horror, slowly shaking his head at what he saw before him and what he could see he was close to becoming. He let the weight in his hand drop and edged back to the doorway.

'Well go on then! Do it, Sullivan! Pull the trigger. Or could it be you can't?' Sullivan merely shook his head again and lowered the pistol to his side.

'You did it once, do it again. What's the matter, Sullivan? Lost the taste?'

'You're not worth it. Nothing is worth it.'

'A noble man? I should have you framed.'

Sullivan paused in the doorway and his gaze fell fleetingly to the floor, to the point where Kendrick had motioned just a short time ago. A shiver passed through him, a cold energy, and then he was turning in the doorway, offering Kendrick a final, almost apologetic look and then running from the room.

'You sanctimonious wretch!' Kendrick bellowed after him. 'There are no prizes for being the better man. No one cares Sullivan. Compassion isn't a competition any more!'

'Kendrick? You there? I heard gunshots.'

Kendrick looked around the office, momentarily perplexed, convinced he was hearing things.

'Kendrick? Come in!'

He recognised Maddox's voice and looked to the doorway, half expecting to see the brute standing there swinging his rifle. It was only after Maddox's third attempt to rouse him that he remembered the walkie-talkie and shoved a hand into his jacket to retrieve it.

'Kendrick? What the hell's going on? I heard shots. Come in!'

Kendrick took up the small unit but paused with it at his lips, his thumb stroking the button whilst his mind worked over the situation.

'Maddox?'

'What's going on? Talk to me!' Maddox shouted back.

There was an emotional resonance to Kendrick's words, betraying the blank look of an unwavering decision that was painted across his face.

'Oh, Maddox. The most horrible thing…Davenport, my dear friend…Sullivan has shot him. Took my pistol and shot him dead. Find him, Maddox. Find them both. Sullivan and the girl. They must be stopped.'

'Permanently?

'They have betrayed the Party. Both of them. This cannot stand. Yes. Permanently, Maddox. Kill them. Kill them both.'

4

Sullivan staggered along the corridors, one hand running along the jet-black walls as the other played in his scorched ear, waggling the index finger as if trying to dislodge a ball of wax. The silence in the ear seemed to pulse, it was a thick and gloopy nothingness trying to push deeper into his head, an alien life that wanted to birth. He could hear little more than tinny clanks and sighs; he was submerged in an invisible pool, unable to break a surface that seemed intent on swimming away from him at every push forward.

There were vibrations in the wall; short, frantic shivers as if a huge vehicle was passing it on the other side. The floor too was not still, it seemed to shift from under him, like it were loose carpet and he were barefoot. He wanted to give in, to drop to his knees and hold his hands up, and to succumb to the prison and his jailers once more. Too tired to run, too broken to care. Yet something pushed him on.

I love you Daddy…

She was still within him, somewhere. He knew it. Could feel it. Yet as he tried to wallow in the perfection of her image it was Mia that he saw. It was her that he heard and could feel tugging at his arm. He couldn't leave her here, he had to protect her and not allow her to fall to the intentions of posturing, evil men. He didn't want to care, couldn't afford concern, but she wouldn't leave him, wouldn't give him peace.

He ran down a corridor he was sure he had just been down and turned a corner that led him back on himself. He felt certain that at any moment he would see himself up ahead.

'I saw this thing on the TV daddy, men had rats in a maze, they would tease them with food to go through certain gates in the maze, tricking them, they would make them enter this cage. They were doing it for research, what were they researching? I knew rats were clever, why didn't they? Then another man…it was horrible…' She cried into my shoulder then, soft and gentle hands closing to fists. *'They were putting things into the rats' eyes. Blinding them, they said. They made them stumble around in that maze without their eyesight. Then another man…'*

'It's not real, darling. It's all make believe.' She hadn't bought that lie. She was clued up. Intelligent. She'd go far.

There was another way out, that was what she had told him, his daughter – no, not her, the other one. Mia? She had said there was another way out of this nightmare. A door, it was a door to another world. No. Don't be stupid. A hatch. It was a hatch in a turret. Was it called a turret? How the fuck should I know?

He started searching the ceiling, looking for anything that seemed like a door, a hole, or an exit. That was where she would be. If he found that then he would find her. He would get her out, save her from this place and these people, and everything would be okay again. They could live out their time in blessed memories and willing delusions. Somewhere a sun was shining.

Coldness belched through the empty space in front of him and suddenly he found he couldn't move. Not a finger, nor an eyelid; he was frozen to the spot whilst a great, piercing energy passed him. He could see images at his eyes, coming through them and forming in his mind; faces, and bodies, small and large, young and old, each seemingly tethered to each other as if the shapes were but one and it was a morphing, shifting, creation of his imagination. Yet his imagination was dry, and parched. He felt only the burning embers of his dream. He saw only her. Them. Thought only of his survival and her escape. What he saw was not real, and yet because of that knowledge, what he saw was twice as vivid.

The coldness became an impossible calmness, both soothing and achingly beautiful. He welcomed it and offered himself to it. For brief, tantalising moments he felt both young and free again, suddenly imbued with an ethereal brightness that was as magnificent as it was out of place. Light had penetrated the dark maze, lit him from within, bouncing and reflecting off his bent and broken edges, and illuminating that which he had closed off, showing him the way around the dead ends.

'Leave,' he told himself.

His response to his own demand was a face drifting through his vision, yellowed and rotten, a summer moon reflected in a dark, bottomless winter puddle. It passed through his eyes, and became the space ahead of him.

Mia's scream came as if cued up ready for him, and then he was moving off, finding strength in his legs and direction in his mind, and as he ran through the shadows, under the darkness, he felt it turning to him, watching him and judging, waiting to see what he did.

Mia tied the second holding strap to the hatch handle and wrapped the slack around her hand, tugging it lightly twice and feeling its strength. She seemed pleased, encouraged. The makeshift stand wobbled beneath her trainers as she shifted herself around to get a better position. She waited, gathered her breath, and focused on the strap and the small, circular handle. It looked so weak and pointless, an afterthought of design. Her hand was bigger than it, almost swallowed it up when she touched it, yet despite its appearance it held strong and firm, keeping the large metal door in place in the ceiling with an unwavering stubbornness.

She began to tug at the strap, waited to feel the reassuring grip around the metal; little tugs at first but gradually increasing in strength as she worked herself into the task at hand. She gently rocked back and forth on the stand as she forged a rhythm like a small piston, sucking in a lungful of air before squeezing it out sharply between gritted teeth.

There was no give at the handle, the hatch remained firmly locked. White paint flecked from it and dropped to the floor, some fell into her hair, some on to her face. She moved more quickly, gave more, pulled harder.

Nothing. Her eyes watered with the effort, her chest bore a stitch and her fingers began to throb, the knuckles growing out like eight new pimples. She suddenly felt stupid, embarrassed, like she had been deceived and shamed, but still she wouldn't quit or slow her efforts. Beneath her the bedside table creaked under the strain as the wood bore a thin, sliver of a crack. She paid no heed, refused to hear it or allow it.

Mia pulled her body down, swung it to the left and then the right, each time pulling on the strap as she moved. Sweat had broken on her forehead, zigzagging its inevitable pathway to her already stinging eyes. A muscle strained in her shoulder, another in her back, but she was oblivious to it all, unable to acknowledge anything but the handle and the hatch. She imagined she could smell the air up above; she longed to feel the snow flecking her face again, to taste it on her tongue. Even that old tent, her home for so many numberless days, seemed warm and welcoming. She would get to the valley this time, and then she wouldn't stop walking. There would be somewhere safe out there, and she would find it. At that thought, that certainty, she pulled down with everything she had, and finally, unmistakably, there was give at the handle. It came with a squeak like a large mouse and was followed by another shower of white paint and from somewhere in the back of her throat, a satisfied gurgle of triumph.

Her hands jumped for the handle, the fingers

wrapping around the metal, and then she was turning it, slowly at first, like a rusty tap handle, but the further it turned the easier it became. Her eyes lit up with an unbearable happiness, her heart bloomed, pushing out the stitch, pushing back the feeling of despair, and then within seconds the handle was spinning between her hands and she was laughing and the laugh was joyous and full.

When finally the hatch yawned to its release, it was so sudden, the change in pressure at her hands so extreme, that she lost her balance on the stand and tumbled to the ground, landing with a thud and a yelp on her backside as the bedside table sheared in two at her feet. Still she was laughing. Looking up at the bottom of the long, silver tube stretching through the building to its other hatch at the roof, she acted as if it were the funniest thing she had ever seen.

She was still laughing as Turtle appeared, standing over her. At first she didn't seem to see him, he was another warped and grotesque shadow, a figment of her imagination, and even as he spoke and bent down to her with an outstretched hand, none of it felt real to her.

'Mia? Are you okay?' He grabbed a slender wrist and began to lift her, his eyes moving from her to the base of the turret just above. 'You were right. You said.'

He looked different. She couldn't place it. She could feel the shaking in his hand as he hauled her to her feet, but it was more than that; it wasn't any outward display, more something that he had lost. She could smell the traces of soap on his skin, the delicate perfume, and it seemed ridiculous. He continued his greedy gaze up at the turret and she saw the light of hope in his eyes and at once she knew whose screams she had heard.

He snatched up the chair and turned the legs back to the floor, instantly he was standing on it and grabbing for the base of the ladder that ran up the left hand side of the shaft. He was too short for it, shorter even than Mia, stubby fingertips just scratching at the bottom rung, tickling the metal.

'Help me up, I'll go first,' Mia said, feeling somewhat affronted by the unfolding situation, as if Turtle had queue jumped her. It was a feeling out of synch with the circumstance but she couldn't deny it, nor could she stop the urge she had to laugh again at the sight of his short and eager little arms flailing around above him in a hopeless fumble.

'No, no I need to go first…these hatches, they are tough to open…'

No shit chef. Thank God, I've got all these men around to help me.

His eagerness had nothing to do with the hatch, nor anything to do with chivalry or Mia's safety, she knew it, and let him have it. It was impossible not to see the truth in his face, and she wondered what he had seen, what he had sensed. At that consideration she turned to the corridor, looking left and then right, staring deep into the gloom, suddenly expecting to see something there. Somehow the calm that seemed to have settled, the complete emptiness of it all, was more ominous and felt more of a threat. Mia knew they were being watched. In her mind she could see the eyes, and they were unblinking and angry, and worse than that they were patient, because they were no longer human. Their watcher had time, never-ending time.

Turtle bent his legs and then jumped, his right hand slapping hard on the lowest rung of the ladder, his fingers coiling over the metal, holding firm. For a couple of seconds he hung there, swinging back and forth, and then his left hand went up to join his right and then he was slowly, methodically and with considerable difficulty, pulling himself up into the shaft.

The hole was barely five feet across, and the ladder was thin and narrow, the rungs giving barely enough space between for his shoeless feet to slip in. His body blocked out the hatch high above as he shuffled up, and then Mia was underneath him, on the chair, bending her knees, wiping off the sweat from her hands on to her trousers, fixing her focus on the lowest rung of the ladder.

'Hurry!' Turtle said over his shoulder. 'We must hurry.'

Mia lunged forward at the ladder with a satisfied grunt and her palms slapped down hard on the metal, her fingers closing around it as the momentum swung her legs forward. She moved her left hand up to the next rung, and then her right, strengthening her hold and delicately yanking herself in. Again she laughed and the laugh echoed back, a hundred Mias all experiencing the same unconfined joy. The other ninety-nine were still laughing as she stopped, and then as she screamed, they all screamed together.

Hands gripped her ankles, dangling at the tip of the hole, and she was pulled off the ladder with one quick, powerful jerk, slipping out of the hole and landing in a crumpled heap on the floor. Thick and heavy boots were in front of her. A rifle barrel was teasingly brushing her face and then the smell of stale cigar smoke was wafting at her nose. Her heart sank and she closed her eyes, the brief dalliance with hope a nasty and spiteful dream. He had a hand at her hair, and then the elastic band holding her ponytail was yanked off and he was lifting her to her feet, moving his great boulder of a face to hers, breathing his stale scent all over her, and moving in for a kiss.

'Not right to run out on a date when he got all cleaned up specially.' Maddox licked her chin and then clamped his mouth over hers, pushing her into him, chewing and biting at her lips. She pulled away and spat in his face but he seemed only to enjoy it more. 'Fight, Mia. Please…'

She screamed as she tried in vain to release herself

from his hold. She shouted Turtle's name but he made no move to look back or even acknowledge it. He was far above them now, growing smaller, getting nearer to the hatch at the roof.

Maddox pulled her over to the hole and stared back up through the turret.

'Hey, short arse, where you going?'

Maddox's booming voice echoed like canon fire around the shaft and Turtle stumbled on the ladder, swinging out on one hand before throwing himself back and regaining his hold. He climbed on, a hand reaching up for the handle at the top hatch.

'You two sneaking out on us? Where'd you think you're going? You two got a little thing happening here, huh? Tell me.' Maddox pulled Mia's face into his own and flashed her the baby blues. 'Troublesome little lady aren't ya?'

Turtle was at the roof hatch and short determined grunts were wafting down the shaft as he yanked and pulled at the handle. Again Maddox moved under the hole and stared back up at him.

'Hey, Turtle, you clear this with the suits? What you doing up there? Where are your boots?' Turtle's short arms were pumping back and forth at the handle, the grunts of exertion getting louder as the handle began to give to him. 'Answer me, Turtle! What you doing?' Maddox swung Mia back to him and pulled down hard on her hair. 'The fuck you two doing here? What are you up to?' He lifted up the rifle and prodded the barrel against the underside of Mia's chin, pushing in hard. 'Am I gonna have to shoot you before we've even had chance to have any fun?'

The top hatch opened high above, and through the shaft came a shriek of tired hinges and a triumphant yelp of excitement. Beyond them was the wild and untamed howl of an unforgiving winter wind. Maddox looked back up the hole and saw Turtle half in the hatch and half out, one foot on the ladder, one on the wall of the shaft, as his upper body and head leaned over and looked out. He seemed frozen in the position.

'Turtle? What the fuck is going on here? Huh? Someone want to give me some answers? Am I gonna have to get angry?'

Turtle was suddenly pulled out of the top of the shaft, his little legs flopping up over the edge and then disappearing from sight with the rest of him. Maddox rocked back in surprise, the rifle instinctively swinging away from Mia and thrusting up through the hole. Snow skittered down at him through the shaft and with it a few stones came like an afterthought, clanking against the metal and dropping at his feet.

'Turtle?'

Mia slowly followed Maddox's eyes up through the shaft, and then both of them were gazing back at the hole of sky; the dirty and thick white smeared with daubs of diluted blue. The light was starting to close off and give into evenings hold. There was a muffled sound across some unseen horizon, carried in broken pieces by the wind. Above them Maddox's rifle held rock steady, his index finger finding the trigger and stroking its gentle curve.

'Turtle?'

There were small pops in the distance like fireworks, and then through the shaft a howl like a ravenous animal, yet it was too deep, too human. The sky seemed to suddenly be eclipsed by a cloud, something cut from the deepest night, and then the cloud was thinning, cresting the edge of the roof and dropping into the hole.

Turtle's stocky body tumbled forward through the top hatch, struck the ladder and then fell through the shaft, bouncing from side to side in a series of dull, aching thuds before landing with a harsh crunch on the floor at Maddox's boots. High above them there were now heavy footfalls on the ladder and then loud, triumphant shouts coming in waves through the hole. Three bodies were climbing down the ladder, descending through the shaft, fast and assured. Two more were climbing over the open hatch and getting a foothold. There was a gunshot from high above, and then Maddox was responding in kind.

6

Kendrick stood alone in the middle of the first floor corridor, his feet frozen in a stride, one hand up before him as if in greeting. Beyond and above him was the huge sealed entrance, and just to his right the partially opened door to the communications room. He saw the small blood pool gathered on the floor, Davenport's right hand slapped down in the centre. He saw the open bedroom door to his left, the room he had put Mia and Sullivan in. The scratches were unavoidable along the walls, the sheared straps too. Yet it was none of these things that had stopped him mid-stride.

For several heavy minutes his mind sought to deny it, until it came again; it was a noise just below him at the base of the stairs. It was a shuffling sound at first, scuffed shoes skimming the floor, and then beyond it there slowly came the unmistakable sounds of sobbing. It was a young child's broken tears and they were coming from somewhere behind him. He suddenly felt his jacket move, just briefly, as if something were there tugging at it, and the sensation was enough to shatter through what held him rapt. He spun around on the spot and prepared to greet whatever was there with a heavy sweep of the arm but as he swung he combed through thin air, lost his footing thudded into the wall and then fell to his front on the floor. He ignored the pain and shoved himself back, hauling his body away from the stairs. His eyes darted across empty space. There was nothing there, nothing to be seen or feared.

'Get it together, Joe. Get it together,' he mumbled quietly to himself.

At first he refused to see what was lying on the ground just before him. Closing his eyes tight he gently moved his head from side to side, and then peered out again through small slits. It was still there.

'No,' he demanded of himself and shuffled back on the floor even further. 'No, I don't think so.'

Again he looked back, and again it was there just before him as if it too had moved across the floor. It was a small cut of rope formed into a tiny noose at one end. The noose was big enough, just, for a grown man's wrist or the tiniest of necks. Kendrick glared back as if furious with its presence. His head was still shaking as he reached out across the floor to touch it. The rope looked old, felt fragile, the thickness somehow a deception that would wither if held. His fingers ran quickly across a few frayed strands in the knot and then lightly around the edge of the noose. His overworked mind was sat on his imagination, holding it back, working desperately to offer a rational reason for it, sure that there was something obvious that it had missed, yet the more Kendrick caressed the noose, the more his fingers played around it, stroked it and picked at it, the less he had to offer as explanation. Then, suddenly, all logic blew out of his mind as the noose yanked closed around his hand.

He tried desperately to get to his feet, but the noose jerked back as a force took hold of the base of the rope and pulled him roughly forward across the floor. His other hand shot out and felt for the noose, the fingers pulling at it, yet the more he fought the tighter its hold grew. He was yanked ungraciously to the top of the stairs and then with one hard and vicious tug, he was pulled over, moving off the steps and then hitting the air, arching over and then finally smacking the bottom step with his back.

Whatever had held the rope was now moving over him, pushing against his face; an oppressive, suffocating and invisible weight. Fingers seemed to play around his eyes and his nose, and then they were tearing down his cheeks and ripping into the wound on his face. He screamed into the air, as something seemed to enter his cheek wound and run through to his teeth. His hands batted aimlessly around in front of him, like he were trying to swat a cloud of flies. He swung himself to his left but the force brought him back. He felt as if he were sinking, pushing through the base of the stairs ready to be swallowed up by the floor itself.

There were noises far below him, gunshots, he was sure, and now similar sounds were coming from just above, pulsing along the roof. He struggled for breath;

the air that hung above him was empty and thin, the ceiling seemed to be lowering, the shadows growing nearer, brushing at him, and pushing him further down. Once more he shoved himself to his side and this time he wasn't fought back. He flipped over on the stairs, moving to his front in one clumsy motion and the force lifted off him, moved through him, and died away amongst what was left of the air.

Kendrick stumbled and swayed back up the stairs, tottering out on to the landing and pinballing drunkenly between the walls towards the partially open door of the communications room. The sounds he had convinced himself he had heard on the roof now seemed to be at the door, the heavy steel vibrating at the mercy of thunderous blows. He fell into the room, shoved Davenport's' prostrate arm to one side and then kicked the door shut.

The knocks at the door came instantly. Small rhythmic taps evenly spaced like a heartbeat. Kendrick was up again, falling into the control panel and rolling the chair to the door, over Davenport's arm, and wedging the back under the handle. The knocks grew louder, became thumps and as he began bellowing through the microphone, the door began to sigh at its hinges and splinter at the handle.

'Safe house compromised! We need immediate evacuation. Request next team's status. Over.' The microphone crackled like applause and then fell to silence.

'Come in! Request next team's status. Talk to me! Is there anybody out there?'

He found himself drawn to the small monitor just before him, and what seemed to be a huge eye dominating the screen, looking into the camera outside. It blinked once and then the image broke apart, sucked into a blackness before that too disappeared and Kendrick found himself looking back at a screen of interference.

POSSESSION

1

Sullivan ran at the scene unfolding in front of him, a stranger invading another's dream. The steady hollowness emanating from his blasted ear had knocked him off balance both physically and mentally and now nothing seemed to make sense; the bodies dropping out of the shaft, the bulky man fighting them off, the girl lying huddled in the doorway, the lump of bones and limbs on the floor that used to be Turtle, and especially the stupid little pistol he had held up before him. As he pulled up next to the chaos he felt ridiculous, conspicuous – wrong man, wrong place, wrong time. He looked across at Mia, not a look of comfort but a look of questioning. Someone was advancing on him, a small man clothed in rags, smeared in dirt. He was waving a crudely taped cricket bat above a face contorted in fury, yellowed teeth gritted together, and he was pulling back, readying the blow. Sullivan jerked away from him, his hands moving up in an indecisive gesture of submission and protection, and the pistol exploded in his hand, taking him by surprise. The shot hit the stranger in the leg and instantly he was on the floor, the bat skimming across to where Sullivan had come to a cowering stop.

Another body lay prone on the floor next to Turtle, a rifle shot neatly centred at his heart. Two more danced between the bodies as they punched and clawed and kicked at Maddox. Mia was now up in the open doorway fending off a young, withering branch of a boy, coming at her with a makeshift hammer of stone and wood, swinging slashing arcs at her retreating body. At the hole Sullivan heard more voices and the heavy clanking of footsteps and then two more strangers had dropped down to the floor and were charging his way. His instinct turned straight to the cold certainty gripped in his right hand, yet his hand was a rock weighing it down and he couldn't seem to lift it. Hatred grew in him, erupted above his heart and oozed its choking thickness down. But it was a perverse hatred. It was hatred of himself – at the ease of instinct, and the animalistic practicality of the kill. But worse than both was the undeniable, horrific pleasure he could feel in that instinct; bought in the moment, paid out over the years.

He let the pistol drop from his hand, refusing its approach, and reached down for the bat, prising it from the fallen stranger. He batted the first of his attackers in the side, knocking him into the next, and then swung back and brought the bat down hard across the second man's back. The body already at his feet was now grabbing at his trousers, pulling at him, trying to get a grip. Sullivan jerked his right hand to his side and brought the bat across the man's face, splintering off a small chunk of tape and wood from the end. He was suddenly picked up and carried along, embraced by the swirling, manic heat of the moment. He turned to the open doorway, to Mia and what he had to do, and moved on.

Maddox fired off another rifle shot and one of his attackers was blasted into the wall. Above him a pair of legs was dangling from the hole, ready to jump down. Maddox swung his other attacker around, moved into the shot and fired the rifle's last bullet between the legs of the body at the hole sending it down on to the steadily growing mound of rags and limbs. Pushing away from the other he spun the rifle butt around and cracked him across his skull putting him on the floor. He jumped forward, lunged his great, bulky body at the ceiling and grabbed the edge of the open hatch. Above him they were pouring through the shaft, the narrow metal turret packed with bodies as even more spilled over the edge at the roof. He reached his hands up, and slammed the hatch on to a woman's foot, pulling it out again before forcing it back into place. He spun the handle, and felt the lock ease itself into place. At his feet one dazed attacker had hold on one of his legs and was moving in, trying to bite through his trousers. Maddox jerked his leg up nonchalantly and knocked the man away, bringing the boot down hard on to his face as he landed back amongst his fallen comrades.

Mia had been forced back into the bedroom by her

attacker, the stone head of his cobbled-together hammer slashing across her right shoulder and drawing blood. He was grabbing clumsily and chaotically at the outsized fatigues, lunatic's eyes, leering and leching as they moved over her. Sullivan ran into the room, and swung the bat low into the boy's ribs. The stranger gave one ugly roar before rolling off Mia and turning his focus on to Sullivan, the hammer swinging in front of his face with such speed and venom that he lost his hold on the handle and it launched itself against the wall, shattering.

Sullivan was moving back, preparing another swing of the bat when the boy came again, leaping forward, charging him down. They collided with a hefty thud, slow dancing to the doorway where Sullivan managed to pull away enough to aim a fist into the side of the boy's face. He gripped the bat and got ready for the stranger to come again, but instead the boy was suddenly yanked away from him and Sullivan swooped hard and fast through thin air, pirouetting on the spot before spinning back around to the open doorway and staring ahead with a slack jawed gait of incomprehension. The stranger was before him but was motionless, cuddled into the enormous frame of Theo Maddox, as blood gurgled over his quivering lips. Maddox was slowly, methodically, drawing his hunting knife up the boy's back, from the base of his spine to the top of his neck.

Sullivan backed off, taking slow unsteady steps to the bed, the bat still in his grip but growing lighter by the second.

Maddox pulled the knife clear with a delicate flick of the wrist, an artist's final brush stroke, and then kicked the opened carcass of the attacker to the ground. He raised tired eyes and stared absently at Sullivan and then at Mia like a doorman assessing their clothing. Momentarily he looked sad, and with a slow shake of the head came a sigh and the sag of his huge shoulders. Turning in the doorway he wandered casually back to the mound of bodies in the corridor. Hands were rising, legs twitching; garbled noises were seeping out of those that still clung on. Maddox straddled the nearest body and then quickly plunged the knife through his heart, drew it out and then moved to the next. One by one each fallen body, the ones alive and the ones dead, took a knife to the heart or to the neck, Maddox robotically going about his business with a clinical efficiency that had long since sucked out any meaning.

Sullivan felt a hand touch his back as Mia shuffled off the bed and stood at his side. The coursing anger that had carried him into this self-imposed trap had now deserted him. He felt numb. Somehow it seemed inevitable. He scolded himself quietly for not seeing it.

"Anger is a trap, what does that mean Daddy? I heard Mummy saying that to you. What does it mean?"

"It means there is no way out of anger."

"I don't understand."

"Me neither."

She could see it in my eyes. My wife that is, yes, she knew. She knew in that moment when I pulled the trigger that I had enjoyed it. It was so cheap. But so costly. It was horrible but felt so good. It was an affair. A capitulation to the base level. Always crying out to us, always wanting us to give in.

It felt right despite being wrong.

Yes. It was a trap.

The bat in his hand felt puny and pathetic, like it was wilting. They had trapped each other and there was nowhere else to run to. Watching Maddox just beyond the door he quickly had the notion that they could charge him, swing left or right in the corridor and then escape, outrun him, but the idea was fleeting and half-hearted. She was pushing herself into him and the weight was unbearable, but then suddenly she was moving past him and nudging him to one side.

'You have a gun?' she whispered.

'No. No, I don't…' *Because I have morals. I'm the better man.*

You're a dead man, daddy.

Sullivan felt his blood chill. 'I'm sorry, I'm…'

Maddox started wiping down the knife. He was resting on his haunches and gazing back into the doorway, assessing them.

'I want the girl, killer. What do you say? You don't try

and stand in my way and I promise I will drop you quick.'
Maddox swung the knife through the air in one clean arc.

Mia was now in front of Sullivan, her hand reaching
for the bat.

'What are you doing?' Sullivan whispered into the
back of her head, his hand tightening around the handle,
fighting her grip. 'He's going to kill you!'

'He's going to kill us both but I'm damned if I'm
dying on my knees.'

She had caught Sullivan off guard. She fumbled the
bat from him and moved it out in front of her.

In the doorway Maddox was standing, a smile
creasing his lips that managed to be both patronising
and proud. 'That's my girl.'

'Mia, please…I came…' Sullivan lost the words before
they could form. In his frantic mind he pieced them
together and heard how stupid they sounded: "I came
here to save you!" That was what he had meant to say,
and what a damn fucked up attempt at that he had
made. She seemed to hear him, her eyes finding his own
just for a second as she edged around the room.

'No you didn't,' she said, and turned back to the
doorway and to Maddox who was now in the room,
blocking their only exit and waiting patiently for Mia to
come to him, the knife solid in one meat slab of a hand,
the blue blooming again in his eyes.

2

The door to the communications room stood hanging from the frame in two large, jagged pieces. Beneath it, Davenport lay in his bloody puddle. Beyond it there was nothing, a sheer, deep, consuming nothing. Kendrick sat staring at the empty space and couldn't stop laughing. He held his arms across his stomach as the merriment started to cause him mini convulsions. His eyes watered, his nose ran. It was the funniest thing he had ever seen. He was looking at nothing, and nothing seemed to be hilarious.

He could hear his own laughter from beneath a thick surface. He looked around into the gloom and tried to see himself, but instead he saw nothing. That wonderful nothing. His body felt as if it were imbued with air so light and gentle that he wondered what kept him anchored to the ground. Something did. A heavy weight from somewhere there in the darkness, an unyielding pressure on his head, something kept him out of sight and out of his own body, something impossible. In that moment he felt himself stand up and smooth down his clothes, yet it wasn't him, it couldn't be him. He turned to the control panel and listened intently to the voices coming back at him.

'Second team en-route. ETA...'

He wasn't listening. Something was, but it wasn't him.

'Hold position. Await second team's arrival.'

He started playing with buttons and switches and suddenly the control panel was alive with light and action. He tried to look out, to feel beyond the sensation of what surrounded him. He told himself he were in a dream and was merely sleepwalking. He had done that a few times as a child. That made sense to him and that was good enough. It added credibility to his wilful deception.

'Come in. Report status. Kendrick? You there?'

He heard himself responding to the voice through the microphone, yet he knew he hadn't spoken the words himself.

It wasn't a dream. It was manipulation.

His body turned from the control panel and looked to the door, staring out through someone else's eyes to the emptiness beyond. He was a balloon being bent, and squeezed and forced into impossible shapes. Now he was walking off, climbing over the body of Eddie Davenport and moving into the corridor outside. He had no choice other than to let his body walk and try and stay with it, to try and see through the dark and to try and not float away. His screams were like rolling thunder across a faraway horizon and at each came a voice in his ear; deep, inhuman, impossible, and spiked with venom.

Nothing.

He heard himself laughing again.

3

Sullivan could feel his blood within him like it was a growing skin. His damaged ear prickled and itched. His eyes watered. He shivered but it felt good. He was back home, one final time, floating through the scene. Breathing in the old feeling. It came back to him so easily. It wanted to be found.

> *"Why do they kill the rats, Daddy?"*
> *"They think they are doing it for good reasons."*
> *"How can there be good reasons?"*
> *"There can't. There are just bad people."*

The scene slowed in front of him, just for a moment. Mia and Maddox were moving in a Hollywood slow motion, their actions somehow matching the mushy, slurred sounds that were feeding into his deafened ear. She was charging him and he was letting her. For the sweetest, most blessed of seconds Sullivan was a mere spectator watching it all play out from behind a screen. An audience of one for a show he hadn't paid to see. The deception was brief and all the more crushing for it.

The bat sheared in two across Maddox's chest and then Mia was knocked over on to her front by one large backhanded slap. Maddox was then bearing down on Sullivan and the knife was slashing through the air. Sullivan ducked the first swipe but the second caught him across the thigh. Maddox was on him, over him, swallowing him up. Sullivan took a hand to the clenched fist holding the knife but instantly his arm buckled back against the force and he was toppled over on to the bed as the knife was shoved crudely into his left arm. Sullivan jerked his head forward and brought his forehead across Maddox's nose. Maddox mimicked the move and Sullivan felt the bone in his nose shatter. A giant hand now covered him, eating up his face, the palm pushing down on to broken bone, manipulating it one way and then the other. The other hand sought out the knife and pushed it down deeper, moving the blade from side to side, opening up the wound.

Mia regained her feet and jumped on to Maddox's back, her teeth biting down into his neck, ripping and tearing at the flesh as her hands wrapped around his throat. He found her hair and pulled hard and fast, yanking her off him and then swinging her around so she faced him on the ground. She spat back what she had bitten off and then brought her hands to his throat again and then his neck, her fingers searching out the wound and pushing in. Maddox roared at the pain, the sheer affront of her actions and rolled his giant bulk on top of her, his hands grasping her at the elbows, pushing at the bone and the joint until she had no choice but to release and succumb to his strength. She screamed and she shouted, but it was defiance and not submission; as he pushed his groin against her, rubbing and grinding and growing, and as the piercing blue deepened, she still had the fight and she let him know it.

The pain from Sullivan's flattened nose was a sharp icicle through his head, his left arm an infernal, raging fire, yet still he pushed through. His right hand was gripping the handle of the knife, ready to pull it free. He tried to look at it but as he did he saw nothing but a blur. "Pull it quick, that's the way," Wiggs told him from somewhere. "Yeah, I know. I'm not stupid," he responded. "Sure you are, Sullivan. You're in jail." Sullivan gripped, then tugged and prised it free, waving it around above him like a trophy, a message to the voices in his head. He could feel an ugly belch of blood gush down his left arm and imagined how it might look and then saw the big mouth of the hole in his mind. It would be grinning, he decided. He turned to the bodies before him, the blurred mound, defined only by the giant, rock of Maddox's head, and then lurched from cotton ball knees, the knife up in the air, held tight by his trembling hands. The blade connected before he did. He felt it sink in, could feel something give to its demand, and then he was on Maddox's back in a clumsy half-hug as blood seemed to explode in his face.

It was easy. It was too easy.

"Why is anger so easy if we know it's a trap?" Wiggs

was asking, and for the first time the old sage sounded genuinely perplexed.

"Shut the fuck up, Wiggs."

Maddox suddenly reared up on to his knees, taking Sullivan with him, his big, beefy hands flapping at Sullivan's own, now gripped around the handle of the knife buried in the back of his neck. Mia seized her chance and shuffled out from under him, kicking out one foot into his gut as a parting gift. Sullivan pushed the knife further, pulled down on it, then pushed again, forcing it up. Maddox made a sound, a gurgle, and then he tried to speak but his words were swimming in blood and what came instead was no more than a choked warble. His hands started loosening their hold, dropping from the handle to Sullivan's wrists before slipping silently off and flopping down at his side with two hearty slaps. He seemed to be breaking down in stages; his body jittered and jerked and then started bending forward as if he were bowing to Mia. As the gurgling stopped his breath eased out like the air from a punctured tyre. Finally he tilted forward and thudded to the floor, face first, and remained still. Sullivan gave himself a moment of contemplation and then joined Maddox on the ground.

'Get up! Get up damn it!'

He could hear how frightened she sounded, how her words were trying hard to spike with authority and command and how instead they just sounded hopeless.

She was tugging at his right arm, pulling him a few feet and then bending down and shouting into the bloody pulp of his face before trying again. He fought her, yanking his arm free of her hold and waving her on with a gentle brush of the hand. She wasn't having it.

'Get up, Sullivan! Please. Get up! Come on!'

And go where? He heard his mind saying as he fought her off for the third time. *Besides, I came here to save you dear, I've done my bit. Now let me die. Let me be alone to find them. That's all...*

'Get up! Don't leave me alone. Don't leave me here. I need you. I need you to get up...please...'

She started pulling him by the hair; hard and purposeful tugs, yanking him from Maddox along a wide blood smear on the ground, like a grotesque slug trail. She moved him to the doorway before he found the energy to fight back.

'Leave me! Get off me!'

'You saved me, now I'm saving you. Get up!'

'I don't want to be saved,' he said it without consideration; it just tumbled from him in a short, snappy, bark. 'Please, just...just leave me girl. Will you just leave me?' He could taste the dull metal blood flavour in his mouth, and swallowed hard, coming empty on what felt like a rock in his throat. He pulled away from her and slumped against the doorway. 'Enough,' he moaned, hoping it would be.

It wasn't.

Mia was tearing at one arm of her fatigues, pulling the material down, and ripping it at the shoulder. She dug her fingers into the tear and prised it open, yanking the material off in one clean swoosh of the arm. She bent down to him and wrapped it delicately around the bloody grin on his arm.

'This is going to hurt,' she said apologetically and he laughed. She finished wrapping the tourniquet and made a loose knot with both ends, slowly pulling it tight across his arm. The flame of pain licked up high and bright down his left hand side and he screamed and started batting her away from him. 'Let's go,' she said and began tugging at his shirt.

'You stubborn girl, you stupid, stubborn girl!'

He pulled away from her again, but this time she moved under him, her head pushing up under his shoulder as she clumsily moved him to his feet and turned him out into the corridor. He could feel the last vestiges of what he held fall down into his boots as he swayed against her. The pain was all, the cuts and bruises, the gashes and breaks, all at once connecting up like a game of join the dots as each and every one ignited within him, pulling him towards submission. She got him no more than a few feet before he collapsed against her, slipped down on to buckling knees and fell amongst the bodies on the floor.

'No, no you don't do this to me! Please!'

Tears broke her words. He felt another piece of love

shatter in his chest and closed his eyes to her face. There was nothing to be gained from any more guilt, he told himself, no further to fall. He held a hand up and tried to find her face. She came to him and rested a burning hot cheek against his palm, her hands cradling his wrist. He heard a whispered plea, and he shook his head to it and then squeezed her cheek letting the index finger push up and wipe at the salty sting that came.

'Let me die,' Sullivan said and then gently repeated the words in case she thought it was a question.

'No...'

'Yes, Mia.'

'I need you.'

'No. I needed you.'

'Your family? Please, Sullivan, don't give up on your family.'

'They're dead. I killed them. Both of them.'

'What? You're not making sense.'

'I'm a murderer. Can't you see it? I fell over the line and there's no getting back. You don't cross back, Mia. It's just a question of how long you have before it finds you. Time, Mia. Time.'

'You didn't kill your family. You don't know what you're saying.'

'She came to them because of me. She offered herself up and they took her. I can feel her. I can feel her here. It's okay, Mia. It's all okay. My wife is here and it's all okay.'

'I don't understand.'

'You don't need to. You just need to live.'

'How do I do that?'

'You do what you have to do.'

'What does that mean?' Her hands were on him, pulling the sides of his jacket together as if she were about to shake him. 'What do I do? Please tell me what I do!' She pulled him up and leant him against the wall just beneath the hatch, her hands went to his face and turned it to her. Still he wouldn't open his eyes. 'What do I do?'

A small line of blood dribbled from one corner of his mouth as he spoke and when the single, solitary word came it was so quiet, so detached, that it seemed to come from a different world. 'Time.'

'Tick-tock, tick-tock.' It was another voice, someone else speaking from a far away place. The voice was low, and broken, mocking yet inviting and as it came again, the words seemed to ooze over her, making her quiver against goose bump skin. The voice was coming from over her shoulder.

Sullivan pulled his eyes open and rolled his head against the wall, looking past Mia and down the corridor. He squinted and then blinked and then his eyes dropped to the floor, moved through the blood and bodies, and came to rest on the pistol just beyond him.

'Face me, child,' the voice demanded in a distorted growl. 'Face me!'

Mia turned slowly, craning around on the spot. Kendrick was standing in the middle of the corridor about twenty feet away. His eyes were rolled back in their sockets, the whites shining like two opals, suspended in the hugging gloom.

4

The thing that stood before her made no move as Mia got to her feet, merely smiled expectantly. Her body was alive, jarred open by a fear that seemed to want to eat her; the goose bumps felt as big as pebbles, the piercing cold wave that had started at the tip of her skull was crashing down, rooting her to where she stood. Kendrick's face blurred and shifted like a reflection in rippling water, slowly washing away and then swimming back as it spoke again. Each word that came to her was a pulse, a gnawing rhythm that started at her heart before travelling to her mind.

'Mia. Child. The girl that came back.'

The voice wasn't Kendrick's. It was her father's, but only fleetingly, just enough to get further inside her and hold her rapt.

'Who are you?'

'Who do you want me to be?'

'You're not my father.'

'Daddy dear. Dear Daddy. Daddy loves Mia.'

'You're not Mr Kendrick, either.'

'I never claimed to be. Though he is here. In the mix. In the pot. In the stew. No one would choose this hollow carcass. This useless vessel. You should hear how he screams. You should taste his fear.'

Something clicked in Mia's throat and she held a hand up as if she was going to choke herself. 'Please don't.'

'Don't what, child?'

'Don't hurt us.'

'Us?'

It turned its empty gaze on to Sullivan and broadened its smile to a ridiculous width. At Mia's feet, Sullivan was hunched over, reaching for the pistol, coughing back blood at each failed attempt. 'I see only you, Mia. Sullivan is already dead. He is beyond hurt now. Look how he tries to get that weapon. The weapon that killed him. Curious how he finds solace in something so pointless, isn't it? Such a desperate and meaningless act. Such a weapon changed the course of his fortunes, and yet still he flails around for it, hoping to find answers. Death is all around him. He reeks of it. He is soaked in it. Yet still he comes. His judgement was made a long time ago and yet he doesn't seem to realise it. Judgements were set on all of you. All but you, Mia.'

'I don't understand.'

'Did your father never teach you about fate, child? Did he never show you how all your paths were already planned? Did he never share his dreams with you, Mia? Such a dereliction of duty.'

'Please…'

'Please? Such manners. Such innocence. Such purity

of heart. You don't belong here, Mia. He should never have brought you, and you should never have come back. You were warned, but you chose to ignore.'

Her right arm suddenly flared as each lettered scar carved there threatened to rip open. She swallowed a scream, refusing to give the hideous thing in front of her the satisfaction she knew it was searching for.

'Do you not understand, Mia? Don't you know what this place is?'

'I know what went on here.'

'What happened here, Mia?'

'People died here.'

'No. What happened here, Mia?'

'They used to kill people here. People were executed.'

'What happened here, Mia? What happened here?'

'I don't...I don't understand?'

'Of course you do, Mia, of course you understand. What happened here, child? What happened?'

She met the shifting face before her and slowly breathed the word he wanted to hear: 'Judgement.'

'The sanctimonious good judged the irredeemably bad. Fate, Mia, people felt they had the power to decide the fate of others.'

'I understand.'

'You do? Yet still you are here.'

'I had no choice! Don't you see?'

'I see everything you stupid child! You have no idea what I can see and do!'

'It wasn't my choice!'

'Choice?' His voice shifted, curdled, and started to snarl. 'None of us had choice you naïve and foolish child! What makes you so special?' Kendrick grabbed at his head and shrieked, forcing the snarling voice away. 'Everyone…everyone wants to speak. How tiresome.' The deep voice was back, the shining eye whites fixed again on Mia. 'They called me mad, your people. They decided I was insane. Those great arbitrators of right and wrong. Whilst they continued destroying people here, they decided I was the madman. Look how far you have all progressed. Look at this civilized world you have created.'

'You are thirteen?'

'BH13' Sullivan said through a croaked whisper at the wall, unheard by Mia and ignored by the warped mimic of Kendrick before them.

'It is easier to discard a number. That was the brand they gave me. Your people.'

'These aren't my people.'

'Your father was an assassin. A butcher. Are you so sheltered as to really not see what is so blatantly obvious? A sin remains a sin no matter in whose name it is committed. There will always be people to judge your sins. But your people were looking the wrong way. Your people feared the living. What a delicious irony.'

'I had no part in coming here. Neither of us did.'

'But yet you are here.'

'This place is evil.'

'No. No child. This place is judgement. Evil is up to you.'

'Let us leave,' Mia asked softly, taking her right hand from her side and holding it to Kendrick in a show of submission. 'Please. I don't want to be here. We don't want to be here.'

'Should I open the door?' He laughed at the look of horror that sprang to her face, his own shifting again, blurring like an image behind a rain-lashed window.

'Please…don't do this…'

'Do you doubt me? Do you question that I could?'

'No! Please…please listen…they made me…'

His voice broke into a weedy, blubbing mimic and repeated the words like a parrot. The voice was her father's.

'Stop it!'

'Why come back child, why do that?' The growl had returned. 'I walked with you. Don't you remember? I walked through you and the smell of fear was ugly. I smell it again now. Why child? Why? I showed you compassion by showing you death. We thought we were rid of you. But no. Not this girl. The girl who came back.'

'Who are you? Tell me. What is your name?'

'Who are you? That's what should be asked. Why never ask that?'

'I asked you a question.'

'So many questions.'

'No answers.'

'It is not my job to satisfy you. It was you that came to me. You were not invited. You were not welcome. Yet still you come…'

Kendrick raised a hand up, turning the palm to the ceiling. Above them the hatch handle started to turn, just slightly, the hideous metal squeak of its release shrieking and then dying, like tyres screeching to a stop. The sound made Mia jump, her hands instantly gripping her sides as she fumbled her stance and swayed uneasily on her feet. Kendrick's smile grew. He seemed pleased with himself.

'Please…please don't…'

'Does it not impress you?'

'Clever. Very clever.'

'A gift, Mia,' his words were slow and controlled and carried an arrogant pomposity. He shot a hand out to one side and suddenly a line of fire erupted along the wall, just beneath the hatch. 'I've been in your dreams. I've looked into your soul. I know your fears.' He laughed manically as he looked into the dread in Sullivan's eyes as the fire bent its course above him. Kendrick turned back to Mia and his voice dropped further, each word vibrating through her. 'I can smell your fear, dear. Your fear is near, dear and I can smell it again.' Kendrick threw his head back impossibly far, his throat seeming to bulge as he did. 'The girl that came back' he said to the ceiling as he started to rise off the ground. His arms moved out to the side and seemed to extend, the fingers on each hand splaying wide like twigs growing from a branch. 'Daddy is so disappointed in you.'

'You're not my father!'

'I'm everyone.' He moved back to the ground slowly and brought his arms out in front of him. His left wrist began to turn as the hand moved completely around and then started to bend back on itself. 'You should hear how this wretched little man screams inside me. What end for this horrid little man called Kendrick? Should I make him face his fears too? Is that how he must meet his judgement?' He pulled his right hand to his shirt and ripped it open, poking and prodding Kendrick's bare chest with one long finger. 'Tell me, Mia, by what means should we carry out Mr Kendrick's sentence? Because if I made him face what he fears most I would have to open the doors and let the living in. It is they who he is most scared of, those that seek to destroy what you have all created. You should hear how such a thing makes him scream. Should I let them have him, Mia? What should I do, child? Tell me.'

'Stop this! Please! Stop!' Sullivan was screaming towards the pistol on the ground, his voice broken and weak like a crossed phone line. He made a lunge for the gun and crumpled into a heap next to Turtle's bare feet.

'I did it for you darling, I need you to believe me.'

The voice coming from Kendrick was suddenly high and light, a female voice, gentle and loving. The thing was looking down at Sullivan and Kendrick's face was slowly floating away again.

'No,' Sullivan said in a shattering whisper. 'No. No!'

'This guilt, darling. This guilt will kill you.'

Kendrick's face had been replaced by that of a woman, her beautiful features dancing over Kendrick's head like a super imposed photo. Mia stared back in a stunned reverence, her mouth hanging open at one side as her teeth started to grind together. She had seen her before. The woman's face had been etched on her mind; her body lying over the barbed wire of the pen outside, slain trying to escape. Now the face was turning down to Sullivan as Kendrick's body crouched low and his long fingers and arms wrapped themselves around his knees.

'She asks for you often. I don't think she can see you yet. She doesn't belong here.'

'Stop it!' Sullivan shouted, a hand shooting to his one good ear and slapping a blood drenched palm over it as his other hand continued to fumble for the pistol.

'It was an accident, darling. You know it was. You were trying to save us. You did save me. You were protecting us. She moved behind him. She was running from him, not you. You couldn't have seen her. In that split second, you couldn't have known. She doesn't blame you. There is no blame. She only wants to speak with you again and tell you that she loves you.'

Tears were pouring from Sullivan's eyes, flooding the bloody mush of his nose. His fist was clenching around his ear and then slowly beating against it trying to stop the words from hitting him.

'Daddy?' Kendrick asked in the voice of a child, tilting his head to one side and staring out through those empty holes in his face. 'Why did you shoot me daddy?'

A roar suddenly erupted through Sullivan, and Mia felt it tear into her, sealing off the fear that had exposed her. The gunshot that followed sounded like little more than the popping of a champagne cork by comparison. It happened so quickly that Mia took a moment to process the information before her. She was looking between both bodies; the bloodied mess of Sullivan and the corrupted shape of Kendrick, now lying flat on his back, rolling from side to side in agony as a blood smear grew out of a charred hole at the top of his shirt, and still she couldn't seem to grasp what had happened. Kendrick's neat little hands were up in the air, reaching for her, like the hands of a child demanding a hug. The horrid watch waggled around on his arm, broken of its clasp.

'Help me! Please! Oh, someone…' It was Kendrick's voice again.

Sullivan wasn't moving. Mia dropped to her knees and ran her hands over his back. He was breathing but it was slow and weary. His eyes were unblinking, fastened on Kendrick, drinking in the sight.

Kendrick rolled to his side, his pleading eyes finding Mia again and widening in hope, as his hands grabbed out to her. She looked above him, then beyond, convinced there should be something else to see. She stared into the darkness, then up to the ceiling. She looked behind her and then back to Kendrick. The fire still burned its amber streak down the wall but it wasn't enough.

'Hello?' she found herself saying.

'Hello? Mia? Help me...' Kendrick replied.

Mia stood and stared off down the corridor. 'I asked you who you were,' she said into the empty corridor. 'Answer me!'

The response came from behind her; an ear-piercing screech at the ceiling as the hatch handle eased itself slowly around, turning against an invisible pressure before springing the lock and letting the hatch yawn open to hands and legs and bodies, tumbling out of the ceiling. High above her she heard another noise, a heavy rumble like the heavens themselves were passing comment on her, and in her mind, in the small piece left to carry her from this spot and move her on, she saw the giant entrance door sliding open and a hundred bodies charging through. She heard muffled voices coming together, the steady blooming screams of triumph and the sharp blood curdling wails of an old and empty rage and then all the sounds were one and it blew through the never ending corridors of the safe house like a howling gale, searching her out, looking to sweep her up along with anything else in its path. Mia turned and began to run.

5

They were a river in the corridor, a chaotic tide that swamped all, pushing through the empty spaces. Kendrick drowned under their force. Hands and legs found him, fists and feet broke him. He was lifted up between them like rubbish as wave after wave probed him and crashed through him. They were in his mouth, blasting through his eyes, cresting his chest and stomach and looking for a way in. He screamed one final time and then he felt his mouth ripped open and he gave no more. Further down his chest had let the flood in. The river dropped him down and then tore him apart.

They landed on Sullivan, body after body dropping on to his back or trampling over his outstretched arms; just one more part of the grotesque carpet along the corridor marking their way. He lay still, letting the last shallow breaths leave him in their short, jagged sighs. He saw a blur of feet and legs move past him and the wild jerking frame of Joe Kendrick beyond rolling helplessly on the floor. Then the bodies and the legs had become one and drawn a darkened veil over Kendrick's body and Sullivan closed his eyes, fell into the emptiness and waited, letting another darkness take him to his own ending.

Mia ran until it hurt, moving around the ends of corridors before pounding the next and repeating the process in a blind and hopeless effort. How ugly the place looked, she suddenly thought. It was a bizarre thing to allow herself to contemplate in the circumstance but she couldn't help it. For the first time since she had stood at the entrance and let her mind wander the shelter, she was actually taking stock of just how unedifying the scenery was. She had heard it described as a tomb, a prison, and a maze and it was all of those things, yet something more too. Those things suggested an ending, and yet to Mia the building was just a beginning, a prelude to the running down of a clock.

Tick-tock.

Time he had said. Just get as much of it as you can. She could hear a dull ticking in her mind. She was running out of time and running out of space.

The sounds of the others pressed around her. She could hear them above and behind, getting nearer, footsteps across the floors like encroaching thunder. She was running in circles – she knew it, she knew this place – and sooner or later she was going to be closed off. But what else was there but to run? To grab whatever time was left?

She looked ahead of her at another sharp turn and pushed into her memory, planning her move. Past the next corridor her path would split in two, feed left and right and then she would be faced with a decision. Time. Which would afford her the most time? Her mind felt frayed, a tenuous notion, it was flattened and worn and gave her nothing. Tears were pins in her eyes, skewering the last of her resolve. She wiped them with a clenched fist and as she turned the corner and hauled herself on she let her memories snap free and drift away. She had no time for such an indulgence.

At the split in the corridor she took the right hand path. Ahead of her orange light caressed the walls, twinkling and dancing its colour from the floor to the ceiling. A line of doors stood open along one side and each was emanating an impossible glowing life from within. The corridor shone and its brilliance was suddenly overwhelming, a lost sun on the deepest winter night. Mia was at the first door before she realised her mistake. The light was changing, shifting, flicking and popping and growing brighter. She could feel the heat from the first door reaching out to her and then the heat was a long tentacle of flame, bending around the frame, crawling up the wall and smearing along the ceiling. She stumbled back, turned sharply and retreated, running back the way she had come.

At the intersection she could see the end of the first corridor coming alive with figures moving forward as if falling from the shadows. The gathered roar was almost deafening but Mia refused their advances and carried on through, running at full tilt down the left hand path of the crossroads. The flames came again almost instantly. They bloomed together in front of her, drawn out of the walls. She ducked the first but couldn't escape the next and she felt her bare arm singe as it cut through the dancing licks. It was bending and stretching, arching over her and jabbing forwards as she passed it. Behind her she heard screams as the oncoming invaders found themselves greeted by the enveloping amber rage; figures were dropping to the floor, rolling back and forth as they batted hopelessly at the pulsing flames. The rest of the pack were backing off, turning into their neighbours and fighting as they tried to push away as one from the fire. Gunshots sounded behind them and more people fell. Mia felt something pass her cheek and explode at the wall to her right but gave it little heed. She was fully held by what was happening in front of her.

She pushed on again, stumbling past doorways and leaping wayward over small patches of fire that seemed to be bursting up through the heavy set floor at intervals. The heat was immense and suffocating, it looked for her, chased her down and taunted her. Once more a flash of amber erupted in front of her, slicing over her head like a giant arm, and this time she was knocked off her stride, dropping hard to her knees before tilting forward and seemingly falling through the floor and into thin air. She turned in the emptiness, spun over through the blackness and then thudded against an uneven, lumpy ground.

The empty hole in the floor above gazed down at her, a lonely moon slowly swallowed by the sun. Streaks of orange stroked at the space as the flames above her started moving together, bending and wrapping around each other, pushing up, growing out and looking down. For a brief moment, held suspended there above, the flames seemed to form a figure but they broke apart as soon as the idea came to her, pushing out to the walls and the ceiling again and submerging both, sealing off the open hatch. Gunfire tore through the emptiness, the loud cracking pops and bangs like a private fireworks display she couldn't see. She could hear them screaming and shouting high above her and in her mind she could see the blackened and defeated bodies on the floor, eaten by the flames or dropped by a bullet, and yet she could feel nothing. There was no pity and there was no revulsion. There was just nothing at all. A part of her had already escaped.

The smell where she lay was pungent and sharp. It was in the walls and the floor, infested in the darkness. She had smelt traces of it wafting through the corridors above and now here she was at the source. It was the first time since arriving that she was grateful for the shadows and the gloom. She saw edges of shapes, dull, partially defined suggestions at the walls, yet what troubled her lay not at the walls but beneath her, amongst the ragged, perversely misshapen floor. A hand was against her cheek, she was sure of it, the rigid, bony ends of fingers tapping at her skin whenever she moved her head. She shifted her feet, feeling and probing at the uneven surface, and then her hands began to ease out to the sides, gently touching whatever they found, trying in vain to give her answers that would disprove her fears. But her grabs at a wilful delusion were hopeless. She knew where she was. She had been here before. Someone had shown it to her and left it hanging in her subconscious.

He had called it the chamber.

This is where they stick their dead

A light bloomed to her left, seemingly halfway up the wall, and slowly revealed itself to be the heart of a giant furnace – a big, charcoal black monstrosity taking up almost the whole wall – small flames jumped and jerked within it, gently etching the room in a cosy autumnal hue. Rags lay before it, bones inside. A pair of legs was dangling out of one corner, separated from a charred husk. Pipes ran from its bulk into the walls, up through the ceiling, blackened arteries from a diseased heart. The shapes around her were slowly painted in and given definition; hooks hanging from the walls, body bags draped over short struts of wood, and beneath her, as she had suspected, as she had known, the floor was stacked high and wide with corpses.

Mia eased herself forward like she was sitting on the

most fragile of glass. The mound shifted under her as shapes and lumps moved against her hands and tumbled down with her to the floor. High above the roar of the invaders came again. The noise was starting to build and this time it seemed to come from all sides. Gunshots. Screaming. Triumph and defeat. She was in a trap within a trap. A coffin within a tomb. She moved slowly down to the floor and regained her footing, standing against the rebellion in her legs and looking out across the room.

Bodies were stacked on all sides, some wrapped in body bags, most just dumped uncaringly in a heap. She lifted the top of her fatigues and held it to her face as she wandered the room, past the furnace and the hanging bags, turning a full circle around what floor was on display, looking for another way out, yet knowing there was none. On the floor, underneath the hole, a ladder was snapped into several pieces, the wood chipped and splintered and drenched in blood. She could see faces in the flickering orange light, grotesque features gawping at her from the piles of bodies, watching her as she fumbled around hopelessly.

She moved back to where she had landed and was instantly caught by a light from above – it was piercing and unnatural, strong and penetrating, and her hand left her face and shielded her eyes – she was suddenly bathed in a spotlight, a turn without anything to say or an act to perform. She ducked away from it and shot back across the room, moving in behind the lines of body bags, out of reach of its searching probe. She heard whispered voices, feet on the floor above, and then beyond both the steady thump of bullets. They were coming, breaking her trap. The light turned and suddenly went out and for a moment there was nothing beyond the alien clanking from the furnace, then the voices came again and were followed by two light thuds as something, someone, dropped through the hole.

Mia drew down to a crouch and shuffled against the wall, peering out from under the low swinging body bags and across to the furnace. Two long shadows crested and then bent along the ceiling as footsteps crunched across the floor. The light came again, and this time it was coming from the room, sweeping around like a searchlight. She pulled herself flat to the floor and began to crawl under its beam. There was no space, and nowhere else to go; Mia moved to the nearest mound of bodies and pressed herself in. There was give instantly, several corpses sliding from the top and tumbling down in a horrible crunch to the ground, opening a greater space for her to shuffle in. At the sudden shift in position the top of the mound fell in on itself and Mia was quickly smothered; skeletal bodies and broken limbs caving in on her, and holding her where she lay. The trap had been sprung and she had nothing to do but wait for the kill.

It wasn't real, she heard her father saying. None of it

is real. He sounded as if he meant it, and he would never lie to her. *It's not real,* she repeated, interlocking her fingers and cupping her hands over her face, trying to shield what was left of her from the stench of what they wanted her to become. The footsteps came on again, muffled from where she hid, yet she could tell they were slow and purposeful, untroubled and in command. They would not turn away until they found what they were looking for. *It's not real.* The footsteps stopped and she could feel them through the lifeless bodies piled over her. There was movement, voices, disgusted words, and then the light again, peeking in through the hideous jumble of death. They were moving through the mound, discarding what they found, getting closer to her.

As the light flashed across her face, she felt something smother her, a cooling force that promised to shield her from everything and take control. It wrapped her, embraced her, and danced through her. She was far away. So very far away. She heard the sounds of the room and let them fade. She heard the rhythm of her heartbeat like it was the ticking of a giant clock and yet she knew it wasn't. Then, finally she was staring up at a huge white light, as large and piercing as the moon always was in her dreams. She gazed through it and felt its beauty. Felt its hope.

EPILOGUE

DEPARTURE

'I said the Party loves you, Mia.'

'She's out of it, chief.'

'Mia?'

'How'd you know her?'

'She's Lucas Hennessey's kid. Get that damn light out her face.'

The man to his left pulled the spotlight away and let it hang at the wall. His boss stepped forward towards the crumpled heap on the floor and sank to his knees.

'Lucas Hennessey's girl, eh? No shit,' the man with the light said.

Mia felt him touch her neck and feel for a pulse. She heard the gunfire above and around her. People were running back and forth in a controlled chaos. They were in a corridor that had not so long since been aflame and the walls were an impenetrable black. She liked the way the man's hand felt, it was strong and secure, purposeful.

'You want me to get her out of here, chief?'

'No, go help the others. Clear this floor. Make sure the fires are out then get word to the top. I want a post set up before we lose the last of the day. And switch that damn light off!'

He duly obliged and scuttled away with the spotlight.

Mia saw the man leaning over her reach for a walkie-talkie clasped to his jacket. He spoke from the side of his mouth, his eyes never leaving hers. 'We got a Party member alive down here. Gimme the status on the medics.'

'We still got some stragglers in the woods, chief. Can't risk the truck getting hit,' a voice came back.

'Tell him to prepare himself, I'm bringing her up to him.'

'You got it, chief.' Mia heard several popping sounds on the other end of the radio and then the other man was gone and the man above her was reaching under her body and lifting her up.

'Hold on there, Mia. We're going to get you looked after.'

She felt like she was floating up on the air, drifting away, bobbing along. He held her strong and tight and yet she felt small. Her head was flopped to the side and each corridor came to her at a skewed angle. People filled the space in front of her. There were bodies on the floor, bodies moving through them. From time to time more shots came but they were few. There was a sharp taste of smoke in her throat and she could see the wisps of its trace on the air.

'Get that damn fire out!' the man bellowed at someone else.

They moved up a staircase and then another and she started to taste something else beyond the smoke and as she did her heart leapt. It was air; clean and crisp and sharp. She could feel the dampness and the moisture and she tried to raise her head up and look for snow.

'I know your father,' the man suddenly said.

Mia heard him plant a foot through the snow, heard the deep, reassuring crunch, delighted in it, then fell back into the blackness again.

The darkness was like velvet and Sullivan let it cradle him as he held his wife. They were sitting together staring out across a misty lake as their daughter ran up and down the bank with a long stick in front of her like it were a sword, swooshing it back and forth, scything through invisible enemies. They had been here so many times before over the years; first date, the proposal and also, yes, she had always claimed this was the place where their daughter had been conceived too. Sullivan had never been sure about that but liked the idea and hoped it were true. There'd be symmetry to it, were it true. Either way it was a magical place. It was their place; the lake, the lush grass and the trees – especially the giant old oak where they now sat – everything was theirs as far as the eye could see.

She moved into him, her head against his heart and for the longest time they said nothing, yet said much. Too much probably. Sullivan watched his daughter against the misty glass of the lake's surface, shining against it in her white dress, muddied and dirtied by one too many adventures. He felt his heart leap, just for a moment, and against it his wife shifted. She was looking up at their daughter too now, both of them sat there with stupid, beaming smiles and gawping, empty eyes. Their daughter stared back, questioning their look with a narrow gaze and then a roll of the eyes, the child's rebuke of the stupid parent.

Across the lake two lights shone through the mist, combing over the water, moving back and forth before going out.

'Our place,' his wife said and squeezed his hand, forcing their fingers together.

'Our place,' Sullivan replied.

'Even in the dark…' his wife said and then stopped.

'What?'

'Even in the dark…it's even beautiful in the dark.'

The smooth, velvet hold grew tighter and Sullivan could only nod in response to her. Across from them the lights had come again and they silhouetted their daughter.

'What are those lights, mummy?' she asked, pointing the stick in their direction, moving it back and forth in time with them.

Her mother merely shook her head and held a hand out to her, beckoning her over. Her daughter stood her ground.

'Come on sweetheart,' her mother said and tapped her watch.

Sullivan stood and dusted himself down, brushing fallen leaves from his lap. He approached his daughter with his arms outstretched, despite the heaviness they carried, and went in for a hug. He felt her in his hold, that familiar weight, and delighted as her hair flopped over and tickled his skin. He could feel her breathing against him and could smell her most wondrous and perfect aroma again. Even as she passed by him, passed through him, and ran up to the great oak tree and the secure embrace of her mother, he could smell her. Feel her. Need her.

Sullivan stood at the edge of the lake, the mist drifting out, gently wrapping around him, and stared off across the water and then up to the searching brilliance of the lights. Back and forth they went across the lake, slowing their movement, gradually becoming one. They didn't break the darkness, they magnified it, and yet, as they found Sullivan and he gave himself over, the light broke him easily. It shattered the little man and plundered his big heart and then swept up every loose piece, and dragged them away.

The headlights of the medical truck clicked on and off in rapid succession, two yellowy beams breaking the forest gloom ahead and lighting the snow road before them. Mia was entranced, her eyes blinking in time to their coming and going. It was several minutes before she realised it was her that was making them do it. She stared down at her freshly bandaged hand and observed her fingers pulling back and forward on the lever. When she finally took her hand away she brought it up to her face and gazed at it as if seeing it for the first time.

The noise from behind her, back down the hill, came intermittently – the familiar popping of gunfire, the detached shouting of threats and orders. She looked through the rear view mirror and watched the scene play out – strangers, all of them, playing their pointless game. Kings of a castle that could never be conquered. They would try, she mused, they had to try, it was what people did. But they would fail and they would fall.

She thought of the nice man that had carried her out of that place and brought her, through the snow and the threat of gunfire, up the hill to the truck. How long would he be nice? How long could he hold that small goodness? Then there was the medic who had tended to her and regaled her with tales of her father and their time together in the Party. He had been good to her. She took no pleasure from what she had to do.

'I'm sorry,' she said to the windscreen.

Turning to the medic, sat there in the passenger seat, slumped against the bloody smear on the window, she repeated her apology but it sounded flat and false.

'You shouldn't be here,' she told his lifeless body. 'We shouldn't be here.'

Mia flicked the headlights on full and stared ahead into the forest, along the snowy road. A single balloon rolled across in front of them, carried by a small breeze. It turned and tumbled, bobbed up and then swept away into the trees where it popped against a sharp nub of branch. She eased her foot to the accelerator and the truck lurched forward. She fed it up a gear and moved on.

The light was piercing Sullivan's eyes. He blinked rapidly and yanked his head away. He waited for the pain to flare once more but nothing came. He was numb. He rolled his head back to its original position and gently opened his eyes. A figure stood before him dressed in white, in his hand he was rolling a small torch between his fingers and scrutinising Sullivan's face. He smiled lightly and raised his eyebrows. Sullivan tried to move his arms but couldn't, he felt held, like an invisible force was pinning him down. It was only as he looked at his arms, and then his legs, also stationary and immovable, that he realised he was lying in a bed.

'Try not to move too much. You need to try and keep still. Rest. That's what you need. Good old-fashioned rest and recuperation. Does wonders for a man, no matter what…he has been through.'

'What?'

'We've tended to you as best we can. Sorted out that nasty wound on your arm and re-set your nose. Wasn't easy, we're missing one of our medical supply trucks, but we did what we could. Been through the wars haven't you? Not to worry, you're quite safe now.'

Sullivan felt like he had been woken from a dream and he wanted desperately to fall asleep and try and catch it up again, but the more the man spoke, the more Sullivan took in of the room, the more awake he became.

'Do you have a name? You're a Party man I assume from the clothes. Good. That's good.' The man wandered to the side of Sullivan's bed and took a seat on a gurney next to it. 'Party looks after its people. It's all okay now.'

'I don't...' Sullivan paused mid word, his eyes widening around the scene before him. The walls, the floor, the ceiling, everything suddenly looked familiar. He jerked his head to the side and saw a small man in army fatigues wiping down a huge smear of blood from a wall. To the man's side a body lay under an old and bloody dustsheet. 'No!' Sullivan suddenly wailed, 'no! NO!'

'Yes, you are one of the lucky ones. We arrived just in time. It was touch and go for a while but we brought you back.'

The door in front of them opened and a man strolled in, bound up in an expensive suit and a neat hairdo. He smiled broadly at Sullivan and jutted a hand down to him.

'He can't shake your hand, sir,' the man in white said, nodding to Sullivan's bandaged arms and hands.

'Oh, of course, silly me. How thoughtless. Do forgive me, won't you?' the expensively attired man said with a small laugh.

'I should think the new Prime Minister could be forgiven anything, sir,' the man in white said, returning his laugh with one of his own.

'New to the job, you see?' The Prime Minister said to Sullivan, with a casual shrug of the shoulders. 'Haven't yet learned who the victims are. Anyway, it's good to see you back with us. What happened here? Can you remember? I guess it may take time. Not to worry. No, don't worry about it. Don't talk. Plenty of time for stories later.'

ACKNOWLEDGEMENTS

With huge thanks to the following for their support -

David Baker, Tom Bromley, BubbleCow, Amit Dey,
Ruby English, Gary James, Hilary Johnson, Angela &
Arthur Millie, Graham Millie, Gary Smailes,
Stew Taylor, Jeremy Thompson & all at Matador

The Party loves them all